THE COME UP

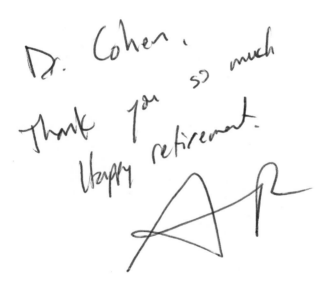

Dr. Cohen,
Thank you so much.
Happy retirement.

Gregory Rossi

First Edition: November 2014

Rossi, Gregory
    The come up / Gregory Rossi.—Street Edition 2.
    ISBN 13 978-1512396256

Printed in the United States of America

Cover design: Anselm Dästner. Interior: Amanda Gentry.

For Yuliana and Veronica

prologue

I only glanced down for a half-sec to bump the volume up a click on my car stereo.

When I looked up, she was there.

She walked in front of my car close enough to graze the bumper. Her left hand dangled a set of keys. Her right hand swung limp from her wrist.

Then on her last step in front of my car she swung that arm, whipped that wrist, and tapped my hood. I sat up in my seat. My eyes drew a line from my car to the Ford F-150 diagonally across the street that I was watching.

She swayed with a gentle tick-tock and walked that very line.

Her body in motion reminded me how much I wanted to play the drums.

The keys in her left hand reflected light off the street lamps. Like a cymbal ringing, the keys didn't propel the beat of her walk — they just hung in there, necessary. The quick switch in her shoulders hit with the snap of a snare drum. Her head remained still, counting time. And the power and drive of the bass drum started where her backbone ended. Her bottom rocked hard, and drove a beat you could sample for a great rap song.

Even in the shadows she cut a vision of pure ebony. She sported all black All-Stars, black jeans, and a lightweight black sweater covering skin that maybe, maybe was a shade lighter.

I liked the colors.

I liked the walk.

I didn't like much else.

The Ford F-150 was parked on the 6300 block of North Kenmare. I knew the block. The F-150 was parked in front of my mom's old building. The one she lived in when she came back.

I was on day six of trying to clear my oldest friend Lenny from a murder rap. History meant nothing to me, even on that sixth day. But like my mom's old building, it lurked hard in the background.

Earlier today I got a call saying if I tailed this particular truck from this exact block, I would find Lenny.

The meeting was bogus. That was a fact. Nobody could show me where Lenny was hiding. Because I was the one who hid him.

The woman walked directly to the back of the F-150 and hopped onto the curb. I recognized her as a kindred spirit. She navigated the street with the style of a true MC. Fluid. So I knew where she was going, but with her flow I just sat back for a moment and witnessed. She quickly tiptoed along the curb like it was a balance beam and trailed her fingers along the truck's perfectly buffed maroon paint job.

She raised her left hand and hit the button to unlock the doors. The F-150's cabin and headlights lit up.

I started my car; turned my lights on.

She didn't even sniff in my direction.

No doubt, it was a set-up, just like everything else in the previous six days. Except this time I came prepared.

I waited until she bound around the front of the truck.

She pulled out the side-view, opened the driver's side door, and climbed in.

I reached over and opened the glove box. The door swung open to reveal a nickel plated thirty-eight. Yup, still there. It had better be, I just picked it up on the way over. It shone like a buffed out katana. I snapped the glove box shut before the steel mesmerized me into a feeling of raw power.

Pulled my car up next to the truck and pinned it into its parking spot.

Bobbed my head as I turned the music down. I was listening to "The Genesis." It was the first song off Nas' classic debut *Illmatic*. "The Genesis" started with the sound of a subway car rolling on elevated tracks. Perfect start. Every cheap story about Chicago started with the El train rolling in the background.

It'd be a sucker move to follow this F-150 on an anonymous tip. I knew that. But I could play along if I did it my way. Bobbing my head to silence was just me being me.

It was open season in Chicago. The city had spent forty-three of the last fifty-odd years under the rule of one family. Now with their reign ending, Chicago was a city for sale. Lately it felt like even the streets could be sold out from under me.

When I looked over at her, the truck's windows were still up. The truck stood higher than my car, so she was looking down at me.

Everything changed the instant our eyes connected. I knew this woman. If she was my adversary, then I better pay attention.

I rolled my window down and mouthed, "Not your car."

I got a good look at her while her window slid down. Her face recalled an Egyptian princess with purple eye make-up streaked back to her temples. Her skin wouldn't even recognize a blemish. Her bright lip-gloss glistened with the reflection of streetlights. Everything was set in these high, regal cheekbones that angled inward to a narrow sharp chin. Her whole face refused to reveal a hint of emotion or thought. Cold.

With her window fully lowered she asked, "Excuse me?"

Her name was Gesso. She was a Chicago street legend.

"I said, that's not your car." I ran data after the phone call, and knew the truck belonged to a guy in Hegwish — at the opposite end of the city.

"That's right. You know why you're here, Bones." She said my name like it was familiar. She softened her tone, but not her face, and said, "Now come along; let's go."

"No," I said.

She didn't react.

"I'm not following anyone anywhere," I said. I decided to play dumb for a minute, and act like her legend didn't precede her, "Unless I know who you are and where we're going."

"I'm the blank slate," she said.

"Got an awful lot of paint on your face to be blank," I said.

"You got game, Bones." She said my name again and again made it feel natural.

I got the feeling she was trying to lull me into feeling familiar. Familiar wasn't a feeling I did well. I said, "I'm deep enough in this to know you're not taking me to Lenny."

"No, no I'm not," she said, "I came to talk."

"This street is as good as any," I said. I kept my left hand on my steering wheel. My right hung limp in my lap.

I was too impatient to take this conversation a breath further. I had walked into two ambushes in the past couple days. I decided to stay ahead of this one.

Reached over and flipped the latch to open the glove box. I made sure I moved slow enough to not trip up. Put my hand in the open glove box and real slow like pulled out the gun. Second time I held it. Second time I held a gun of any kind. Checked the safety and pointed it at her.

I swear I saw her right eyebrow give a faint lift, and her lips a quick, taut smile.

"Now," I said, "I'm done playing. Give it to me simple."

At that I put my thumb on the thirty-eight's hammer. Except, I didn't want it to go off. I didn't know what would happen if the hammer slipped from under my thumb and clicked back to its resting position. Instead I just rested my thumb across the hammer, tried to make it look natural.

"Easy enough, Bones," Gesso said, her voice sounded simply satisfied like she was choosing between two colors of nail polish. "I came to deliver a message," she said, "It's your life. Or Lenny's. You decide."

PART I: **THE GENESIS**

one *Six days earlier.*

My phone rang first thing Friday morning.

"Bones, yo." It was Lenny.

"Working?" I asked.

"Yeah, waiting on JB."

After his last stint in county, Lenny landed a job working for JB Foster's holding company. Talked his way out of the mailroom and into being JB Foster's personal driver. Lenny had been on the job just over a year, and that surprised me by six months. I thought he'd try dealing casual drugs to his co-workers and be locked up again or back on the street. Instead he got promoted.

JB Foster was a hot name around town. He was a South Side success story who donated money by the truckload and attached his name to all sorts of status.

"What're you up to tonight?" Lenny asked.

"Bartender. Dorothy." I could tell Lenny six times in six days my plans for the seventh and he'd forget.

"Oh, yeah, you're locking that down tonight?"

"Or something."

"You should've been with me last night," he said, using his second favorite conversation starter. He began the phone call with his first.

Lenny continued, "Bottle service. Honeys in the bathroom."

"You're done with the pee tests, right?"

"Just," he answered.

Lenny's latest parole was still in effect but thanks to budget cutbacks he only had to fill the cup for sixteen months after his last release.

"So what? You're not comfortable peeing alone in the bathroom any-more?" I joked, "You needed the company?"

His voice sounded like he spoke out the side of his mouth, "I was the guest of a remarkable lady from –" he paused so his brain could claw through last night's haze.

"Forget her name too?" I asked.

"Nah, I got it in my phone."

"Stepping out that quick, huh Lenny? What did you do, ride some rails?"

"Nah, I decided to limit myself to pills," he said, "Easier to manage."

Adderall, no doubt.

The jokes were good. But I didn't like talking until I had two cups of coffee — unless I had a girl next to me.

"What's up, Lenny, you need something?"

"Yeah, uh," Lenny said.

That 'yeah, uh' negated everything we just said. It made our little chat a preamble to his ask.

He said, "Are you watching the news?"

Current events weren't Lenny and my thing, so I asked, "Why?"

"Uh, something's going on."

"On the news?"

"Up here. At JB's. I picked him up in Kenilworth."

JB Foster had an estate in Kenilworth. I find that word "estate" a bit whack, but it definitely fit a house like his with the expanse of Lake Michigan behind it.

Lenny continued, "He got a phone call on the drive in. Said hold off on going to the office. Told me to drive to his loft. Didn't say a word after that."

The old money estate wasn't enough for JB. He also had a new money party loft in the city. It was in the old China Club building.

"Cops were here before us," Lenny said, "WGN just rolled up."

"Who's the reporter?"

"Couldn't see, they're around the corner."

I walked to the living room and turned on my TV. My antennae took a minute to digitize the signal. Lenny was talking about how JB acted seriously strange after the phone call. Didn't say a word to Lenny.

"There's a lot of cops there, Lenny."

"No shit," he shot back, "What are they saying?"

I couldn't listen to the TV and Lenny at the same time. But. They had the news scroll on.

"Hold on." I listened, heard a name. The scroll at the bottom read "MURDER."

"Bobby?" I asked.

"Bobby?" Lenny asked back.

"I heard the name Bobby," I said, "Someone in the building. His first name was Bobby. Bobby something. I'm trying to listen for his last name."

I watched the images on the screen. I wasn't just watching the field reporter. WGN already had b-roll scrolling to help put the story over the top.

"How long you been there?"

I could hear the wheel of Lenny's lighter spin. Then the click. He was quiet for a second — inhaling his cigarette.

When he spoke while exhaling, it had that sound like his mouth was partially paralyzed, "Half-hour."

The images on the TV started to tell a story. Picture by picture. JB Foster with woman after woman after woman. Then the story switched. They showed pictures of JB with the same woman again and again.

First I mouthed, 'Oh, no,' to myself, and then I said, "Aaaaahhhhhhh, not Bobby. Babi."

A couple things surprised me. I was surprised I didn't hear Lenny's chin hit the ground through the telephone. I also couldn't believe Lenny waited a half-hour to call me. Lenny was an instant gratification kind of guy. He couldn't wait for anything.

He waited thirty minutes to call because he had something to think about.

He still hadn't said anything.

In many ways, I stood in my house that day because of Lenny. Because when I was a kid, his family provided a pathetic smidge of comfort in my life. They didn't do enough to make my life turn out better. But it could've been much worse. His mom helped me with stuff like nice hot meals when my mom wasn't around. Or when I got tired of filling up on free refills at Burger King. Basically, when my mom didn't have money in her purse I couldn't steal it. So I went to Lenny's house after school and hung out until dinner.

I carried a primal debt to Lenny for the simple fact that his family fed me when I was hungry. I realized that Lenny was cashing on the favor he had done me as a kid. He just couldn't ask, and his silence was shocking. Lenny could explain or justify anything under the sun. If you knew Lenny like I knew Lenny then you knew his silence was really a question. He was asking if I'd help him.

He knew I would never say no.

I said, "We need to talk. Right?"

He exhaled. Again I could hear how he was speaking through a cloud of smoke.

He said, "Right."

two

Lenny wouldn't give up any information on the phone. I walked him down a line of questions. Tried to get at his involvement in the murder of Babi Patras. He talked as I walked him and then he just stopped.

I cut him loose, "Call me from a pay phone when you leave the station. A pay phone," I enunciated, "I'll pick you up."

Click.

I wore boxer briefs and my ink — that was it. I walked back over to the TV.

Without caffeine I felt like a sack of molasses sat on the back of my head. I was watching TV and drinking water, when I really needed music and coffee.

The reporter on the scene for WGN stayed on camera the whole time. Watching this mega news story from the start was like watching a star implode. Soon enough it would turn into a black hole sucking all other stories out of the news-o-sphere.

I made coffee. I drank two cups while watching WGN. The b-roll featured JB Foster and Babi Patras. Her first name was something long and Greek. Everyone I knew called her by her shortened nickname, Babi. That was back when her and Lenny dated.

She was six feet tall, and could inspect Lenny's scalp over his slouch.

She possessed a deep down beauty that would sound trite when describing a dead woman. She was twenty-four — three years younger than us. Lenny knew her older brother.

Babi Patras took a big step on the social ladder after meeting Lenny's boss, JB Foster. Good-bye to Lenny with his messy hair, slouchy-posture and washed out clothes. Her and JB Foster got serious quick.

I needed to get to work, so I went into the bathroom for a shower.

Whenever I stood before the mirror shirtless, my eyes went straight to my ribs and stomach. At sixteen you could play my ribs for a xylophone and hit all the notes up to my armpits. I was a forgotten kid: crazy mom, middle brother a runaway, my oldest brother murdered. Couldn't even speculate about my dad. Forget about nurturing, nobody was around to even put dinner on the table. As a result I nursed myself on fast food and Ensure. When I didn't have money, I just went hungry.

Bones. That's all I really was back then, a six-foot-two stack of bones. When I was twenty-seven I still wore my nickname like a battle scar.

three

Usually, I rode the Halsted bus to work. That day I drove. I planned on picking Lenny up from the cop shop.

I grabbed a metered spot because I didn't want to pay the full fare at a parking lot.

I ran credit reports for department store credit applications. Anyone who's ever filled out a form to get a fifteen-percent discount at the checkout counter has worked with me. I loved the job. It wasn't that I liked credit reporting, or working with numbers in particular. I liked working and accomplishing shit.

The information told a story. After I learned the ropes I started putting those stories together — a person's address and their credit score were enough information to tell if a particular consumer was a slave to credit or independent minded.

At a party one night, I told a buddy about what I learned at my job. I was twenty-five at the time. He hired me to find out information on his parents — turned out his dad had stolen his identity and taken out a loan.

It just happened naturally. *Hey, uh, Bones, do you think you could.* It started like that. *I could,* I said. Give me a social security number and I could do anything.

After the first job, another friend hired me. I never thought of myself as a fixer or a pro snoop. I did favors for friends, and I ran it like a business. I wasn't interested in a license, or an office, or working with other people. I had no desire to be legit. I just liked the work.

That Friday I got tired of feeding the parking meters by lunchtime. The vampire nightmares of all Chicagoans came true on the day the parking meter contract took effect. They've been sucking the life out of us ever since. By the time I dropped twelve dollars into the machines, it was too late to move to a parking lot. The worst part was orange envelope anxiety. Each time I left my office I ran to the meter to avoid a parking ticket.

I was getting squeezed in the office too. My boss has a quota and a slate of performance statistics that measured his manhood. Lucky for him, work kept my mind off speculating about Lenny's trouble.

Eighteen months on my job and the work was cake. I could pump out results two times as fast as my co-workers. I had the eye for it the way a hip-hop producer had an ear for music. A decent producer could hear a melodic line in a song, between the beats. He could take a three-second sample and match it with a drumbeat he had created himself (or sampled from yet another song). Hip-hop was about layering. The guys who made the music and built the beats and crafted the melodies could tell a story by weaving the layers together.

At the credit-reporting agency that was me. I knew the job so well, I could do two things at once.

All afternoon the harder I worked, the further I could see my boss sink back into his chair. I ran enough data by five o'clock to make his weekend a little less stressful.

As I walked out the door, my mind returned to the thing I was avoiding: Lenny.

I checked my phone for the thousandth time: no call, no text.

At my car an orange envelope was hooked under my windshield wiper. I was two minutes late because my boss kept asking me shit. Fucking parking ticket. I stomped up to my car and whipped it off. I was about to kick the car's fender.

That's when my phone vibrated.

A text.

From Lenny.

I needed to read it twice.

"At home," it said.

Lenny sent a text that he was at home.

I could already hear his excuse about no payphones even though the kid just spent a day in the only place guaranteed to have them.

four

"See any old friends?" I asked standing in Lenny's living room.

"Looked around but, nah, not in homicide. They escorted me pretty quickly through the place. PD is on a mission on this one. Homicide's going to cash in."

"You were supposed to call from a pay phone."

Lenny dragged on a cigarette.

He said, "It's a circus over there, news trucks everywhere. I'm guessing they pulled in every detective to get briefed on this thing. They even had some quiet guy with a suit that followed me from room-to-room."

"Internal affairs," I told him, "Dotting i's and crossing t's."

"Strip-searched me. Printed me even though they got me on file. Seven fucking hours. No smokes." he took another drag.

"Hospitality isn't their strongpoint."

"I wonder how they treated the maid who found the body," Lenny speculated, "Probably had immigration crawling up her ass."

Lenny's voice had no bite in it. His storyteller's charisma was exhausted; there were no comedic hooks or questions in his voice. Used them all up at the PD.

He was hung over from last night and exhausted from the session at headquarters. That was fine. A packed bowl sat next to his cigarettes. That wasn't.

I opened up my phone, and finally replied to his 'At home' text.

I typed, 'Cool. See you tomorrow.'

As I looked him over, my eyes kept returning to the packed bowl.

His head was pinned to the threadbare fake velvet couch he got when his grandma died. He still wore his black slacks from his driver uniform and a white t-shirt. His greasy ginger hair stood whacked-out from him having nothing to do but run his hands through it all day.

I smelled weed inside the cloud of cigarette smoke, so I walked over and turned the TV off.

His phone pinged.

I said, "That's me."

He picked it up to look.

I grabbed the packed bowl off the coffee table and took a hit.

"Who'd you talk to?" I asked after I inhaled.

"Some detective named Glenn. He was a democrat. He was pretty cool though. His partner was there too."

"Straight up homicide talk?" I asked, then exhaled.

Lenny nodded, leaned up to take another drag off his cigarette.

Then he said, "The usual, you know. They tried to squeeze me for information and I told them I didn't know anything. Said I dropped JB off in Kenilworth, headed right to Onyx. There until three or so. Picked JB back up at seven this morning."

He sounded a little punch drunk going through his routine.

Lenny's talking helped me relax. His eyelids were a bit droopy for my liking, but he wasn't broken by a day with the CPD.

Lenny had stamina when it came to the cops.

He had tried and failed at the grift enough times that he should just forget how to spell G-A-M-E. His small time dealing, stealing and rackets got him landed in the joint three times — everything small enough so they were all Cook County bids. Part of Lenny's luck was that he always avoided the State Pen. That meant the only thing hardened about him were his lungs. Lenny had maintained a steady diet of Marb Reds since fuzz first appeared on his sack.

Lenny's voice, which probably would've been pitched naturally high, reverberated through his tar-hardened trachea and came out in a rasp. The few pockmarks on his cheeks held the potential for making him seem rugged. He wasn't rugged. When I looked at Lenny I thought he could be really handsome if he'd just added layering to his hair and tried on a low impact fitness routine.

"Did you give them anything interesting?" I asked.

He nodded, "Had to tell them I dated Babi, they would've found out. We talked about that a lot." he added, "JB's statement won't help. By his words alone I could come off looking pretty bad."

"Drug test?" I asked. Picked the bowl up again, readied it for my lips.

He nodded during another inhale of his cigarette.

That was bad. I decided to not take another hit.

Lenny let his neck go slack. The cigarettes might have perked him up if it wasn't for the weed and depleted dopamine pulling him down. His head fell all the way back against the couch again. His pupils had pushed everything back, so his eyes were these two gigantic black dots.

"Get suspended from work?" I asked.

I had to wait for him to exhale again.

"With pay," he said, his smile showed victory. "JB had this chick from HR waiting for me when I left the station. I liked her. Cutie from Tinley Park. She was ice cold though when she handed me the letter from his lawyer."

Lenny could've talked more and more about less and less.

I told him, "Lenny, you said you needed to talk in person. I'm here."

What followed was the longest stretch of silence I've seen him have since watching him sleep on my couch.

I had a slight buzz from the weed hit. I sat in a chair and let Lenny breathe and work his way through it. I watched as he lit another cigarette.

I looked around, but checked his face every ten seconds or so. Watched every lip part and raised eyebrow. After a drag he'd use his free hand to aggressively wipe his mouth clean. I knew him so well, I could feel his story being assembled in the silence.

This is Lenny, I kept repeating to myself. I understood the whole of his life better than I knew my own. Knowing the whole, and repeating that to myself, made me feel ready for what came next. When he finally spoke I wasn't as shocked as I could've been.

"I'm in trouble."

I alone could talk Lenny into a corner, and find out whatever I wanted. I knew even the cops couldn't do that.

His dark pupiled eyes were set wide. He had much more than a couple weed hits in his system. He wasn't sniffling or swallowing back his post-nasal drip. It wasn't coke. He also had a strict policy not to puncture his space suit. It wasn't heroin.

In an ideal world, Lenny would be on his game — stone sober. Maybe doing push-ups and all sweaty in preparation for what comes next. But Lenny wasn't the physical type. And his de-facto escape route from life's pressures was always chemically enabled.

Lenny probably figured he needed something to take the edge off after seven hours at HQ. He succeeded on that front. All his edges were off.

He pulled hard on his second cigarette in silence. The ashtray held half a pack of butts and waited for more.

I put my chin in my hand. "Just lay it out, Lenny."

Impatient as I was, the wait didn't kill me. It took forever. It took a half-sec. It didn't matter.

He said, "Someone paid me for access to JB's apartment last night."

"How'd you give them access?"

"Keys. I swiped a set, made copies, and returned the originals before JB noticed. There's a side door along Des Plaines Street that people can use to avoid the doorman and security cameras. They gave me two weeks to give them access or the deal was off. No one was supposed to be in the apartment when they showed up. I had to wait til a night when I dropped JB off in Kennilworth to be sure."

As Lenny laid the story down, I knew it was the first time he spoke those words. If this was a recording studio, Lenny could've walked in, laid out his rap and walked out. First take, nailed. No need to revise. He wasn't confused or hesitant.

"How much?"

"Twenty-five thousand."

"Who was he?"

"This guy Albert Brongel I met at Onyx. Wasn't for him though. We're cool. He was speaking for someone else. I insisted on meeting the guy. He was this older hard-ass looking guy with a dark black crew cut. I saw him last night for the exchange. He's the one that handed over the money bag."

"Check the bag for any devices?" I asked.

Lenny was sitting forward, elbows on knees, inhaling again.

He nodded.

Lenny aided a break-in. The break-in led to a murder. Lenny went to a club to spend his hard-earned money. I wanted to believe him, but it would only be a good alibi if the murder occurred late enough.

"They say what they wanted?"

"Information."

"What kind?"

Lenny shrugged. It was beside the point.

It was all beside the point except for Lenny's involvement.

I stood up and went to his kitchen to boil water. The kid didn't even own a teapot. I used a saucepan: filled it, set it on the stove, and watched. I stared into the aluminum pan and thought about what it would be like to stand inside that water as it went from cool to a rolling boil.

I could almost feel the burn on my skin when the water in the saucepan started to shimmy. When I knew it was hot, and ready to boil, I dipped my fingertips in and quickly drew them out.

Lenny was on the run. That's what I decided watching the water get hot. He just didn't know it. Lenny had twenty-five grand and was in the early stages of ingesting his escape. No, Lenny would never do suicide. Just the opposite. He was ramping up to a bender that would occupy him til the investigation ended.

Lenny didn't understand that, for him, his game was over. At the sign of the first tiny bubbles in the saucepan, I went back to Lenny.

He was still sitting on the couch, another butt in the ashtray.

I said, "Please tell me the money isn't here."

Lenny shook his head.

"Can you get to it without anyone seeing you?"

He answered, "Yeah, I got that all covered, no worries."

"How much did you blow last night?"

"Thousand or so."

That converted to two grand at Lenny's rate of exaggeration. He would have attracted a lot of attention. The kind of attention that came with bottle service and women crowding up his booth like he was in a music video. It would be money well spent if it paid for his alibi. He shouldn't count on it.

I went back to the kitchen. The water was boiling, so I turned it off.

Found the Folgers crystals in his cabinet and made him a cup, plenty of milk and sugar.

I brought it out, laid the coffee right in front of him.

"You're going back to jail, Lenny," I said.

"What're you talking about, Bones," he said through a slight slur.

"They did a pee test. Parole violation. You're done."

He fell back into the couch, said "Shit," paused, "Didn't think about that."

As if it was just that one detail he didn't consider.

"I suggest you pack a bag and leave," I said.

"Where can I go?"

"You should hide deep til they find the murderer. Because whoever did it is going to come looking for you."

He tried to put a look in his eyes that suggested clarity. I watched as the flight instinct shot through the chemicals and herbals in his blood. Lenny didn't know how to fight.

I asked "Can you get the money easily?"

He moved his lips, "Yeah," but didn't make a sound. After a quiet minute, he said, "I don't know what to do."

I paced through his house eyeing the things he should pack. In the back of my mind I needed to decide if I was helping him, or he was using me.

Next to his TV he had a cheap stereo rack — the kind with detachable speakers. One speaker rested sideways with CDs stacked on it.

I saw the case to Nas' *Illmatic* on top. My CD. He borrowed it last time he got out of county and whenever I visited him here I usually got high enough to forget about taking it back.

I picked up the case, and opened it.

It was empty.

"Bastard," I said about Lenny. I hated when people stacked CDs on top of each other and didn't put them back in the case. I started fingering the pile of naked CDs.

"It's in the player," Lenny said.

I turned on the stereo to marry the CD with the case. Then I thought of a simple test.

"Let me see your phone," I said.

I navigated his screen. It was six-forty on a Friday night.

I scrolled through his recent calls. A bunch of neighborhood guys had called — they knew he had dated Babi. I then looked at only the outgoing calls. My name was the second of three calls he made today. Just shy of eight this morning. The call previous to mine was to a girl at two-thirty in the morning. That would be Lenny at the club entering a girl's number and making a test call.

The call after mine was made this afternoon to another old friend of ours, The Roach. That explained the weed.

I was his first call this morning. If I was second or third on his call log today, it would've been different. To me, that would've meant he wanted to use me, and I would've let Lenny flutter in the wind. But he called me first, and that made me feel important.

I turned his phone off, but kept it in my hand.

"Do you want help?" I asked.

Lenny was busy inhaling his cigarette. It was good cover for him. Kept him from saying, *yes, I need help.* Instead he just nodded his head in a quick line of tight nods.

"Okay," I said, "Then take fifteen minutes to pack a bag. After you leave, go get the money. Order a pizza at Lina's and sit at a table reading a paper while they make it. Leave your car out front with the flashers on. Order it at seven-fifteen. Read all about Babi's murder in the paper and talk to the guys behind the counter about it. Leave at eight when the pizza's ready. I'll be just down the block. I'll pull out when you do, you just follow me."

"Where am I going?"

"I'll know at eight," I said.

"Do you know what you're doing?" Lenny asked.

"Not yet," I said.

Lenny was putting out the cigarette and spilled a few butts over the side of the ashtray onto his coffee table. Again his head bobbed and nodded in agreement.

"I'm keeping your phone," I said and pulled out the battery.

five

I left Lenny's house expecting to see him again in seventy-five minutes.

I drove up Ashland Avenue to Taylor Street and the row of restaurants and bars by the university. I made this drive every other week to visit with friends. That night, I made the drive blind. I found a parking spot close to Hawkeye's Bar.

I could find what I needed inside Hawkeye's.

Before I climbed out, I put the battery back in Lenny's phone and turned it on. I opened up my own phone and held them side-by-side. The two screens lit up my face in the dark car. I scrolled through Lenny's phone, then entered a couple of numbers in mine. Albert Brongel — the middleman — interested me the most. Entered his info first. Then I found the number for the girl Lenny called last night — his alibi — and entered hers.

In the two short minutes it was on, Lenny's phone blew up with texts. Before I accidentally hit a button and answered someone's message, I pulled the battery out again and put the phone in my glove box.

Hawkeye's Bar was a neighborhood institution for the university and surrounding medical campus. Since there weren't any normal sports bars around there, the crowd was a decent mix of North and Southsiders. Wherever I went I always rocked a White Sox baseball cap. That way everyone knew I rep'ed the South Side.

I kept my chin down and I navigated the crowd.

I hooked around the bar, walked up on Scotty Smuda as he drained a Miller Lite bottle.

"Frankie just left," Scotty said, "I'm heading out too."

"Let's talk here for a minute," I said as I tapped his shoulder with the back of my hand.

Scotty raised his hand into the bartender's sight line for one more beer.

"Water," I said when the bartender looked my way.

"What are you up to tonight?" he asked.

"Got a date later," I said.

"What color is she?" Scotty asked. That was the first question the guys always asked me when it came to girls.

"Lily white, Scotty," I said. The veiled racist comments always made me cringe, "She's a bartender up on the North Side."

"Oh, coming home are we?" he joked.

"Maybe just a visit."

The dating conversation had to be done. That's just the way we talked. I liked how we looked like old friends talking in a bar, nothing else.

I cut to the next topic of conversation, "How's the rental market these days?"

Scotty Smuda was the one rich kid I knew. His dad helped him buy a decent inventory of buildings across the near South Side. He also ran a contracting business — mostly kitchen and bath remodels — on the North Side.

Scotty had apartments, Lenny needed a squat.

Between swigs of beer he admitted he did have one empty apartment in a Canaryville three-flat. He said, "Rent's cheap and the neighborhood doesn't justify a rehab. So the place is kind of shitty."

"Been vacant a while?" I asked.

Scotty nodded.

I knew I was playing it overly cautious. There wasn't an obvious need to speak in code with Scotty. Nobody watched us. Nobody followed me. But Lenny could be a murderer as far as I knew. It made sense to tip toe into the conversation.

He raised an eyebrow and nodded back, "You want to check it out?"

I didn't want to fake like we were playing spy games or some shit. I didn't want to toy with him. I told him, "Nah, I don't want to check it out. Lenny needs a squat."

Scotty was two inches taller than me. He wore a black White Sox cap like mine but the brim on his was curved and worn. I replaced mine on Opening Day every year.

He looked up over my hat, scanned the room and asked, "You want to talk about it here?"

"Sure," I said, "Nothing to worry about."

His eyes darted to the bartender, "Nobody's listening?"

I laughed, "No, Scotty, nobody's listening," and pointed out, "You hear anyone else's conversation."

Still, he dropped his voice before asking, "Nobody's watching?"

"Nhhho," I laughed again, "Nobody's watching. You're here every Friday. You couldn't even count the number of times I met you here over the years. So there's nothing odd. Nothing strange. Nothing out of the ordinary."

Scotty glanced sideways at the bartender. Then looked back at me and asked again, to be sure, "We can talk straight?"

"You think he's gonna say something?" I asked, pointed my thumb over my shoulder to the bartender. "Your tips probably paid for half his tattoos. So, no. No need to creep around like you do with your secret lover."

His eyes popped. He couldn't control the goofy smile that overtook his face. He tried to get composed, swallowed his beer hard.

Scotty said, "What are you talking about, Bones?"

"I could care less right now Scotty," I told him, "I'm sure nobody else knows. But I can tell. You've been talking about women differently and less often. Just slightly. And you know I'm always paying attention."

It wasn't just Lenny that I felt like I knew better than I knew myself. When I came up I valued Scotty's, Lenny's, and Frankie's lives more than my own. They had families like I wanted. Because of that fact, I assumed they were better people than me. So I watched them intently, and ever since I was young I felt in-tune with their manners.

"Don't worry about it," I told him, "Whoever you're creeping with, it's on the DL."

Scotty took a drink from his beer. It was clearly a stall tactic. He wanted to change the subject.

Scotty put the beer down and asked, "I'll do you this favor, but you just know that by saving Lenny you aren't straight in my eyes. And I know you can save Lenny — put your mind to anything, Bones, and you got it. I've always known that. But you better think about upping your game and finding Vanni."

My oldest brother was officially a missing person. But everyone knew that wasn't the case.

Scotty nodded. He asked, "What if the cops find Lenny in my building?"

"You left the door open. Lenny got in on his own. I'll return the key to you so the set isn't missing," I told him, "and there won't be a copy to be found. Anywhere."

That wasn't far fetched. Lenny had worked for Scotty plenty of times. When he couldn't find a job, Scotty'd always hire him to paint and fix simple things in his buildings.

Scotty seemed to accept that, so I added, "If you're cool with it, give me the key and I'll drop it back with you later. Then you forget you saw me tonight. We talk again in a week or so."

Scotty took two long pulls off his beer, cocked his eyes so he could see me over the side of the bottle.

He set the empty bottle down. Looked at the bottle, then at me.

Scotty nodded as he stared at the empty brown bottle. Used his thumbnail to scrape a thick piece of the label off. Then his nod slowed to a stop.

Looked up at me and said, "Got a set of keys in my truck. I'm on Lafflin south of Taylor. Give me a minute, I gotta take a piss. Pull up alongside me in five."

"Make it three," I said. I still had two errands to run.

six

Forty minutes remained until I met Lenny again. First I needed to head home. On my way I swung by the pizza shop I had told Lenny to order from. I slowed my car to a crawl as I drove past. His car wasn't out front with the flashers on. He wasn't perched at the one table inside either.

Twice today I had asked Lenny to follow my lead - call me from a pay phone at the police station and then order a pizza and wait. He had ignored me both times.

I sped up and navigated the one-ways and the traffic lights to get across Halsted to my house. I turned down my alley. That's when I realized how fast I was driving. The tight space amplified my speed as I shot through the gauntlet between garages.

Turned my car off. I sat stunned inside my garage. Here I was hustling around to help him out, and all he did was whatever he wanted.

I decided right then and there - this was the end of his line. I wasn't helping him again. I would be at the pizza shop at eight and if he wasn't, we were finished. If he was there, then I'd take him to his squat. If he violated any of my arrangements — like no leaving the squat, or no phone calls — then that was it. Only Lenny could decide how long this went on.

I could never deny that Lenny's family fed me when I was hungry. That's why I answered whenever he called. This was a murder rap though. This wasn't stealing my bag of weed, or taking my CDs. This wasn't hitting on girlfriends or leaving me stranded at a party when I didn't have a car. This wasn't juvenile. This was my work, and that was the difference.

Before I jumped from my car and ran into my house, I made that decision. Before I grabbed my sleeping bag and two towels and a sheet and a bar of soap from my closet. Before I sped to the grocery store. And before sweat dripped down my back as I reached into the grocery store freezers to grab enough frozen pizzas and burritos for a week, I decided as I sat in my garage. This was it for Lenny. This would be my final payback.

seven

At eight-eleven Lenny pulled his car off the curb and followed me.

With the right pieces in play I finally relaxed enough to slide Nas' *Illmatic* into the player. Long time no listen. I obsess over great albums. When I was a kid, I did a stint with *Illmatic* when I listened to it once a day forever. After two years this joint was part of my DNA.

Lenny followed me a mile west to McKinley Park. We stopped on a half-empty side street on the far side of the park.

Before Lenny could budge from his seat, I climbed and marched to his door to prevent him from getting out. Whirled my finger for him to roll down his window.

I could hear the rock station blaring through glass.

"What?" he said when his window lowered.

"What'd you do, Lenny?" I said, the accusing tone reaching out ahead of me, "I drove by Lina's and you weren't parked out front."

"The fuck you talking about, Bones, I saw you there. I followed you here."

I didn't yell. Neither did he.

"Seven-twenty-five, Lenny," I said, "You weren't there. Neither was your car."

He squinted his eyes hard, like he couldn't comprehend. "I had to get cigarettes. And went for the cash. And picked up some fucking food, dude. You think I had time to just sit there?"

The coffee I made Lenny, and the time, had done him well.

I gave up on pressing him. I didn't want to argue and attract attention. I said, "Just pop your trunk," and walked back to my car.

The spare tire in my Camry was housed under the floor of my trunk. The floor was made up of industrial grade carpet on top of a piece of heavy-duty plastic. Like with most cars, the plastic floor of the trunk lifted up to reveal the spare tire. I reached in and held the plastic down with one hand and peeled back the carpet with another. The strips of Velcro I had installed ripped apart and the carpet peeled back to reveal a display of Midwestern license plates: Wisconsin, Indiana, Ohio and Michigan. Last summer I followed the White Sox to some away games and picked them up as souvenirs.

I chose Indiana.

Lenny sat in his car smoking until I wiped my prints from his license plates and tossed them into his trunk.

I pulled two grocery bags filled with chips and cookies out of his trunk and told him, "There's another bag. Grab it," and walked to my car.

The hideout apartment was in Canaryville, the neighborhood to the south of Bridgeport where I lived.

Lenny and I drove in silence.

eight

Inside the squat, I loaded up his freezer with burritos and pizzas while he got the bedroom situated.

When I finished stacking the food I said, "Alright, let me see the money."

Lenny came out of the bedroom and placed a plastic grocery bag on the kitchen table.

"No paper sleeves holding them together," I said, "That's good."

The money was all worn bills rubber-banded together in sloppy stacks. Not at all like a thin brick of crisp new money. Made sense. Serialized bills could be traced. Whoever paid Lenny didn't want the money to leave a trail. Still, I wasn't going to take chances. I needed to do my own laundry.

I checked the clock on my phone. I had time to run to Gary, Indiana and wash a couple of thousand bucks. Then I could jet right back to Dorothy's restaurant so we could hang out after her shift ended.

Lenny sat at the kitchen table and picked up a square of Lina's pizza. I went into the bedroom to check on his set up.

My sleeping bag lay open on the floor. Lenny had spread the sheets out on top of it. The TV was plugged in and the towels I grabbed from my house sat folded on top of the TV. Nice work.

I stood for a minute and looked it all over. Lenny couldn't leave. He couldn't move around too much. He was basically going to sit here and watch TV for the next week.

"You'll be alright, Lenny," I said as I walked from the bedroom. I stood over him and scooped a square of pizza off the cardboard. "Reminds me of that time when my brother Stephen ran away and my mom went off the deep end."

During the span of two days my middle brother ran away and never came back. The next day my mom took off to England — she had this schizo thing about thinking she was Lady Di. Vanni had been murdered a year earlier. At twelve, I was abandoned and alone.

I had been forging my mom's name for years, so I sent a letter to school and spent two weeks watching TV. When I returned to school, I wasn't the same. I couldn't say my childhood before that was any good. Not that I had actual feelings about this at the time. The effects of abandonment remained invisible to me for years.

At twenty-two I landed my first salaried job. A little at a time I started to show signs. I was in control and could thrive on my own. I began to let my guard down.

There were a couple things I mastered being abandoned and hungry at twelve. I knew survival. I also became an expert on other people's lives.

At twenty-seven I could honestly say I was insane for most of my life. That's when I was coming into my own. Working for a living made me feel like it was my time to shine.

I couldn't tell if Lenny was coming down from his high, or just not listening.

I peered into the bag of money again. I pulled it out. I re-stacked it. I didn't have to re-stack it, but it was fun to handle. Then I peeled off a G and handed it over to Lenny. Put the rest back in the bag.

I truly hoped the murder case never touched Lenny. I hoped the CPD would find and book the murderer. If they booked JB Foster it would be a trial for the ages. But regardless of what happened with Babi Patras, the next time Lenny popped his head out the CPD would slip cuffs on his wrists. Lenny told me it usually took four to five business days to get his pee test back. I figured he had until tomorrow morning.

"Hang tight, Lenny," I stood up and offered up a fist bump.

He offered up the back of his hand because his fingers were too sloppy from the pizza to make a fist.

I told Lenny I wouldn't be back for seven days. Next Friday night. Not a word. Not a visit. Nothing. No phone calls. Don't even take the garbage out.

"If you run out of toilet paper, just use the bar of soap," I said, "Don't go out."

Lenny seemed distracted and didn't have much to say.

I turned and reached for the door.

"Why now, Bones?" Lenny asked.

I was standing with one hand on the doorknob.

I turned back around, "Why now what, Lenny?"

"Why are you helping me like this now? After all these times? After everything I pulled. After county. I'd go smoke crack in the ghetto and you never said a thing. You'd just make these comments. *I'm glad I'm not you*, and shit like that."

I hated history. The last thing I expected to hear with his survival on the line was this one thing I had said to him when I was eighteen.

I said, "Lenny Supinski. Get your head in the game. This game right here," I pointed to the ground, "You said after the last time you got out, that you're never going back. Did you mean it? Bringing up anything we did or said when we were eighteen isn't going to mean a thing right now."

I paced in front of him.

He looked too tired to argue. He needed to swing his head in a big swoop to help whiplash the words out, "Oh, you're so fucking self-righteous, Bones."

"That's right," I said, "I consider it a major accomplishment."

He didn't say anything to that.

A Coke can ashtray was on the table in front of him. He pushed the cigarette around the opening, used the razor-thin tin to slice the embers off. Dropped the butt in and I heard the embers fizzle in the dregs. Once the can was filled with ashes and butts, he couldn't take it to the alley. He couldn't even throw out the garbage for fear of being spotted. This little shithole was Lenny's ecosystem for the coming week and he was filling the air to his liking.

Lenny twisted his panties up and said, "So, I'm supposed to feel blessed now? Mr. Holier-than-thou decides to come off his perch to save me?"

Sarcasm was new to Lenny — like the rest of us he was a natural.

"You know, Lenny, thankful and appreciative would be a good start. But don't worry about that. You called me; I answered."

"And now you're walking out with my bag of money," he said.

"Jesus Christ," I said and held the bag up for him. "Want to get caught with it? Or do you want to just go back to your apartment? We don't have to do any of this. Not a thing."

He spat out the word, "Shit" with a big puff of smoke.

We both sat silent for a minute. The conversation had gotten away from us. It had come to the point where we said exactly what we were feeling. Neither of us was equipped to do that.

I figured sitting here with a carton of smokes and the TV would be the easiest time he'd ever do.

I headed for the door a second time.

"What are you going to do?" Lenny asked once I had it open and was ready to step through.

I looked up at the ceiling and said, "Everything I can."

I didn't want to ask if that was enough for him.

nine

I took the streets of Chicago personal. That's why I felt betrayed by the Skyway.

The Skyway was a stretch of toll road that connected Chicago with Gary, Indiana. The toll kept traffic light. That was nice. It was rarely policed. That was a bonus. What I loved about it was the landscape.

The Skyway hung over the skyline of South Chicago. After the toll-booth and the down slope from the bridge, the Skyway came to ground among Chicago's industrial wasteland.

As my car sprinted toward the casinos in Gary, I reveled in the familiar scene: a fossil fueled power plant. Small-scale oil refineries. Steel mills. Manufacturing sites. The surrounding land was filled with all the smelly necessities of city life that people downtown in the Loop worked so hard to keep out of sight. Water inlets wove through the landscape too. I usually drove the Skyway in the early mornings or late at night. Regardless of the time, a handful of trawlers were always fishing catfish in the still waters off Lake Michigan.

The Skyway was exactly the same as it had always been. Except the city sold it a couple years back to make up for budget shortages. I never minded paying tolls to the city, or the woman working the tollbooth. After the sale, I hated paying tolls to a corporation for the privilege to drive on a road.

My nightmare had come true — the streets had been sold out from under me.

It was still the quickest route to Gary. I drove it right to a casino.

At the blackjack table, I laid out two hundred bucks. The dealer was a scrawny middle-aged black woman from Gary. She had a nice smile. There was a couple of button-down preppies I figured had just rolled over from Munster. And a gelled-up dude who looked like someone from Hegwish should look. The Hegwish guy had enough gel in his hair that you could see his scalp through the spikes. His girlfriend saw his gel, and matched it with a spray tan. I nodded at the two of them. The yuppies from Munster kept to themselves.

I had to wait three hands before I won. Then I won another.

"Here we go," I said aloud and pulled the roll from my pocket.

I laid out two grand. Everyone looked.

I wore my typical outfit: black and red Jordan Flights, dark jeans, a black long sleeve T, and my black White Sox cap. White T shirts were my thing, but I had the black long sleeves on to cover up my tats while I moved Lenny earlier. I kept the sleeves on here in the casino too.

I kept my chin down, letting the brim from my cap hide my face.

I won another. Then lost two.

"That's it for you, lady," I said, smiling at the dealer. I tossed her fifty bucks of Lenny's money, swept up the rest, and walked away.

I played roulette and fifteen minutes of Caribbean Stud. I had bought four grand in chips, and cashed out thirty-six hundred. Forty minutes later I drove back to the city.

ten

"No hat?" Dorothy asked when I walked in.

I threw my thumb over my shoulder, "In the car."

This was my fourth time there. I sat at the bar with a view of the TV. The Bulls game had two minutes left. They were away against the Nuggets.

The restaurant had a French name, but everyone called it The Promenade.

Dorothy left me as I settled in. She stopped four spots down the bar for a quick chat with a couple on a date. There were only a few tables with people still eating. It was eleven at night.

I was here at the perfect time. I could grab the last food before the kitchen closed. It made me feel everything regarding Lenny had worked out perfectly earlier.

"Yeah," Dorothy said when she came back. She held a tight smirk on her face. She dropped her chin to her chest, mocking me. Then she repeated my order from the very first time I stopped in, "Lemme get a fruit cocktail."

"And a glass of seltzer," I tacked on quickly.

"Sounds like a real man to me," she said and laughed.

"Except make it a burger, medium." I was starving.

"Now that does sound like a real man to me."

It was rare finding someone with a quicker wit than mine, and Dorothy was fast. Dishwater blond, tall and fine; she made a lot of tips.

Got her number last Friday and texted back and forth a few times before agreeing on a drink when she got off tonight. My mouth can get the best of me, so I didn't count on the drinks until we were drinking.

I don't drink much. I'll sip a cognac, especially when I roll up and watch the game somewhere for three hours. On a sixteen-dollar Hennessy I tip one hundred percent for the three-hour perch. I rarely have more than a drink or two in a night. But I always pack my one-hitter.

The couple at the bar saw I was cozy with Dorothy and tried to chat me up.

The guy was a funnyman. His hands were always waving while his shoulders perpetually hunched up. He kept his head still.

He waved Dorothy over for his latest. I decided to listen.

"Right?" he asked Dorothy, "Women are like cats." Then he lays a palm out to Dorothy asking for her agreement, "Right? You can't just reach out and grab them. They've got to come to you."

He was on that dog versus cat analogy I had heard a thousand times. He set it up nice: good pacing, decent diction. He kept it going and the women giggled as he riffed. He was having a great time in his blue velvet sport coat and button down. Northsider.

When I watched people have fun like that it usually pissed me off. I'd normally be like, what the fuck does this guy know? Think to myself that he learned this funny armchair philosophy in the pages of Details Magazine or some shit like that.

I didn't think like that that night. I was hyped to hang with Dorothy, so I didn't let those thoughts take hold. I thought about having fun, and not killing my chances too soon.

Instead, I nodded. I was with him.

He continued riffing. He mimicked a dog sniffing, talked about crotches and armpits. He did a decent job entertaining Dorothy and his date for a few minuets. They were both laughing at the sniffing part.

But he couldn't get past the initial metaphor. It was all about approaching women, and letting them come to you. Problem with the routine was it didn't go anywhere. It felt like an MC who wasted a good opening line.

I just had to chime in. "It's a good analogy, no doubt," I said, "But it goes further than that. Once the cat starts rubbing up on you, you've really got to get under their fur. You can't just pet nicely on the surface."

The girls nodded. The guy listened.

"You've got to get up in the cat's business," I continued.

I had dated girls with cats. I knew how it went.

I strung the riff out a little bit. Described feeling a cat's musculature below the coat of fur and thick skin. They giggled, so I knew it was working.

"You're right though," I said pointing at the guy, "You don't get anywhere without the right approach." I had to give him his props, it was the right thing to do.

Then I finished by saying, "But to really get over you've got to know how to pet the pussy."

Game over.

Dorothy's sparkling green eyes bugged out in surprise. She kept them on me the whole time she laughed.

The guy's date laughed too. After her laughter calmed down, she lifted up her martini glass and tilted her head to the side and mouthed, 'True.'

The guy gave me a fist bump.

Dorothy's laughter calmed to a giggle. Her great eyes were still blazing though. She twisted her tongue into a corkscrew and clamped down on it with her teeth. Then she walked away.

That was it. I had danced at the edge of appropriateness and yet kept it from achieving all-out vulgarity. I'm always on that edge of appropriateness. Sometimes it doesn't come out the right way. Tonight I brought it home.

I waited at the original Bar Louie while she finished work. At the bar she drank two beers, and I sipped another cognac.

I kept her laughing and interested enough that she invited me back to her place. I didn't push it when I got there. After forty-five minutes of some serious kissing and heavy petting, she kicked me out.

eleven

Saturday morning there were two things I couldn't do. I couldn't check on Lenny. And I couldn't wait around. Waiting around was a sucker's game. If I decided to wait, it seemed like the only thing I'd be doing — waiting for the cops to hang charges on Lenny. Then what? Waiting to see what evidence they had? Then I'd have to wait for them to test the evidence to see if it held weight. If I was a lawyer, then waiting would be my game. I wasn't a lawyer. I wasn't anything.

Still, I didn't know what to do. So I talked myself through it as if I were a baby.

If I was a friend of Lenny's (I was) and if I was concerned about him (I was) and if Lenny had texted me last night that he was at home (he did) and if I texted him back to say I'd see him today (I did), then I guess I'd have to go see him today.

Point by point it made sense.

So I went to Lenny's apartment.

Lenny lived on the other side of the neighborhood. It wasn't quite a mile away. I should've driven and saved the walking time. I didn't. I walked up to the Dunkin Donuts, grabbed a coffee, and headed down Thirty-First to Lenny's spot.

A squad car was parked in front of Lenny's apartment, next to a gun metal grey Crown Vic.

Lenny lived in the refitted office suite of an old warehouse. The warehouse was the size of a three-car garage. The space was too small to be really functional in today's economy. A Northsider rented the warehouse space for his carpentry shop.

When I walked up to the front door it was wide open.

I stood in the doorway and yelled in, "Hello."

"Who's that?" a loud voice boomed.

"Name's Bones. Lenny here?" I still couldn't see who was talking.

A uniformed cop came out from the back of Lenny's apartment.

He thrust a flat palm at me, "Stay there."

"Can I come in?" I pretended like it was cold. It was November in Chicago, not cold.

"I said, stay there," again his hand jutted out to re-assert his authority.

"What happened? Is Lenny inside?" I asked.

The cop just walked away. I should have walked too.

A minute later a detective walked out from the back of the apartment. His afro was cut short. He was smaller than me, maybe five-nine. Looked muscular but not muscle-bound. He had a long face that was mostly jaw.

"I'm Detective Glenn," he said through his upper lip. He tilted his chin down, like me, when he spoke.

I nodded, "Lenny here?"

"What's your name?"

"Bones, everyone calls me Bones."

"Okay, Bones," he shifted weight, between his feet, "No, Lenny's not here. Were you expecting to see him?"

"Yeah, I told him I'd stop by today. I wanted to talk to him about Babi." It was best to appear up-front.

"Babi Patras?"

I hunched my shoulders, like, *who else?*

"When was the last time you saw Lenny," Glenn asked.

I played the part. And at the same time I was the part. Took me a minute before I could come up with an answer, "I dunno man. Maybe a week ago? I don't see him too much anymore. We're just old friends."

"The last time you talked to him?"

"Yuh, yesterday," I said, "He called to say he was going into the police station."

Glenn shifted his weight from one balanced position to the next, tilted his head in interest, "Why would he call you yesterday?"

I told Glenn the real deal — that Lenny wanted me to check my TV when the news crews showed up in front of JB Foster's loft.

"Why would Lenny call you?"

I could feel Detective Glenn lifting up a kind of leverage bar with his words. Ready to bring weight down on me. I stood up on my toes, looked over his head, and changed the subject, "Lenny's not there is he? Are you guys searching his apartment?"

"Early this morning someone spotted a man forcing his way into the apartment."

"Someone broke into Lenny's apartment?"

"You know a lot about Lenny then?" Glenn asked.

I shrugged, said, "And Lenny isn't in there?"

I pulled out my phone like I was going to call him. I didn't ask for the cop's permission because there wasn't anything to ask. That's how I acted. I threw my eyes in Glenn's direction as I walked away. I didn't want to act like I had an exaggerated need to cooperate with or avoid the cops.

"Bones is it?" Glenn said as I walked away.

I turned back and put the phone to my ear, "Yeah."

"I'll find you when I need you," he said.

That's when I realized I should've left as soon as I saw the squad car parked out front. I had acted right with Detective Glenn, no doubt. But suspicion was his game. I just became a player.

twelve

I walked home and looked through my phone for the name and number I entered last night. Albert Brongel, that was it.

Yeah, I had a house. I bought it last year. It was the first thing I ever considered my own and I held an unhealthy amount of pride in that fact. I earned the right to buy my house, no doubt. But I give a lot of credit to Bridgeport; in a way it was a gift from the neighborhood.

When a Bridgeport house east of Halsted went "For Sale by Owner," it meant two things. The most obvious reason was that people could sell without paying a broker fee.

In my case, the guy selling was this old cop on the brink of retirement.

Initially my lawyer tried to talk me out of the purchase. The lawyer said the cop was untrustworthy – he had committed an unspeakable crime.

Face-to-face the cop seemed harmless. We had exchanged neighborhood names. We both knew people. Neither of us put those names on a pedestal. That sat right with me. He also knew about Vanni and expressed sympathy. Another thing that sat right was the house's illegal apartment. The cop wanted to rent the basement out from me for a year. He was living full time in Michigan City then, and needed the Chicago address for twelve months until he retired.

We Southsiders call a spade a spade. I straight up told the cop what my lawyer said.

The old cop told me that he was a young beat cop in the Robert Taylor Homes. A couple homicide detectives wanted to pin a murder on some nineteen-year-old black kid. He had refused to back up their testimony. The kid went free and the detectives' reputations took a hit. The only person who got punished was the old cop. When I met him he'd been at a boring desk job, with no overtime, for twenty years.

His bungalow was "For Sale by Owner," following neighborhood custom. The house already had an offer in on it from a Chinese family. Chinatown was the next neighborhood to the north, and more and more Chinese were moving into Bridgeport.

The old cop let me underbid the Chinese, and sold the house to me.

That's when the neighborhood "gift" came into play. I bought the house. I earned it. I paid for it. But I didn't get the house because I was the highest bidder. I got it because I was the whitest.

I found the number and called Lenny's middleman, Albert Brongel.

After six rings Brongel's phone went to voice mail.

"I'm a friend of Lenny's, we might have met once," I lied, "When you and Lenny were hanging out together. He's not home, so I wanted to see if you knew where he was. You've got my number, call me back."

I was on-edge after my talk with Detective Glenn; I moved quickly when I arrived back at my house. I walked into my garage and pulled everything out of my car related to Lenny: his car and house keys, his phone, the bag of money, and the key to his squat.

Inside my house, I went upstairs and turned on my stereo. Put the bass on thump.

Downstairs in the laundry room, I could hear the music throbbing from the floor above me. There was a tool room next to the laundry area.

Behind one wall of the tool room was my stash. I still hustled a little; I only sold to friends. So I didn't buy a ton of inventory — just a couple of ounces at a time. It was nothing at all, really.

I had maintained that small hustle ever since Lenny got in the game. He was the first kid we knew who made big money dealing in high school.

The walls of my tool room were black-stained beaded board — that kind of wood that looked like corduroy with all its vertical lines. I cleared off and removed the shelf I had installed on one wall. When I took the shelf off, it revealed the horizontal seam I had cut into the wood. The vertical seams blended in naturally with the wood's corduroy wale.

I took an Ikea hexagonal tool out from my toolbox and slid it into the seam. Most of the guys I grew up with were in the trades. I had designed this stash box. Then got a carpenter to help me build it. Pressure held the access panel into place — no nails, no screws.

With the Ikea hex tool in the seam, I turned it and pulled. Butter.

The panel opened up on a hidden hinge along the bottom edge. Inside the panel were shelves made from small baskets. My stash was empty.

I opened the plastic grocery bag with Lenny's money in it. I pulled out the four stacks and placed them neatly on the shelves. I wiped down Lenny's keys, phone, and the keys to the squat and set them all in another basket.

Pressing the panel back in, I hoped Lenny was just as safe in his squat. I wanted him to feel as snug as the wood I slid back into place.

My phone rang. Blocked number.

"Yeah," I answered.

"Who's this?" the guy asked sounding vaguely tough and unconvincingly Italian.

"Who's this?" I asked back. I knew it was Albert Brongel. I wanted to delay the conversation. The tool nook shared a wall with the illegal basement apartment. After the old cop retired a couple months ago, I rented the place to a drunk forklift operator. His hangovers kept him incapacitated most weekend days. But it didn't disable his ears.

"Did you call me?" Brongel said, trying to soften up his voice a little.

"Did I? Who are you?"

"What's your name?" he asked, put on his best tone yet to get me to answer.

I walked up into my kitchen and shut the door leading downstairs.

I didn't say anything.

"Hello?" he asked.

I hung up. I walked to the living room and turned down my stereo.

He called back.

"Yeah," I said again.

"This is Albert Brongel, you left me a message about Lenny," he said with a pleasant voice.

Thought so.

"He with you?" I asked.

"No, why would he be?"

It wasn't a stretch to ask. Lenny often partied until he passed out. A lot of nights he wound up on people's couches.

"Just checking. I'm an old friend," I told him, "Wanted to find out the deal with his job. I'm kind of like his AA sponsor, wanted to see what happened with his work after yesterday. You heard about his boss' girlfriend right?"

"Uh, yeah of course."

I couldn't tell Albert Brongel that I wanted to meet. I needed to get him to suggest it. Only then would I have a chance at finding out who had paid Lenny the twenty-five grand.

"How'd you get my number," Brongel asked.

"I think he gave it to me a while back. We were all supposed to meet up at a party or in a VIP room somewhere. We've met before right?" I asked.

"I don't think so," Brongel said.

"I keep tabs on Lenny," I said to move on, "Help him stay straight for his parole officer. The kid's a walking violation, you know?"

I laughed at my joke. He didn't.

"But you said you're an old friend."

"Right," I said. I wanted to say more, but I didn't want to push.

"Listen, bro," Brongel said. Maybe Brongel was a sales guy. He wanted to use my name, and it was the perfect time for it in our conversation—except he didn't have my name. So the 'bro' fit in as a substitute. "We should talk," he said.

That's when I realized I didn't have to play coy. Since I called him, I now embodied the connection between Lenny and Albert Brongel. If the cops came to me, I could lead them directly to Brongel. There was never a chance of us not agreeing to meet.

"Bones," I said, "Everyone calls me Bones."

"You got a real name?" he said.

I could picture him poised with a pen—even nodding to someone else in the room.

"Yeah," I said, spat it out so he'd know it was a stupid question, "I just told you. Bones."

By the time we finished we agreed to meet later that night at some bar on the North Side. That meant I had time to run data on Albert Brongel. And I had time to think through how I'd get info out of him.

Before we hung up, he asked, "How will I know which one is you?"

I smirked to myself. I always felt like I stood out on the North Side. I didn't dress preppy and I didn't talk about stock options. I only accented the differences by always wearing my baseball cap.

I used a line from an old White Sox billboard and told him, "Good guys wear black."

thirteen

At six o'clock I left home and headed into work. When I had a side job to work, I went into the office when nobody was there and ran data.

I focused on Albert Brongel. There was a handful of them in Chicago-land. I wrote down the address of three and figured the guy I was look-ing for was the one who lived on Racine by Wrigley Field. The address put his apartment close to the bar we were meeting at later.

I researched Brongel's vitals. By the looks of it he made about eighty-something a year — pretty good bank if he was twenty-seven like Lenny and I. No mortgage. He had a car payment going to GMC Finance every month. He didn't carry any credit card debt.

Four addresses back on his credit report he lived in Downers Grove on Maple Street, which was the address of another Albert Brongel — his dad. I tried to find a financial tie between the two of them — a co-sign on the car. My data had limits. If I wanted to fill the picture in more, I need-ed to hit the streets.

I liked work. I liked playing music and digging the data. It kept my mind off Lenny.

When the time approached nine o'clock, my research trickled to a drip. That's when I started reading the newspapers on the internet.

Babi Patras was gorgeous. The papers told the story of a girl who moved to the city for college and earned a degree in business adminis-tration. Her uncles owned a couple of suburban Greek diners. The pa-pers said she grew up in Palos Hills, a suburb with a Greek church that drew Greek families. I knew her brother from the party circuit when we were younger. Their family moved out to the burbs before Jim Patras would have to attend Bogan High School. Jim had a city edge; I figured Babi did too.

Babi worked in PR for a high-end restaurant group. The unspoken narrative was that she struck the lotto when she met JB Foster. Looking at her pictures, I could tell she struck the lotto at birth. The quotes from her family showed them to be proud. They spoke as if her and JB were equals. The storyline became The Princess and The Mogul.

The newspapers did their job. Even though I only culled surface facts, they made me feel like I could talk with authority about Babi Patras.

Lenny Supinski didn't get a mention. Yet. No doubt, a reporter knew about Lenny either from his source at the CPD or one of his interviewees. A good reporter or editor would know when to put Lenny's name out there. Not on the first full day of newspaper coverage. That would taint the picture-perfect world they created in print, just so they could shatter that world in the days to come. That's how I figured they'd monetize this story over the next two weeks. Serialize it like a soap opera and inject new characters and evidence whenever the story felt slow.

fourteen

We were meeting at this bar called Red Rocks on the North Side at Sheffield and George. I knew the location. Despite a series of name changes over the years, the bar had always featured the same stuff: cheap beer and cover bands that kept the post-college crowd dancing.

I drove past it. It would be noisy inside; the noise would be good cover. I turned into the neighborhood to the west of Sheffield until I found a parking spot. It took thirty-minutes, I would barely be on time.

I spend plenty of time up here, on the North Side. It's not that I don't like it, but I couldn't live here. I date North Side girls, and whenever we hang out during the day there never seems to be any old people or children. These people had no worries, I always thought. They didn't know stress. Their first couple years' rent was subsidized by their parents. Their cars were too nice. What it came down to was, it cost a lot of money to live in a neighborhood without poor people, or brown ones.

I left my coat in the car.

There was a big North Side vs. South Side divide in Chicago. I think most of the hate traveled upward. The Northsiders I've met just ignored the South Side. They didn't have a chip on their shoulders or speak in awed tones of real estate prices down by me. Southsiders spend a lot of time thinking those things. And that was just the harmless kind of talk.

When I rounded the corner onto Sheffield, the first thing I noticed was a bar called Vaughan's. There were a couple of these around the city. The original South Side spot was legendary for cheap Guinness. All the Irish tradesmen I knew did time there. The same family opened up this North Side outpost. Took advantage of North Side profit margins.

Two doors down from Vaughan's was the spot, Red Rocks.

Chin down, I walked up and noticed a stocky bouncer at the door outside and another inside with a black light scanning IDs. Right there I should've known. It should've been the other way around. You scanned an ID with the black light first. Then entered to pay the cover.

I didn't notice anyone else.

The stocky bouncer out front wore Doc Martens and tactical gear like he got hired from a bouncing outfit that took itself too seriously. I started to breeze past him and get my ID ready.

The guy outside the door stepped up. I should've looked at him. At six feet, I shouldn't have had to look up at all, but that's the way it was walking with my chin down and my White Sox cap on.

People poured into the bar. The crowd wasn't much different from the college bars I never went to when I was in school. I was smart enough to get a degree because that's all college was for me. I was a guy studying so I could get a job. I didn't quite get college life.

At Red Rocks I stood out because I just looked like who I was. Everyone else looked just like they did in college. Except maybe they had upgraded from the J. Crew catalogue to shopping at the store.

I heard a whistle. I should've looked, too. Instead I tried to ignore the outfitted bouncer who took his job too seriously. I stepped past him in the doorway.

He said, "Bones."

I was too surprised to ignore him.

He stretched out his left arm and caught me before I reached the door. His other hand grabbed the back neckline of my shirt, and he threw a solid hip into me. The bump took me off trajectory. Nudged me down Sheffield away from the bar.

There was a group of guys entering, already drunk, who thought I was being bounced. One of them started to giggle and said, "Dude, djou see that?"

I wasn't scared with just this guy on me. I kept calm and held back any resistance my body wanted to put out.

I couldn't feel a gun at his hip or on my back. I walked patiently with him to see if he'd let his guard drop. I figured if Albert Brongel wanted to bring a heavy for our little talk, fine. I would just make it that much uglier for him.

Behind Red Rocks the train rattled overhead. I figured he would lead me behind the building and under the tracks. I was okay with that too. I just had to get this stocky guy's hands off me before we got there. I didn't rush it though.

Lenny had talked once about Brongel being the player, lady's man type. The guy on my hip wasn't him. I scanned the street. I tried to put eyes on Brongel and see if he was standing out there in the darkness, legs akimbo with a put-on tough look on his face.

I remembered this morning, out front of Lenny's apartment. The cops were doing this case by the book. The profile was too high. They wouldn't enter Lenny's apartment without serving a warrant. The detective, Glenn, had said a neighbor reported a break in. That must've been true. I suddenly thought differently about the guy hurrying me along.

I didn't spot Albert Brongel.

Instead this six-six guy with chiseled cheeks and long hair crossed the street diagonally in our direction. He waved his hands away from the bar, gesturing to the stocky guy at my back to move faster. He was about fifteen feet out.

He was wearing police issue patrol boots. From the pocket of his windbreaker he pulled a Taser. It was a compact model, and it had a white swoosh of a logo on it. The swoosh was like a three quarter circle, and it had a star in the middle.

Instead of tensing, I got loose. Couldn't delay. No amount of voltage was going to stream through my skin. As the tall guy hopped onto the curb from the street to the sidewalk, I fell. Just dropped. I lifted my knees to my chest and brought my legs out from under me. If I kept falling my ass would smack into the sidewalk. The guy behind me clenched my shirt at the collar so it rode up and caught me under the armpits.

The stocky guy couldn't do much else other than hold on tight.

The tall guy was now two steps away. As I fell, he both reached for me with one hand and readied his Taser with the other.

I jammed my leg out and kicked the inside of his knee.

He buckled.

The stocky guy behind and above me held the back of my shirt with one hand and threw punches with the other. The first punch landed on my skull. My hard head and the adrenaline saved me from feeling the blows.

I stayed focused on the tall guy. I didn't want that Taser triggered. He was buckled down to my level. Good. I put a hand on the sidewalk for stability and fucking kicked the motherfucker in the teeth. The side of his head. His cheekbone.

He flailed his arms and tried grabbing my legs. I started whipping them back and forth in full freak-out fashion. He couldn't get a grip.

"HEY!" people started to yell.

I wanted to tell everyone to just leave, but a hail of punches landed around my head.

The stocky guy was pulling me up with one hand while punching down on me with his other. The jerking threw me off balance. I was kicking wildly, his jerking me around made the kicks get wilder.

I couldn't do shit without leverage. My hand bounced off the ground with each tug on my collar. My kicks lost force without having a stable plant, but my foot kept glancing off the guy's face and torso. Finally, he fell back and the Taser skidded into the gutter.

I twisted around to punch the stocky guy in the nuts.

Bam. Solid blow.

Until then all his punches had landed on the top of my head and my forehead.

Dude was tough. The blow to the nuts didn't stop him.

When I twisted to hit him, it opened a new angle to my face. He clocked my spectacular nose, and landed one on the corner of my upper lip.

I started motoring my legs. I wanted to catch the pavement and propel myself back up. My legs thrust awkwardly a few times before they caught the ground and lifted.

On my way up I jammed an elbow into the stocky guy's nuts again. He keeled over at the waist.

If Brongel watched, he'd be running.

I got my feet fully under me, and landed a knee to his chest. He was strong, and only staggered back a couple small steps. Again I went for the knee.

I did a little hop step to close the gap quickly. Jumped up but didn't put too much vertical into it. Kicked as I came down and landed my foot on the outside of his knee.

He fell straight to the sidewalk.

When he fell, I saw a crowd of people standing around watching. It was a bunch of kids my age. They didn't have a worry in the world. This to them would be another story. The time they saw some wigger beat two guys up outside Red Rocks.

I didn't know it then, but those kids weren't anything like me. At twenty-seven it still hadn't sunk in yet. Oh, I knew they were limp. Their lives had enough cushion that allowed them to talk stock prices and sports with a depth that made everything else about them seem shallow to me.

That night they had a show. I clocked time on the two heavies. Nostrils flared. Full exhales.

As I looked at the crowd I noticed how everyone mirrored my expression.

Those kids. My peers. They were afraid of me.

I hop stepped over to the tall guy. He was on one knee, getting to his feet.

I tried to kick the wind out of him.

He grabbed my foot. I could tell he was the tougher one of the two. Things might've worked out different if they had him bring me away from the bar.

I didn't stop long enough for him to get a good grip. I elevated from my toes on the leg he was holding. Brought my other leg up high. Jammed it down in a big stomp motion. The bottom of my Jordans ripped across his right eyebrow.

Guy didn't fall.

I did it again. He fell down a little more.

And again. This time his head bounced with a thud against the sidewalk. When he lifted it up slightly I could see blood on his forehead.

"FUCKING BRONGEL!" I shouted.

The legit Red Rocks bouncer with the scanner busted through the crowd.

I tried making my posture neutral for a moment so the bouncer would see I wasn't the threat. Everyone was already pointing at the two heavies anyway.

I can still picture the looks on all their faces. I was raw. I didn't feel victorious, even with a sufficient beat down issued. The scene on the sidewalk made me think I'd never have a life like those kids. I had too many fights in me.

I looked right at the legit Red Rocks bouncer and shook my head. Don't stop me.

He didn't.

So I ran.

fifteen

It was easy to run. I dashed a half block down, then two blocks over, and up a brick-paved alley. I headed across Clark and east towards the lake. After I sprinted across Broadway I started jogging. The closer I got to the lake, the denser the neighborhood became.

By the time I started walking I was pissed at myself. I should've hid and followed the two guys to their car. I didn't feel happy about escaping; I was mad about running away too quickly.

sixteen

When I pulled my car out and started driving, I just released.

The all-consuming rush of the battle wasn't finished. I couldn't pull the feeling down. After driving a few blocks the tension let loose and I needed to pour the energy somewhere. I turned on the stereo. *Illmatic* popped up like it had been for the past day.

My fingers instinctively skipped tracks until I got to "The World Is Yours." It was so right right then. I screamed my way through a couple of choruses and mashed up all the vocal parts in a way that wouldn't make sense to anybody except for me.

I was too hyped to go word-for-word at first. Then I felt my heart steady as I tried to catch the beat.

The second time through the song I rapped on point with the lyrics. After the song finished, I played it again. I didn't let go. It took me fifteen minutes to get home using the expressway with just that song on repeat — I rapped right along with it — until I pulled into my garage.

seventeen

At home I walked into my bedroom, pulled out my bowl and took two monster hits. The music in the car didn't fully calm me down. Maybe the weed would. More than likely, I'd be up all night blowing adrenaline after the attack.

I put Gtronic Radio on and started to pacing out my house. Albert Brongel. I stepped through the kitchen and to my back porch to check the window. Brongel hired two guys. My music was on just loud enough. Not so loud it bumped the drunk guy downstairs awake. Loud enough so the bass touched my ears in that far corner. I kept thinking of those three people, Brongel and his men. I backtracked through the house and up to the front windows for a look.

When I swooshed down off that first wave of high, I forced myself into the bathroom for an inspection. A nub had popped out above my eye — it'd change colors in a day. The top of my head felt like it was ringed in a crown of lumps.

My blood flowed manic. I knew I wouldn't sleep.

I needed to figure out what happened earlier. Lenny told me a story. He didn't tell me the whole story.

As I criss-crossed my house I realized there was more to it. Most obvious was the fact that nobody dropped twenty-five G on an incompetent chump. Nobody spent that kind of money without doing the job right.

I busted on Lenny a lot, that's what friends do. I also knew Lenny wouldn't fold or faint or cower at the sight of two-hundred-fifty one-hundred dollar bills. He'd made and lost that kind of money a half dozen times since he was seventeen. Yes, Lenny should forget how to spell g-a-m-e, but he couldn't. He played. Besides Lenny would insist on meeting his benefactor before the drop. He had a knack for getting face-time with the boss, any boss.

That insight made me wonder if Lenny was hiding something. His story about getting the money from Albert Brongel and the military guy in the passenger seat was probably true. Lenny purposefully left out the meeting before that, where he met the moneyman. I wanted to know why.

I paced through my living room and kitchen and pulled myself apart.

Tried to tell myself I wanted to go talk to Lenny. But really, I just needed to be out of the house.

Finally after a couple hours of bouncing off the walls, I put on a light flannel and took a walk.

eighteen

I was nine when I first took to the streets. My mom was always gone and I didn't have house keys yet.

First time I got locked out of the house I went to Lenny's for dinner. I remember awkwardly showing up as they were sitting down. That only happened once. Showing up like that felt like asking for a handout. It only worked for me when I walked Lenny home from school and just stayed.

After that I tried sitting in front of our house. That was just okay. My neighbors didn't bother me. They were great at keeping my crazy family out of their lives.

After a few more lockouts I started to feel stranded on the front steps. When I sat there I had nothing to do but wallow and conjure that feeling that always hung in the back of my head: nobody was on my side.

I was getting locked out all the time at nine years old. Soon enough when it happened I would just take a walk. I'd push outward, map a new route on each walk. I'd zig zag up and down the neighborhood streets. When the weather got sub-zero I finally snuck my mom's keys from her and made a copy.

I felt propelled to the streets. Motion kept me from feeling the misery of my house. By the time I was ten I started reading more and stopped going out after dinner. I'd seclude myself inside a book until my mom holed up in her room. Then I'd suit up in street clothes. I was never much of a sleeper anyway. Three, four nights a week I'd just roam the neighborhood from eleven until two or three in the morning. Thinking about it, I realized how strange it would be to see a ten year old kid wandering the quiet streets at two a.m. on a Tuesday. What the hell did I do out there? I walked the blocks with a bop. I made up songs. I sang songs I knew. I heard music inside my head and could walk all night skipping off a beat. At that early age that's when I felt most alive.

That's why I didn't expect to fall asleep that night pacing in my house. I thought about Albert Brongel. I thought about Lenny. But I didn't have to think about taking a walk though — my body wanted it.

I hit the streets around two in the morning. I bopped down to Thirty-Ninth. I was a block from where my grandparents once lived at Thirty-Eight and Lowe.

I stood on the curb where Lowe dead-ended into Pershing. Canaryville began across Thirty-Ninth Street. I stood on my toes, on the curb, and bounced up and down. I looked over the edge of that low curb as if hanging over the edge of a cliff. From that point it was three blocks to Lenny's squat.

Bridgeport featured a lot of dead-ends like that curb I stood on. They disrupted the typical Chicago grid. Disruption wasn't normal for Chicago; the city thrived on the order of the grid.

I didn't flirt with the idea of visiting Lenny. I had a plan, so I turned around and walked toward Comiskey and up along the railroad tracks.

Walking the streets was meditative. My mind separated from my body. I stopped thinking and just moved.

I walked. Then I knew. That's what it felt like. One minute my brain streamed manic. The next I had an idea about Albert Brongel.

I headed for the Dunkin' Donuts at Thirty-First and Halsted at four in the morning. On my early morning walks, I always stopped in here to pick up a coffee.

The usual burnt-out white teenager manned the counter — too young for me to know her. Too young. Also, as usual, there were three or four mentally marginal people in the seats.

After I ordered my coffee one of the crazies asked me, "You been to the airport?"

"Meigs?" I asked. Everyone still talked about how the mayor had militarized a battalion of bulldozers in the middle of the night to destroy a piece of civic property.

"Midway," the guy said. His fat tongue pushed through the slots of missing teeth. "Has it changed since they sold it?" The guy's hair was frizzed-out like my mom's.

"No," I laughed, "people finally caught on with that one."

"Fool me three times," he said and laughed through his broken teeth.

I could imagine this guy with note pads of scribble at home. And a bag stuffed with articles about Midway Airport. His mind probably rocked with the thought of someone being able to buy a piece of the city. He wasn't the only one. The people of Chicago rallied on that one.

He nodded his chin at me. Just like people normally do on the streets. When he closed his lips and hid his teeth he looked pensive.

"Alright man," I told him, "Have a good night."

He looked me in the eye. Clarity. Fear. Gratitude.

nineteen

I drank the coffee as I drove. My research on Albert Brongel sat on the passenger seat next to a couple tools. The papers were held down by a socket and screwdriver set. If my plan worked, I wouldn't need the tools. I cruised with the windows down.

I drove to the North Side past Wrigley Field to get to Albert Brongel's apartment on Racine.

Chicago had two baseball teams which created natural animosity. The North Side Cubs played at Wrigley Field. The South Side Sox played at Comiskey Park in Bridgeport, my neighborhood.

To reach Wrigley Field I had to drive through Boystown, the gay neighborhood. The fact that Wrigleyville and Boystown shared a border was significant.

The knuckle-draggers I knew on the South Side never let that geographical fact fade. Because of the Wrigley-Boystown connect, all the homophobes put the two together. Wrigley Field was the world's largest gay bar, they'd say. And the words "North Side" and "faggot" melted together. Those slurs rolled off peoples tongues.

'I saw Melissa Riley out the other night.'

'Oh yeah, what's she up to?'

'Dating some northsidefaggot.'

I never played that game. We went to high school with a few closeted gays who smartly avoided me and my friends. In college I started to meet a few gay guys at parties. The ones I met turned out to be passionate music fans like me, so I didn't mind hanging out with them.

I parked and approached Brongel's three flat through the alley— hopped the fence next to his garage. Each apartment had a rear entrance onto the exposed back porch. In Bridgeport people encased their back porches in siding to create an extra room on the house. Up here, the open back porch made for easy access. If I wanted to, I could loosen up the security bars on his back window with my socket set. That was my back-up plan. Instead I moved two all-season deck chairs in front of the back door. They'd make a good noisemaker if Brongel tried to run.

I walked through the back yard, up the gangway to the front of the house. I wanted to keep this simple, and not over-think anything. I walked around front and read Brongel's name on the mailbox.

Then I rang the buzzer.

twenty

It only took six buzzes to wake someone up. When they answered, I put on a hushed raspy growl and said, "Yo, it's Lenny."

My impersonation wouldn't pass through another exchange, but it was five in the morning and I doubt they wanted an intercom conversation.

BUZZZZZ.

I had my White Sox cap on as usual. Anyone looking down the stairwell only saw the Sox logo and black cap.

Someone opened the door.

I made a soft whistle, then I inhaled, and let out a big sigh, like a 'oh my goodness I'm Lenny and what a long day I've been having,' kind of sigh. It kept them from expecting answers while I was on the stairs.

At the top of the stairs, I lifted up my chin expecting a confrontation.

The doorway was empty.

I walked in and heard someone pissing in the bathroom. The bathroom door was open.

The living room was furnished with a nice leather couch and love-seat with a distressed wood coffee table and obligatory flat screen. I looked at the couch for a moment. That's where Lenny had slept. On weekends Lenny rarely made it home at the end of the night. He'd carry the party on to a restaurant then someone's house and be too tired to head back to the South Side. Guys from the neighborhood started joking about Lenny's couch-surfing ways. Apparently there were pictures all over Facebook with him on different people's couches.

I walked back to the open bathroom door.

"Heeeyay," the guy convulsed as he walked into me.

I said a curt, "Hey."

He wore baby blue pinstriped boxer shorts and a navy Dave Matthews Band concert t-shirt. Musical taste aside I was certain that any guy who slept in a t-shirt just had to be effeminate. I thought worse things about people who slept in their socks.

He was stumbling as he exited the bathroom, and rubbing his hair, "The Mother Fuck–".

"We need to talk."

"Hey!" he started to shout, "What do you–"

I raised my hand up, "Don't, I'm not hurting anyone. My friend Lenny is missing and I heard him mention your name once."

He quieted down to say, "What the fuck, man," but he still didn't have a clue.

I found it odd that he needed to catch up. Nobody needed to catch up two days after handing over twenty-five grand that was tied to a murder. Nobody needed to catch up six hours after sending two guys to beat up a stranger.

I said, "You're not Albert Brongel."

"No," the guy said.

I stood in the kitchen and could see one bedroom door open. That would be the guy's in front of me. The bathroom door was open.

I pointed to the one closed door, "Albert here?"

"No."

"Fine," I looked right at him, "But you know Lenny."

"'f course," he said.

He couldn't say no after buzzing me up.

He squinted his eyes and pushed out his lips trying to get his brain working better.

"Albert at his girlfriend's?"

"Al has girls, not girlfriends."

So, no.

"Why'd you let me in?" I shook my head in small cuts back and forth, wagging the bill of my White Sox cap at him.

"I thought you were Lenny."

"You buzzed me up because you thought I was Lenny. What got you out of bed?"

I didn't think he came to the buzzer wondering if I was a booty call. The way he offered up his 'Al has girls, not girlfriends' comment meant a couple of things. This guy didn't get the girls. And the slight brag about his friend meant he was too often a tag-along on their adventures. More importantly, I figured he was just like me. He woke up to answer the buzzer because his friend had disappeared.

The kitchen had a nice table with four chairs — looked like a hand-me down from some well-off parents who wanted to replace it with something nicer.

I pointed to the bigger of the bedrooms closer to the living room, and said to confirm, "Albert's?"

He nodded.

"Let's go in," I said.

Albert had a nice bed with a set of sheets and pillowcases that matched. His was the kind of bed girls liked to wake up in. On one wall was a gigantic black and white poster of the Chicago skyline. The skyline sprang from the expanse of Lake Michigan. The framed poster confirmed that Chicago's was the prettiest skyline in the world, no doubt.

"When was the last time you saw Albert?" I asked.

There wasn't much here. A nightstand with a box of paperwork underneath it. The box was one of those wicker baskets with a canvas liner. On top of the nightstand was a picture of Albert with, I figured, his parents. They were on the back of a boat holding drinks. Whenever I see people with pictures like that in their house, it always felt like bragging to me.

The roommate tried to answer my question. I imagined he first needed to remember that he just finished Saturday night. It took him a minute, then he said, "Couple of days, I don't know," he said.

"Thursday?" I asked.

"Probably."

Albert Brongel hadn't been home since Thursday.

He was hiding.

"Same as Lenny," I said and added, "Wonder where they are." As if we were simpatico and just looking for our buds.

I pulled the basket of paperwork and set it on the bed. Mail order catalogues. Credit card bills. A couple Complex magazines. And what looked like a direct deposit pay-stub that arrived in the mail.

"You can't look through there, man." He was coming to life.

"Do you know where Lenny is?"

"No," he said with a smirky grimace on his face that said, 'as if.'

"Then you stand there and watch me, nothing else," I said, and opened up the pay-stub.

"I said, you can't do that," he insisted. When he tried to speak real words it sounded awkward. His tongue swelled from dehydration and he couldn't fully control his speech.

Before looking at the pay-stub, I said, "Albert makes about eighty-five a year and carries no credit card debt. Did you know that?"

He didn't.

"Document Alliance," I said aloud, that was the name on the pay-stub. It had a triangular logo with a series of crossed lines inside the triangle.

"Warehousing," the guy said.

"Odd," I said, "The logo looks just like the Price Properties logo," and dropped the pay-stub back in the basket.

I'm no student of corporate branding but the Price family under their Price Properties Group stamps either their name or logo on everything from hospital wings, university school of businesses, running races and firework displays. You'd have to willfully blind yourself to influence peddling in Chicago to not know that logo.

I returned the rest of the shit I took out back into the basket.

I said, "It might be awkward telling Albert that you let some guy in to dig through his personal things."

I tilted the basket up so everything settled into a nicer pile using the basket's corner as a guide. Then I put the basket back.

"So don't tell him," I said. I figured he might just take that suggestion. "Got it?"

He scrunched his eyes and puckered his lips even harder than before and said, "Just get the fuck out of here."

I had only touched the edge of the basket, and the papers in them. I decided not to wipe them down.

I let the roommate have his moment of pushback.

I got out of there, and wiped the front door down on my way out.

The streets were still empty when I got in my car. I drove down to Belmont and over to the lake. My drive that early in the morning was prettier than the picture on Albert Brongel's wall. Chicago, man, every street spoke to me. Every street felt connected to me somehow. Even driving, all the streets reached out to me like I was a gigantic recording studio mixing board and I was plugged in. Or they were plugged into me. Sometimes I got tripped up in the mess of wires. At other times I could fade each line in and out as desired. I could fade out the memories at will, and pump up the bass line propelling the rhythm and just be there in the pocket, square in the moment.

twenty-one

I slept for two hours after my visit to Albert Brongel's apartment and woke up with Lenny's voice inside my head.

If Lenny ever dreamt of holding a job, then driving JB Foster around Chicago would've been his dream assignment. He only hated one part of it — Sunday mornings.

'They even have curling up there, Bones!' Lenny had said after his first time driving JB on a Sunday morning.

Tar had oozed from his saturated lungs when he said those words to me. His mouth was a dark, black hole. Lenny would've considered himself a prince with a prince's job if it wasn't for the fact that JB Foster made Lenny chauffer him to his Sunday hockey game at nine every Sunday morning. Lenny had to be up at seven-thirty to make it on time.

'I'm not talking about bicep curling here,' Lenny had said and waved his hands in front of his face. 'Not up at the fucking North Shore Sports Center! Noooooo.' He then raised his arms and shook his hand so hard he could've broken a finger.

Lenny had paused for a drag off his cigarette, and exhaled in exhaustion, 'I'm talking about grown people sweeping the fucking ice.'

That kind of curling.

As far as he told me, he pulled up at the Sports Center at eight-forty-five like clockwork — every Sunday.

This kind of knowledge was second nature to me. Ever since I was a kid Lenny's life was a case study. Scotty Smuda's too. I watched them to learn how you might act if you had a family. How being comfortable at home looked — with favorite blankets and pillows and shit. What kind of things did families talk about? How did *they* deal with problems? I learned all that and more, simply by observing these meatheads.

I had internalized Lenny's story for so long that it no longer felt like friendship. It was much simpler than that: his life was my life.

twenty-two

I pulled into The North Shore Sports Center at 9:35. Passed time with Nas and the Sunday papers. Trees had been slain since Friday morning in the name of Babi Patras and JB Foster.

There was an immigration fluff piece on JB's maid — the one who found the body. She was legal, no doubt, otherwise she wouldn't have sat for the interview. In the article she played the role of a humble Mexican maid. She spoke softly to the reporter and made simple proclamations. The article even had one of those paragraphs in italics imagining the life she left behind in the dusty fields of Jalisco. The piece felt orchestrated. There wasn't any reason to be suspicious of the maid. I felt suspicious though — probably a personality flaw on my part. Praise a person too much and I didn't react well.

I was reading a major Chicago newspaper, so the article wasn't too long. *Illmatic's* run time was just shy of forty-minutes. It had just started playing for the second time when JB left the Sports Center.

I slid my car in behind his as he pulled out of the parking lot.

He drove a metallic blue Jaguar coupe. One thing I liked about JB is that he never tried to play up any salt-of-the-earth South Side roots. From the minute I heard about him, he was all cosmopolitan all the time. I didn't quite know what that meant other than that he only rode in European sedans and only wore suits to work.

I glanced back after driving a couple of blocks and saw the black Yukon Denali that had turned out of the bank across the street from the Sports Center. The Denali didn't just hang back. It made steady ground.

I already knew where JB lived. Lenny and I drove up here when he first started driving JB. He wanted to show me his house. He was proud when he first landed the job, and when we drove by Lenny looked at the massive house like it was his own.

Knowing where JB lived allowed me to keep an eye on the Denali. Two blocks from JB's house the Denali came up fast on my tail. I initially thought the guy behind was a concerned neighbor who followed us because I looked suspicious. Then I caught sight of his face in the rearview mirror.

His black hair looked to be as short as you could get a buzz cut, and his face looked like it was made of rocks. He was more of a middle-aged fitness freak than a pasty white titan of industry who clocked forty-five minutes on the treadmill every morning.

The gate on JB's lakefront estate hung open after the Jaguar pulled through.

I decided to let myself in.

The black Denali jumped forward as soon as my wheels turned in the direction of JB's driveway. I turned in and was far enough in front of the Denali that the driver couldn't cut me off before I glided onto the driveway.

JB must've seen the action behind him, because the Jaguar's wheels chirped when he slammed on the breaks.

I came to a stop five yards behind him.

I heard the Denali's engine rev as he jumped through the gate. Then his tires screeched and he halted within an inch of my bumper.

Before I had my car in park he had already popped out.

Definitely not a concerned friend. This guy was hired muscle.

On his walk to me he held a palm up in JB's direction to tell him to stay in the car.

I rolled my window down.

The hired muscle pointed at me as he strode past and said, "You're trespassing."

He strode up to JB's car in his black Tac boots and dark jeans. He also wore a solid black Under Armour long sleeve base layer. His military pension plus good civilian money couldn't take the stiffness out of his joints though. Special services, I guessed.

JB's car was parked just before the outbuilding housing the garage and servants quarters. Mine was behind his, and the Denali parked behind me just inside the gate.

I climbed out.

The security guy flexed every muscle he could during his four strong strides, came up in my face and said, "You're going to have to leave."

I swept my arm as if I was displaying a sparkling black Denali on a game show, "I'm blocked in."

He had to think about that. If he got in his truck, he'd be leaving JB exposed to me for a minute. He didn't look back at the Denali, but we were thinking the same thing.

He should've parked outside the gates.

"Premature ejaculation is treatable," I said, nodded at his truck, "You've got to learn to take your time."

His temples pulsed. He turned and tried to throw a shoulder into me at the same time. I leaned back against my car, out of his way. He stepped to JB's window and started to tell him to pull all the way up to the house.

I walked over and stood behind him, trying to get a direct look at JB.

Peeked around the guard's shoulder and said, "Yo, you get your security service on Groupon, JB?"

The guard turned around, got up in my grill and spoke like a drill sergeant, "Get in your car or you'll be put under arrest."

"No, I won't."

"You are trespassing," he spat, "The cops will be here in three minutes."

His threat carried the suggestion that three minutes would be plenty of time to render me unconscious and tie me up.

I didn't doubt his abilities.

I looked over his shoulder at JB.

JB had his window down, listening.

I gave JB a nod with a little lip curl that said I was down.

He didn't get it.

I spoke over the shoulder again, directly to JB, "The cops come in three minutes. Then the TV news crews on the scanner will be here in twenty."

JB didn't miss a beat, "What do you want?" His voice hung with disappointment. It must've been hard for him to turn down free press.

JB then told his bodyguard to step down.

With that courtesy granted, I took a few steps back toward my car and stood in the gap between our two vehicles.

He climbed out wearing sweatpants and a grey Patagonia base layer t-shirt.

I always pictured meeting him in his office. I never asked, but I was always disappointed Lenny didn't come through with an intro.

JB was a Southsider, so I gravitated to his story. As a teenager in South Holland, in the south suburbs, JB Foster took a job with the sanitation department. Said it was the best paying job available in high school. He moved to a private sanitation company in the city during college.

JB played up the hardscrabble angle and the family who owned the company took him under their wing. After college he stayed on, and by twenty-nine took over the day-to-day operation. Age conspired in his favor. The family had a young son in college, but he wanted to get into real estate. By then JB was almost part of the family. After years of hiding an affair, he came clean about dating the patriarch's daughter. Based on the stories I read, I didn't know if he was really dating her, or just playing games.

He introduced the old-school family ownership to debt. The family took a taste from him but barely nibbled. Floating payroll was about the farthest they wanted to go. That kind of finance was too old school for JB's taste. On the down low JB met with the top bankers in the city, logged time on the phone with New York.

JB's ambitions kept butting up against the family. His first business plan to expand their business was rejected outright. JB didn't worry. He had made enough friends in the LaSalle Street financial corridor that he knew he could jump ship to an investment bank.

The second business plan for the family was an obvious play for a severance package.

JB's proposal had more of what they hated about the first one. Expanded operations. More bidding for low-margin municipal contracts. Union busting. JB wanted to leverage every company asset to the multiplier of ten. The total finance package weighed in near two-hundred million.

Just before JB thought the family lawyer was about to reveal JB's severance package, he shocked them. He said, The debt won't be yours. The statement attained the status of myth around Chicago. *The debt won't be yours.* JB wanted to buy their company. He wanted the family to take the deal and walk away. He asked them to give up sixty years of family legacy. He half expected the patriarch to pull him by his ear and throw him out the door.

They shocked him back and accepted.

This was over twenty years ago. The Price family took the money and invested in real estate during a rock bottom market. Chicago's skyline sparkled with crown jewels of architecture. The Price family didn't build any of those. But two decades into the real estate game they did buy and build enough buildings to be the gold that held the crown jewels together. The Price family buildings weren't pretty, but they were everywhere.

The family has always paid JB the highest compliments, and ever since that day they've said practically in unison, 'We were learning from the master.'

The master walked over to me. His dark messy hair looked magazine worthy.

I looked over my shoulder, checking to be sure the guard was in his truck.

I said, "Lenny is missing. And I'm pretty sure he didn't do it."

"*Pretty sure* isn't descriptive enough," JB said. He was everything I expected. Quick and confident. Even in one sentence he sounded smart.

"It's a start," I said.

"Lenny doesn't work for me anymore. His present whereabouts are only of concern to the police right now."

"And others," I added.

"So few I just started counting," he said without even thinking the word *smirk*.

"Somebody wanted to get to you. They pried Lenny and he allowed them to get access to your loft," I reached into my pockets to see if I had gum. I had drank another big D&D coffee on the way up and hadn't brushed my teeth yet. I didn't think I had gum, but it made for a good break. I pulled my empty hand from my pocket and opened it up.

He looked at my hand.

"Not my words," I said, "I never said them if you happen to relay the story to any confidants."

"You're saying someone paid him," JB followed quickly. He had that perfect boardroom posture. His torso was bolt upright and the only movements came when he extended his arm from the elbow to under-score a point. "You're saying that's how he got the money. Because Lenny would never blow two grand at a club? Lenny tried everything he could to avoid paying for a drink. Is that what you're trying to say?"

"Nope. You just said it," I answered, "Lenny does spend money on drinks, but he only buys for people he likes," I said. "Look, nobody knows Lenny like I do, so I wouldn't be here if this didn't have weight."

"I'll say it again. That's not descriptive enough."

JB didn't play it either way. I couldn't tell if he was interested.

"I have the front," I said.

"The front is nothing."

"The front is a start," I added as if to remind him.

"No," he said, "This isn't the start of some big investigation. It's simple. These crimes are not complicated. Greed or lust. The occasional serial-killer is the exception that proves the rule."

At fifty-four years old late-period JB Foster sounded like a politician. No matter what people asked him, he just stuck to his own agenda. His theory on the murder was a perfect example. None of his claim about greed or lust spoke to Lenny's reality, and I couldn't contradict him without starting a whole different conversation.

I asked, "Are you the same guy who was just asking for more details?"

"I'm not asking for anything, you're the one who confronted me."

He still hadn't moved. I didn't either. The dark stone of his house framed him in his black sweats and shirt.

"Right, lust or greed," I said, "Which one you got Lenny pegged for?"

"Babi stopped being driven by Lenny when she was alone. She started taking cabs. It changed the way we worked together. I couldn't ask Lenny to pick Babi up at work while I finished up at the office. On Wednesday, the day before," he paused, "I told him he was getting transferred to the general pool."

His hands fell to his side once they were finished punctuating.

"Lenny," I said simply, "A crime of lust?"

It didn't take any soul searching to realize that Lenny had lied about Babi Patras — claiming she was just a thing, that it was no big deal. I'm sure at one point in time, that's how Lenny felt. Like any point in time before she started boning his boss.

Realizing Babi was a climber and he just got stepped on could make a dude obsess.

And then he gets demoted.

I said, "You can't put Lenny in your loft that night."

"Like I said, it's not in my hands," JB answered.

His posture gave me nothing. His words gave me nothing.

I decided to put out a flier.

"Explain the twenty-five grand to me?" I asked, "How does Lenny net a bag full of money like that?"

I broke my posture and started to lean on my front fender. I didn't take my eye off him as I felt behind me for the car.

It looked like JB needed a few seconds to think.

Then he said, "My watch."

"What's that?"

"My time-piece. A DeWitt Academia. He could've fenced it. I haven't seen it lately. I thought I left it at the office and kept forgetting to check. But now that I think about it, it's gone."

I didn't believe none of his shit, his facts were backwards.

"You don't fence shit for twenty-five grand," I spit.

For me, where I came from this was a conversation, not a confrontation. But I could tell he felt threatened. JB would be on high alert until they found the killer. Even the PD would keep him on their suspect list until the end.

JB needed a few seconds to think up that line about his watch gone missing. He was selling a story. That's what he did, that's how JB Foster made bank.

After purchasing the sanitation company, JB worked himself out of debt through a new business division—document storage. It was genius. He didn't see himself as a garbage man. He saw his business as one that took unwanted items away from your business. Whether they were garbage bags to a dump or boxes to a storage facility. It didn't matter as long as you paid your bill.

Last year JB won a contract with the city to take over their document storage business. I followed the transaction just like I did the parking meters and the Skyway and Midway Airport. I figured it was a city asset the Aldermen could sell to pad their friends' pockets. The nature of the deal made it difficult to protest. After all people wouldn't be paying for the storage like they did a parking meter or highway toll. The protests came loudly but from too few.

Standing on his driveway JB didn't have anything to say.

"I'll tell you something then," I said, "You think this is all about Lenny. But this is all about you."

He shot back, "This has nothing to do with me."

"Ten percent off your stock price says otherwise." This morning's paper included an editorial about how JB wanted a resolution as soon as possible. His company took a hit in the markets on Friday. JB's image equaled his company's image, so if JB Foster was a suspect, it was only natural that his company's stock was suspect.

"People are fickle," he said, put his hands on hips.

The best time to push is when someone gets defensive.

"The cover up will kill you," I said.

He shook his head incredulously, "You have no idea what you're saying do you?"

I pointed at him, "One of us is spinning a story," then let my finger drop, "and one of us is cracking rocks."

"What's that supposed to mean?"

"I'm working in reality here. The cover-up is gonna kill you."

"Are you threatening me?"

I held my hands up. "A figure of speech. I'm not killing anyone. I'm saving a friend. And you, John Bowman Foster, will likely get off unscathed. JB Foster, this waxed-up creation you're selling, may not fare so well."

"Sounds like a threat to me."

"Sounds to me like you think you can get a quick conviction hung on Lenny."

I showed him I was onto his game. Waited to see if he'd respond.

Lenny had history with the girl. The lust angle was a no-brainer, even if evidence showed otherwise. I got that. Lenny's lust was already proven. Throw in the watch, and nobody could deny that lust plus larceny rolled smoothly off the tongue. JB just needed to keep admitting new threads to his story. He's about to spin his story until it was the only one people remembered.

Why? Quarterly earnings were king.

For JB, the quickest way out of this mess was Lenny.

"Finished?" he asked.

I was surprised he asked.

If my prediction was correct, then Tuesday's newspapers would bulge with coverage that looked like a catalogue for DeWitte Academia watches. They'll probably even call them *time pieces.*

"Whatever man," I said, "I figured I was here to help. You're just taking advantage of the complications."

"Like I said, these things are simple," JB said.

I answered back, "You take lust then. It's a sucker bet."

I stood up off my fender.

When I turned away JB said, "He has your license plates."

I looked back at him.

JB nodded toward the black Denali, "He'll have reports on the shit stains in your underwear."

"Great, JB," I said as I opened my car door, "Don't be surprised if he gets all descriptive with the smell."

I looked up briefly to see if he would laugh. He didn't.

I added, "If he does his job, then next time we meet you might actually know something instead of this mess you're shoveling," and waived my hand in front of my nose.

twenty-three

Late Sunday afternoon I drove to Twenty-Sixth Street. I wanted to talk to the cleaning woman who discovered Babi Patras' body. I was starving, so I decided to eat and figure out a way to find her that didn't involve going in to work.

I needed an ally. Yolanda Duarte couldn't do much for me, but after my failure with Albert Brongel and JB Foster I decided to start smaller.

I settled down with my feast at Los Comales. At five on a Sunday afternoon the local Mexicans in their Sunday finest had gone home. There weren't any little girls in puffy church dresses. No guys in cowboy boots and hats. Everyone had changed back to wearing jeans and a hoodie. I ate a steak torta milanesa and two steak tacos, no onions anywhere.

Chicago named this neighborhood Little Village. The Mexicans who built a new life had their own name for it. K-Town. Twenty-Sixth-Street was the heart of Mexican life in Chicago. Like many immigrant communities they lived apart from us.

This street defined life for many older immigrants. They never went out to bars downtown when they turned twenty-one. They never went to college. They moved near the Two-Six fresh from Mexico, got their first cash-only job, and let their kids and grandkids do all that.

The westernmost blocks of Twenty-Sixth Street got shabby. If English was your second language you probably couldn't keep track of the streets as you drove past them. The street names all looked the same: Komensky, Keeler, Kostner, on down to Kedzie. K-Town.

The article in this morning's paper said Yolanda Duarte lived in the Little Village. I needed an address. In the meantime I got a taco.

K-Town had a definite Mexican flavor. To me the neighborhood didn't seem much different than any other American city. Commerce gave it status. Twenty-Sixth Street generated the second most sales tax revenue of any street in the city of Chicago. The Mexican population was large.

I thought about where the locals spent their money. They couldn't spend it all at the pastry and candy shops. I looked out the restaurant's front window, scanned storefronts as far as my eye could see.

Sunday was a true rest day for the community. The shops weren't too active, even with plenty of people on the sidewalks. I realized that was because the real money was already spent. On Friday and Saturday the Mexican community shaved mad money off the top of each payday. The wires heading down to Mexico burned red hot with remittances to the family back home. Those wires vibrated and played a multi-billion dollar song. All going south.

I wolfed down the torta first. Took a minute. Ate some jalepeno-pickled carrots. Started to pick up a taco when it hit me. The wires. Everyone in K-Town used the wires.

twenty-four

I finished my tacos and walked across the street to the currency exchange. They had a Western Union sign in the window. They most certainly hacen giros, if you knew the lingo. They were just about to close.

I leaned my face up against the bullet proof glass and asked, "If I usually wire money from a different location, can you pull up my records on your computer here? I need to find account information."

"No, we only have customer files for this store," she said.

I took a form and wrote Yolanda Duarte's name on it. Then I circled the address field, and slid a hundred under the form.

"I'm looking for an address," I said, "Nothing else."

She looked up at the security camera.

I didn't think the room would be mic-ed.

"Do you know who she is?" I asked.

The woman nodded.

"Anyone else come here asking about her?"

"No."

"Just the address is okay," I said. I held my wallet in my hand.

The woman walked over to the computer. She clacked some keys. I could see the computer monitor through the glass, but not read any details. I got real curious about the details on screen. Pulled out another hundred of Lenny's money before she walked back. Kept it on the ready.

She came back and slid the form back to me.

I returned the form to her with the second hundred, leaned into the glass and asked, "Can I get a print out of her activity over the past two months?"

My eyes darted down to the second Benjamin. Hers did too.

Three minutes later I stood on the sidewalk of the Two-Six reading Yolanda Duarte's activity report. Mrs. Duarte wired three hundred bucks every other week. The report went back three months, and every other Friday between five and six she'd wire the money south. Except this past week. It was her off-week and on Saturday morning she wired six hundred bucks.

I took the information and went looking for the pawnshop.

twenty-five

"Hey, yo," I said to a few kids. Their heads were shaved to the skin, save for a long crop of hair at their widows' peak. "Where's the pawnshop?"

They pointed west, towards the K-streets. Weekend traffic along Twenty-Sixth was jam-packed from noon to midnight with blown up rigs and squat hoopdies. After six blocks of brisk walking, I finally spotted the Pawn Broker. Even with signage in Spanish, I could tell the spot from the assortment of stereo equipment, TVs, and a couple Flamenco guitars in the window.

Inside, I asked, "You speak English?"

"We closing."

He was five-eight and skinny, he had enough rings and bracelets on to make him look like he should work in a music shop selling guitars. He also looked pre-hardened to any friendly questions from a guy like me.

I slid the Western Union form across the counter and pointed to Yolanda Duarte's name on it, "Did this woman sell anything here in the past couple of days?"

His eyes bulged, "You a cop?"

"No, but I can get them here if you want."

Pawnbrokers stayed away from trouble. The majority of them kept their inventory in a database and shared it with the cops willingly. But this wasn't Chicago's Little Village after all. This was K-Town, a place unto itself. A heavy dose of illegals for clientele meant they kept different rules and different books. Identities needed to be protected in a place where CPD translated to Spanish as INS.

He stared hard.

"I'm not a cop," I repeated, "I'm not looking to make trouble for her," I rested my palms lightly on the counter, "Unless you make trouble for me."

"You want to see the books?" he asked.

"Sure," I said. He pulled a ledger out from under the counter. It was in English. Nice penmanship along the rows listing the necessary information. At the end of each line was a customer's signature.

I closed it almost as fast as I opened it.

"Okay," I said, "Let's say I'm not looking for something on these books."

I didn't want the Little Village English. I wanted K-Town Spanish.

I took a business card out of the display on the counter. I set it before me and pulled out my phone.

The kid was good. While I slow dialed 9-1-1 we tossed a few who's-harder-than-who one liners back and forth. Then he gave in a half-sec before the call got connected.

twenty-six

A thick-necked control freak answered the door with muscles popping out of his tank top and his jaw pulsing.

"What's up, man," I said, "I'm looking for Yolanda."

"Who are you?"

"Name's Bones. I'm looking for a friend who disappeared. He works with JB Foster too."

I guessed he was Yolanda's son. He ground down his teeth at the thought of me talking to his mom.

"Got a badge?"

"No badge."

"Then walk the fuck away," his accent was barely noticeable; I could tell he was raised in an ESL house.

"What's your name?" I asked.

"You don't have a badge, then she doesn't have to talk to you so get off the porch and walk away."

His mom's story was in a major newspaper. They likely had press here all weekend. Snake-charming news producers probably poked around for a new angle on the JB Foster-Babi Patras murder story. Babi Patras was hot enough and JB Foster was rich enough that the story might go national by week's end.

"I don't even have a press badge," I said, "But I do have a word for you: *aretes.*"

"What?"

I yanked this word off the Spanish ledger at the pawnshop. I studied Spanish in school and my annunciation was pretty damn good. I knew he understood me.

"*Aretes,* and I'm not repeating it again."

"What's this about?"

"Ah hah, not expecting that were you," I became friendly-like because I had no beef with either him or his mom. "What's your name?"

"Vicente."

"This is about earrings. Okay? Tell her that and I'll be here waiting."

The way I saw it, I was doing Yolanda a favor. There were no earrings mentioned in the papers. I had no way of knowing if they were a part of the police report. But I figured the diamond studs were Babi Patras' and someone would miss them soon.

Vicente's stare came out ice cold when he returned and opened the door for me.

I walked into the living room, and his mom was standing there, looking very afraid.

"Mucho gusto," I said, and then in English, "Please, nothing to be afraid of."

She stood mute and picked at her fingernails. She wore a blue skirt with a tight-fitting hot-pink blouse. Her head of black hair looked like a Lion's mane down to her shoulders. She got done up for church and left her nice clothes on all day. She was a little chubby, and probably in her mid to late fifties. Her bra squeezed her boobs to make two satellites on top.

Yolanda said something in Spanish to her son. He muttered something back and motioned his hands towards her like 'he's got it.'

I pulled the earrings from my pocket. "Do I need to say where I got them?"

He looked at her. She looked down. He started to talk. Pulled it back and was quiet for a beat.

Then he asked her a question. Her answer included the word *giros*, so I knew she told him she wired the money.

"I'm not here to cause trouble," I said again, "We know she had nothing to do with it, correct?"

They both nod.

"I just want some information. She ever hear of Albert Brongel?"

She hadn't.

"What does she think about the woman, Babi?" I asked.

She tried retreating behind the veil of her son's translation. He asked a clarifying question back at her before he answered, "She seemed nice. On the mornings they were together in the house the girl stayed in the bedroom always. My mom knew better than to go in the bedroom when the door was closed. It sounds like the woman would stay there until it was time to leave, and then she just said goodbye."

Yolanda added, "She always say *Adios.*"

"When you first see Babi in Mr. Foster's apartment?" I said directly to Yolanda. I wanted to keep her talking.

"Eight mounts," she answered.

Which was about the duration of their relationship.

Vicente asked her a question, interrupted the rapport I tried to establish. She answered back in clipped, sharp Spanish. She declared things to him. He kept asking questions. Then she stopped him cold and took her lion's mane and lifted it up.

Ahhh, that's how she got the earrings out of there. I had wondered if she hid them in a bottle of chemicals or in her boob-splitting bra. But no, she put them on and walked them right out JB's front door.

Vicente finally had the answer he wanted, so he turned and talked to me.

"She says she doesn't think the girl had good morals, and that she was very pretty and doesn't understand why a beautiful woman would, would," he paused to search for the word, then said "compromise herself when she could find a nice husband." His head went from her to me, like he didn't change a word in translation. "But," Vicente said echoing his mom's *pero,* "She says she never thinks bad things about her and can, could never hurt her."

"No doubt, Yolanda," I said looking right at her, "I'm not here to cause trouble."

We chatted about JB Foster. She said she knew he was rich, but added she didn't know how much — and waved her hand toward the Sunday *La Raza* on the coffee table.

"Any suspicious people you see come into the apartment?" I asked. I was going through the motions a little bit. It probably reminded her of the cops.

She had nothing.

"And the driver, this Lenny," I asked, "What do you think about him?"

She shook her head immediately and said, "No, I no like him," and did a shove-off with her arms.

I asked why.

She turned to her son and talked rapid fire Spanish. The only word I caught was *cabeza.*

Vicente translated, "She doesn't like him. He came into the apartment once or twice a week and what she's saying is, is that he moved his head too much. He always looked like he's up to something. He walked around the apartment too much. He even took water and food from the fridge like he owned the place."

I wanted to smile, but didn't. In spite of his vanilla looks, this was one reason why Lenny never made it on the grift. He just looked like he was up to something, even when he wasn't.

"That it?" Vicente asked.

"Just so you know, I didn't pay to get these earrings," I said, "the guy at the pawn'll probably come back to you. Now, Vicente, gimme your number."

I couldn't figure out their deal. Maybe she had a husband in Mexico that Vicente hated, and he wanted his mom to keep the money she made to herself. There was a whole world of *maybes* that hung between mother and son. I had no idea.

twenty-seven

"What kind of information?" Dorothy asked.

"Mostly personal finance. For a long time I worked only for friends. Then I started working, like, the street on divorces and shit like that."

"Stuff like that, Bones," she corrects me, playfully.

"That too. That's what I've got to do tonight, later."

"It fits you," she said.

"What?"

"Watching people," she forked through the apple slices and crumbled blue cheese on her salad.

We were at this café by her house in the hipster realm south of Wicker Park. I had been here a couple times. A New York transplant had opened the spot. His press release claimed he was Jay-Z's personal chef for a stretch. The cafe didn't siphon any business from the popular hipster coffee shop on Chicago Avenue just south of here. The place didn't do much business at all. It would close soon, no doubt. But I represented hip-hop so it was my spot for a minute.

It was early Monday evening. After my busy weekend I kept it in stealth mode all day at work. I was hyped for this though, and had been having fun up until she turned our date into an interview.

I decided to play along. "How does watching people fit me?" I asked.

"It's all a big secret, isn't it? You can't talk about it." she looked great in ballet flats, with leg warmers, skinny jeans and a green tank top. She wore a pink cashmere sweater too, but it was hot in the café where we sat. The green tank top made her eyes pop more than usual.

I said, "Oh, I don't know about that, what's there to say about it?"

"Personal finance? Divorce?" she asked, "What's not to say about it?"

"It's what I do," I said.

She wrung her hands together and a sparkle shot out her eyes, "But you're a P.I. like Humphrey Bogart, that's so interesting."

I laughed and shook my head, "No such thing. I don't have an office. I'm not licensed. I don't own a gun. People don't even call me."

"A fixer then," she said, "you're the guy they call in to clean up messes."

I tilted my head to the other side, "No, like I said I don't get phone calls. I just do shit," I said, "Um, things. Neighborhood jobs for neighborhood friends."

"Yeah, a fixer," she said, nodding like she had me.

I didn't like her thinking she had me figured out.

"Look," I laid it out, "I work at a shitty credit reporting agency and I do things for people."

"Things for people," she repeated, and said, "Perfectly vague," she smiled and waited a beat before she added, "Bones."

The shimmy in her yoga-sculpted shoulders said playful. I didn't take it any other way.

I had to respond to her 'Bones' comment, so I asked, "What like all you get is the bare bones?"

"Like you aren't saying much about your job, and I'm calling you Bones."

"You work at a restaurant, and want to act, right?"

She nodded while crunching on a piece of Arugula.

"Is there more that you could be telling me?" I asked.

"I'm in a new show starting next month. I'll be pretty busy."

"What's the show?"

"An adaptation of an Ianesco play."

"Don't know it."

"He's a French absurdist."

"So what's that mean?"

I was a pro at this. I could extract any personal information from people without giving up any of my own. I did know a lot about her. I knew where she grew up and schools attended. Since Chicago was my town I've been to most parts of the city and suburbs and know enough local businesses that I can wow people with my outsider knowledge of their hometowns. She was from Lake Bluff. She has only been to Bridgeport and the near South Side for thrift store shopping. At a bar or party I could do all this and charm someone into a date, or do all this and just move on.

"So," she said to stop the chatter, "Your mom."

"Oh god."

"Did she name you Bones?" she asked.

"She did not," I said, "At one point in time I was a very skinny teenager, like see my ribs skinny," I left out the really bad stuff, "and the name stuck."

"But you also have, you know, a real name?" she asked.

I had never thought about it but it was possible I didn't want to use the name my mom gave me.

"Of course."

"And?"

She wanted to know my name. I didn't really have anything against it, but the direct pressure made me want to keep it off the table a little longer. I'd rather reveal it on my own time, in my own way.

"What's in a name, Dorothy?" I asked.

Mid-chew from the side of her mouth she said, "Apparently a lot,"

"What's in a name?" I sang softly. I thought it sounded good. Sang it again, *"What's in a name?"* a little louder then. Nobody else was eating here so I could get a little boisterous without disturbing folks. I picked up the R&B quiet storm beat in my head and carried on singing with a full voice, *"What's in a na-a-ame? When you have my heart,"* Nice pause for the beat, *"From the ve-e-e-ry start?"* I couldn't pull off the Melisma, but it was spot on for a dude fucking around on a date.

"Nice voice," Dorothy said, "That Usher?"

"That's a Bones original," I said. She was floored. "Just came up with it for you, Dorothy."

"I *like* it," she laughed.

She playfully tried to get my name out of me during dinner. I didn't even think about telling her anymore, I just answered with my newly minted R&B hit.

By the look in her eyes, I was certain that if I had the right connects I could write those lyrics and make a million bucks. But I was far from the right connects.

I busted out the song on the sidewalk after we left the restaurant. I hopped and stepped around her like we were in a video on BET. She played the coy hottie and I played the earnest loveryboy trying to get in her pants, er, I mean win her heart. I was ready to flash to the last scene in the music video where she would be in her white skivvies in a white-sheeted bed. She'd be in gauzy soft focus while the camera would be sharp on me, singing.

"You know," she put a stop to my clowning when we got close to her house, "If you want a girlfriend, you're going to have to tell someone your name."

"Panda Bear."

"What?" she mocked surprise, "Your name's Panda Bear?" And half-rolled her eyes while faking a frown too.

"Naah, not girlfriend, Panda Bear," the idea just struck me. It made complete sense in the instant I said it. I said, "Like if I want a *Panda Bear*, not a girlfriend. You know like Panda Bears are these soft and cuddly other worldly creatures. People have posters of Panda's and keychains and shit like that."

"You want me on a keychain?" she asked like she was the straight half of a comedy duo.

"No, I want that soft and beautiful creature," I said, "But here's the thing. You piss a Panda Bear off and they're known to be pretty vicious creatures — tear your shit apart. Right?"

She shrugged.

I put on my Nat Geo voice-over voice and added, *"Pandas are often associated with the gentle and docile. But they have been known to at-tack humans out of irritation."*

That got me a smile from her.

"Just picture a Panda up in the trees, kinda looking back and forth," I said and switched back to voice-over voice, *"Coveting an orderly home life, the Panda will choose not to mate over inviting the chaotic male presence into her lair,* and the shot would be of the panda looking off into the distance. *She would rather kick his ass to the curb."*

Dorothy's smile turned to a laugh. I continued:

"*Craving a constant companion.* Now the shot is of the Panda peacefully eating a handful of berries but we all know the shot is about who's not there, *the Panda truly aspires to coupledom with a basket of rolled up towels in the bathroom.*"

Her laugh reached her belly and I was just waiting for her to do that thing where she turned her tongue into a corkscrew and bit down on it.

I said, "It's just my way of saying I'm not delusional about the whole thing, and you are beautiful. So maybe you'll be my Panda Bear."

Clowning and acting a fool are not just for the foolish, if you do it right.

I added, "What the fuck is up with the basket of rolled towels appearing in the bathrooms of your close friends after they're married? That some Martha Stewart shit?"

Her ponytail was shaking from her laugh. Her shoulders shook from under her coat and she kept her eyes wide and pinned on me. Through it all she managed to shrug an 'I don't know,' regarding the rolled towels.

It was the kind of laughter that would help nudge things along when we got upstairs.

"I bet you never had someone ask you to be their Panda Bear."

She quickly calmed to a chuckle, enough to ask, "Are you asking?"

I grab her hand and we stop in front of her building.

"Not with me having to leave early tonight," I was having a great time, but I wanted to hit the club Onyx prime time at eleven and see what popped.

"Let's do a proper date later this week," I said, "See a show or something."

We went upstairs for a session of heavy heavy petting.

When we got hot her phone rang. She ignored it.

Then her phone rang again. She pulled back from our kiss, didn't bother looking at the phone and said to me, "Whoever's calling can't be as cute as you."

When she spoke all I could think about was her hot breath.

In a couple different ways during our grinding session she let me know I couldn't hide behind "Bones." That it just wasn't acceptable.

I knew it too. But on a night when I make up an R&B classic and pulled the Panda Bear thing I got a pass. I knew it, because I had pulled similar stunts before.

It was rough peeling myself away. She laid back while I found my shirt on her couch and pulled it on. I laid her tank-top across her belly, which she promptly shuffled on.

As we both started buttoning up our pants I apologized for having to jet on business.

"I'm sure you'll tell me about it later," she said. Her eyes were all smoked-out lusty.

Mine must've looked the same.

twenty-eight

I stood inside the club Onyx at eleven-thirty on a Monday night, feeling a strong connection with Lenny. Him and clubs, man, he never could stay away.

I was here to get eyes on Albert Brongel.

Misguided as the club scene could get, as shallow as the people could be, at least they weren't just taking the stool next to their old man at the corner bar.

I walked through the crowded main floor at Onyx. I had seen Lenny in enough clubs to know he'd feel right at home here.

Instead of the bar, I walked directly over to the DJ booth. The DJ laid down a hype Kanye re-mix I hadn't heard before. The booth was perfectly positioned between the general public and the VIP lounge. I didn't pay attention to the décor of the club, but the layout was nice. The VIPs could be seen only if they stood along the railing at the top of the steps.

The railing was crowded with people who enjoyed looking down at others. Tonight, Brongel wasn't one of them.

According to Lenny, he and Brongel held this spot down every Monday. This was where Lenny dropped two grand on Thursday night.

I knew the DJ. He had spun at a couple private parties I had worked myself into recently. He was a Southsider so I introduced myself. He didn't remember me but was all 'Yeah, yeah, yeah,' when I talked about places I'd see him spin. He liked the club gig, and — based on the healthy crowd - his residency there made it the hype Monday spot.

I chatted him up for a minute until it got uncomfortable. He stopped looking at me, and I could tell he wanted me to walk.

That's when I asked my question.

"Meeting my boys Lenny and Albert Brongel up here tonight," I asked.

His eyes lit up, but not from excitement.

I asked, "See 'em yet?"

I had figured Albert Brongel could still be in hiding and out at the club. Maybe he thought there wasn't evidence or enough intel out there for the wrong people to track him down.

He figured wrong though. I was the wrong people.

The DJ hesitated to answer. Just that briefest hesitation revealed my deeper feelings about clubs. Everyone ran a game. Strivers? No doubt. But nobody was who they said they were.

Based on posture alone, the DJ had his avoidance shit down. The speakers were right over our heads so I didn't know what he actually said. It didn't seem like he said anything at all.

I mouthed "VIP?"

He paused. I took it for a yes.

I pulled out my phone as if I was going to send a text to one of them.

As I started to text, I turned my shoulders slightly away from him. He nodded in approval.

When I moved through the crowd, I imagined Lenny moving with me, guiding me around the spot. At twenty-seven I had been partying with Lenny for over half my life. We had started stealing booze and copping weed when we were twelve. It felt like second nature to navigate a crowded party or bar with him.

Next up for me was the head of security.

I stood in the middle of the crowd. Most everyone had a friend to lean on. That made it easier to spot the head of security. He and I were the only ones standing alone looking out at the room. He wore a black button down and black slacks, like most of the guys here.

He was five-nine with a receding hairline and a smushed nose. Except for the nose he looked all like the other club-goers who had graduated from P90X. There was one difference. The club patrons wore skinny black slacks. This guy's were looser. And his black Sketchers looked dressy but were just glorified sneakers.

I could picture him in the back room practicing high lift kicks to some imaginary guy's chin. He needed the pants to be loose and the sneakers borderline athletic. I used to work out at a gym where a bunch of bouncers and security types held court. It was the kind of gym that trained MMA fighters. I could've been wrong about his clothes. But there was no mistaking his nose. He probably couldn't smell anymore from it being broken so many times.

I rolled up and asked him, "You work out at Chicago Fitness Center?"

He nodded at me. Looked away.

Yeah, club posturing.

"You know Lenny Supinski? Comes here a lot, especially Mondays."

He looked at me hard. I could picture him practicing that look in the mirror too.

"He's my oldest friend, man," I said, "What's your name?"

Nothing.

Maybe I was the problem in clubs. I cared what I said to people, and cared about what they said back. Sure I enjoyed myself if the music was good, and occasionally found a woman who made great company. But the amount of time I spent talking mush with people — that's what I couldn't stand.

I stood there quiet and kept the pauses long and uncomfortable.

I said, "Lenny said he had an epic night here on Thursday, and then hasn't been seen since."

Again he didn't say anything. I had been riding his hip for two minutes and got nothing.

I was getting worked up. The nice image of Lenny hanging at my elbow faded.

"Doing a favor for his Moms, yo," I said, "She's worried."

Still not a word. But his head started to swivel back and forth, mostly forth towards the VIP area.

"Thing is, I'm not sure if he was here or not, you know. I wondered if I could check out the security footage from that night. His old lady is willing to pay for the help."

He looked right at me again. I had done a good job of keeping my words easy in an *it's-all-good* kind of flow. I raised my eyebrows just a little, smiled.

What I really wanted to do was use my thumb as a spike and jam it up in the soft flesh underneath his chin and bring him to the floor. It'd be worth it, but it'd only add to my troubles.

He was on the hook after I mentioned that his mom would pay money. Money meant conflict. I spoke his language.

"Just wanted to see who he was with and maybe get a lead from any friends he had here."

He leaned into my ear. Finally spoke, "Lenny didn't have friends."

"Who am I then?" I asked back.

"I don't know and don't care."

"But you know who he is," I said, I had my head tilted sideways and mimicked his posture, "Were you two friendly?"

We stood shoulder to shoulder and talked facing the crowd. That's the way he wanted it.

He leaned over and said, "Lenny was jealous."

"What's that got to do with it?" I asked.

"He couldn't handle seeing Babi with anyone else, his boss of all people."

Of course this guy knew Babi. JB Foster too. That was his job.

"Interesting," I said, "He said he rode some rails in the bathroom with a few ladies last Thursday."

The head of security just shook his head. He wasn't about to get drawn in.

I tried anyway. "You're saying Lenny and Babi had a thing at one point in time?"

"Aren't you his best friend?" The guy said.

"I said I was his oldest friend." I was trying to confront him while avoiding confrontation, so I didn't lecture him on friendship.

His hands were at his sides. He shifted his weight. I knew he was close to blowing me off and walking away.

So I just had to ask straight-up, "What about that footage? I can swing by tomorrow. Five bills do it?"

He raised his arms, held his hands out in front of him and tented his fingertips together. I took it as a pre-aggression move.

"I do security the old fashioned way here," he said, "the only cameras are on the bartenders to keep them from stealing."

I said, "That's cool," and looked up at the ceiling; I noticed all the mirrored half-globes. A club this size couldn't get insured without being wired.

I didn't say anything else, just hoped that I hooked him.

I walked straight to the exit, stepped outside and waited.

twenty-nine

Ten minutes later Albert Brongel flushed out of Onyx.

I was standing three feet above ground on a loading dock. The roll-up garage door at my back was slashed with graffiti. The garage door was recessed a foot from the front wall so that I stood in the shadows. The edge of the loading dock stuck out over the sidewalk and was lit by a streetlight. Layered tire tread bumpers were bolted to the loading dock wall to provided cushion for the big rigs that still clogged the daytime streets of the West Loop.

If I peeked around the wall of the dock, I could see people leaving Onyx. I positioned myself here because most of the parkable street spaces were in this direction. There were train tracks in the other direction, but all the spaces by the tracks were riddled with broken bottles.

Brongel moved fast. Headed in my direction. I pulled my head back into the shadows. It kept me from watching the front door to Onyx to see if someone followed him out.

I felt comfortable again, had put my White Sox hat on after the club. I stood there the whole time thinking about the head of security. I kept picturing my thumb poking through the soft under-flesh of his jaw. I thought about the vice grip I'd need on his head. Maybe with my left hand I could reach across his forehead and pull his ear out with my fingers and threaten to rip off the ear if he defended himself too well. Paralyzing him from his ear would leave his neck splayed open for my thumb.

That's the kind of mood I was in when Albert Brongel walked right in front of me.

When he passed, I jumped off the loading dock.

"Holy Shit!" he said, put a hand to his heart.

"I'll walk with you, Albert," I said. When we got to the corner I asked, "Which one's your car?"

I had hoped to catch Brongel inside the club. I thought if he had people around him then he might give up information easier. At least he would avoid physical conflict.

"Know who I am?" I asked.

He looked up at my hat. Shook his head.

Brongel had blond hair and blue eyes — real handsome fellow. I could see him having girls, not a girlfriend.

"Good," I said, "Who'd you set up Lenny's meet with? The military type who paid the twenty-five grand?"

He immediately started shaking his head, "No."

"Yes."

"Not now," he insisted.

"Now is the only time," I said.

"Let's go," he said and flung a hand in the direction of his car, "Follow me."

"It took me two days to find you. I'm not letting you go."

"Saturday. That wasn't my idea," he spoke through quick panted breaths.

"Sounded like you on the phone," I said, "We can get to that later. First things first. Who's the guy?"

"I can't get more involved in this. I need to get out," he said. Flop sweat started to glisten on his forehead as he looked over his shoulder.

He added, "I had nothing to do with Saturday. I was forced to set up the meeting."

I shrugged my shoulders and said, "Who's the guy? That's what I want to know."

"Not now," he said and his breath got more out of control. He had to take in a deep breath and huff it out before he could speak again, "Later, we can meet later. I can't talk right now."

I blocked him with my body and shook my head.

"Seriously man," his eyes darted around, "You either have to come with me-"

"That's not happening," I said.

His kept his head moving — behind him and then over my shoulder. "Or go. Right now. Go," he said, "This is serious."

"Maybe for you," I said, "It's been serious for Lenny since Thursday."

"You have to belie-," he said.

It was too late.

His head stopped moving. He held his breath. His eyes focused on something over my right shoulder.

I too turned to look. My vision couldn't register anything except shadows. Both sides of the street were lined with darkened loading docks. They ran around the corner and all the way down to the Lake Street elevated tracks. I put a hand on Brongel's shoulder to keep him from running. Then I turned further around.

Darkness.

It felt like different pieces of the shadow pulled together from the loading docks and from the support for the elevated tracks and from the dark spaces hanging around the warehouses. They formed a force that materialized from thin air. Not since the shock of both my mom and brother leaving me when I was twelve had I been taken by surprise like that. I was too cautious, normally. Suddenly everything around me became a weapon. The darkness was a weapon used against me. Surprise was a weapon. It felt like the air around me was a weapon too, because none of it felt displaced by the presence of this shadow being. I knew a man had to be behind the attack. Yet I couldn't see his torso turn. I couldn't see his arm swing. I heard something move behind me. I just couldn't see through the thick shadows. By the time I began to grasp the vague feeling of a presence — THUNK — I got knocked hard at the base of my skull.

thirty

I didn't black out. Instead my vision clouded up like a mesh screen was dropped on my eyeballs. I fell in slow motion. The ground beneath me turned into a weapon too. I must've smacked hard onto a patch of gravel someone laid to fill in a pothole. I could feel the uneven edges of the gravel press into my left cheek.

I couldn't move. I tried, but my body rang like a tuning fork and my nerves couldn't make out the right pathway to get my muscles moving. All my nerves buzzed from the whack to my head

I steadied my breath to cut through the shock. This deep rhythm boiled up inside. I started to hear music, and a muffled staccato rap. The music and rap rose up like a force propelling me from within.

POP. A gunshot rang clear.

Adrenaline opened big holes in the virtual mesh covering my eyes.

I tried to look passed out. I couldn't battle a guy with a gun. It wasn't a decision to lie there. I was scared. Keeping my eyes closed was the closest I could get to hiding.

Someone lifted up my arm and put a gun in my hand.

I tried to keep it limp and heavy. I focused only on the in and out of my breath. That kept me from thinking about my arm and possibly slipping and tensing it up. With the gun snug in my hand, he pressed my palm and fingers hard into the grip. The strong hand had to be a man's. It felt like he was wearing the same kind of talc dry latex gloves a tattoo artist wore. Then he peeled back my index finger and slid it right onto the trigger.

His finger squeezed mine. My finger squeezed the trigger.

The kickback rocked me.

It was the first time I fired a gun.

With the gun's recoil, I think I must have groaned or made some sound in my chest. I couldn't help it. I was wide-awake with my eyes closed.

I wanted the next thing I heard to be footsteps moving away.

I didn't hear a thing.

I decided to count to–

BAM. A boot slammed into the back of my head. I grunted, couldn't help it. I tried cutting off the groan pushing from my chest. It wouldn't stop. All I did was make my breath choppy and my chest convulse.

A second kick didn't come.

I didn't see the guy or hear him leave.

I counted to ten and got up. The gun was either a nine-millimeter or a forty-five. I couldn't tell.

I put it down for a minute and peeled the gravel off my face. I cupped the gravel in my hand and slid it into my pocket.

Albert Brongel sat in his driver's seat with one eye missing. Whoever shot him didn't want any cranial interference. Whoever shot him did it on the spur of the moment, and had the trained instincts to pull it off.

I never thought I'd be happy to have someone try and frame me for murder. Because in order to frame me, I needed to be alive. At least that's why I think he left me there.

Sirens started calling in the background. They weren't close. I didn't see any flashers. It sounded like the sirens needed to travel up and over buildings and far down open avenues. I had a minute.

I wanted to run.

Instead, I walked.

First I crossed the street. I would have jetted two blocks north to the west side rail yard and pick up the tracks heading out of town. That was the easiest and most unobstructed route out of here. If I could get to the tracks and circumvent the neighborhood, then I'd spend the next three hours walking home.

But my car was here. The metered spot would get ticketed in the morning. That was acceptable even with my vile hatred for the parking meters and their license to suck money from my pockets. I'd pay the ticket with a smile, if it weren't for one thing.

The entire neighborhood would be a murder scene for the next twenty-four hours and any car parked here would be suspect.

Instead of heading north across Fulton to the railroad tracks, I skipped south across Lake Street under the El. I headed another block south to Randolph. Randolph was the main traffic vein westbound out of the Loop. It was always well lit, but thankfully empty that Monday at midnight.

I could hear the squads behind me. They were probably three blocks back on Fulton at the club. They would have to find the bouncer who issued the "shots fired" call. Then they would have to find the body. I sprinted across Randolph.

Everything from here to Onyx would get sealed off first.

New siren sounds began popping up in the air around me. They were converging from all points to swarm the neighborhood inside a minute. I had less time than expected.

I had parked three blocks south, on a short, empty street called Rundell Place.

I didn't take the long way around. There'd be six or ten squads here and stopping every body still giving off heat.

The sirens grew louder. The cops weren't squawking their sirens just when they blew threw intersections. The sirens wailed and echoed off the flat front of the warehouses and restaurants. The sound ruined the normal order of the night. That's when I knew they were close.

After I crossed Randolph I felt like I could see the sirens' sound waves as they spread through the neighborhood. They traveled like a sonic blob until they filled every street.

With the foremost sound wave catching up to me, I started running. The intensity of the sirens created a pressure at my back. The sound wave hit me. I didn't resist. I let its edge push my hip. The waves' push added speed to my run. When I reached the street my car was parked on, the wave pushed me hard enough that I had to wrestle with it to break free from its current. I thrust myself sideways and stumbled through the turn.

Luckily, I wasn't the type of guy to valet park at clubs. I naturally preferred a few block walk to my spots. This one was a winner. It gave me access to a southbound street, but dead-ended before it reached Randolph.

The sirens' scream was muffled by the buildings that formed the dead-end.

I sprinted the last twenty yards in complete control. I slid across the asphalt to my car door and put the key in the lock.

I stayed calm in my car. I walked myself through the steps of starting and breathing and putting it in gear and breathing and pulling the U-turn and breathing. All the while I imagined squares of the neighborhood being blocked off one by one as new squads got added to the grid. Two more minutes and I'd be sealed in, no doubt.

I exhaled and jetted south. I glided down the on-ramp to the Eisenhower Expressway and slid into the slipstream.

thirty-one

Back in my garage, I turned my car off and sat for a minute. The only sound at two in the morning was the car's exhaust pipes ticking off heat.

I cleared the inventory of out-of-state license plates from my trunk and went inside.

I reluctantly gathered all my weed and paraphernalia.

I took out the gun and wiped it down before wrapping it in a hand towel. I tried not thinking about it too much, just focused on the movements and making sure I wiped the gun down thoroughly.

I pulled out the earrings I had lifted from the K-Town pawnshop.

They were just props now. That's how I decided to think of them. I ignored the fact that the earrings and gun could tie me to two murders.

Downstairs, I opened the panel in the old coal room and stacked everything inside.

thirty-two

There were two guys I knew who could get what I needed. One was an old friend turned adversary. The other an old adversary turned friend. I woke up at six-thirty that Tuesday morning trying to decide between the two of them.

I wallowed in bed long enough to pick which guy to approach. Took me twenty minutes.

At seven-ten in the morning I pulled into the McCormick Place Convention Center employee parking lot.

The Roach was a union electrician here. The Roach's dad and uncle were also union electricians here. Nepotism and the labor sector didn't interest me.

The Roach was my supplier. Everyone called him Eric now.

I checked the rear view mirror. The left side of my face was dotted with bruises from my fall onto the gravel last night.

Four minutes into the wait I saw his black FJ Cruiser turn into the parking lot entrance. He whipped it tight around the corner. He jetted straight to a parking space and turned his car off.

I pulled up behind him.

The Roach had started his union job the week after we graduated high school. Ever since then no matter how far the night stretched into morning we needed to dump The Roach at seven-fifteen.

He climbed out of his car and glared at me. The Roach was an all-black-everything kind of guy. Black coat. Black fleece. Black boots. The only color on his whole person was the small red Dickies label sewn into his black work pants. He wore his black hair in a ponytail.

He looked at his watch.

He only had ten minutes. I needed five.

"Bones," The Roach said and began walking towards the door, "Not here, I don't have time."

The Roach left work at three-thirty every day for his other job. Mostly he dealt weed and coke. He also pushed a decent volume in Percocets and Vicoden to his tradesmen buddies with chronic back pain. I calculated that he netted an extra forty to fifty grand a year.

"Keep walking, Roach," I said and walked with him, "I'll follow you right inside."

He stopped.

"I wanted to ask you about Lenny," I said since it was my standard opening from the weekend, "You seen him?"

"Nope," he said and started walking again.

"Don't," I said with a tone of caution, "Don't do it."

He stopped. He turned around and said, "I haven't seen him, what else can I say?"

"When was the last time you did?" I asked.

"I can't even remember," he said and shook his head in long swoops.

"C'mon Roach," I said, "You tell me that Lenny's ex-girlfriend is murdered inside of Lenny's boss' house and you haven't thought exactly when you saw him last? I haven't seen Lenny all weekend. I think he's hiding. And I know exactly what I'm going to say when the cops come knocking." This wasn't why I was here, but I realized we better talk it over. I could feel the tight squint around my temples ease the more I tried to figure Roach out. "You don't have a better story than, I can't remember?"

He said, "Last week sometime."

"Let's try Thursday to be exact," I said, "Lenny said he was using Thursday night at Onyx," I added. "Did you meet him there, or did he swing by before hand?"

"Between you and I?"

I didn't answer

He shook his head, "I met him at Onyx. He was raging and I didn't stay long. It was one of those nights you just need to steer clear from Lenny. Already had some trashy girl on his arm. Indiscreet, if you know what I mean."

"See him at all on Friday?" I asked. I had been suspicious that The Roach had picked Lenny up from the police station. Lenny had weed on him. After Thursday Lenny would need to cop again on Friday because he didn't hold while on parole.

"Not at all," The Roach said, and asked "How about you?"

"He called me Friday morning," I said. I told him about our conversation. That we talked before Lenny went in for questioning. I mentioned I had a date Friday night. Everything else I told him about Friday between the call and my date was a lie.

Then I told him about the scene with Detective Glenn at Lenny's apartment on Saturday morning.

"They had a warrant already?" The Roach asked.

"Nah, they said someone reported a B&E. The door was open when they got there, so they walked in."

The Roach nodded. It made sense to him.

Sure it did, that's why I told the story like I did.

I didn't trust The Roach as a friend, because we were no longer friends.

"Nice face," he said and lifted his chin in my direction.

"You're not worried?" I asked to avoid explaining my face.

"About what?" he said.

"About Lenny."

He shook his head and said, "Bones, I don't think he did it, honestly."

"I'm not talking about that. Do you think he'll give you up if it keeps him out of prison?"

"The fuck you talking about?" The Roach asked, "I had nothing to do with Babi Patras. Her and I messed around when I was like twenty-two. That thing was long over." he shot his hand out and let it sail away. "Moved on."

"Idiot. He's still on parole," I said and gave it a beat to sink in, "Cops probably gave him a pee test when they brought him in. Parole violation means he's going back up."

Comprehension made The Roach's face go slack. He put both hands behind his head to stroke his ponytail and blew out a breath.

"Unless," I said indicating with silence that Lenny would go back to jail *unless* he tried to cut a deal by offering up his supplier.

It hung between us until The Roach picked it out of the air and nodded, "Unless."

"Something to think about," I told him.

I didn't reassure him, that wasn't my job. He alone needed to wrestle with the idea of Lenny flipping on him.

At the end of high school The Roach basically stole Lenny's business. Lenny earned big money throwing parties and dealing to high school kids. Back then The Roach dealt steroids and supplements out of the gym—small time stuff to non-athletes that wanted to look ripped. The short of it is that I stopped being friends with The Roach after I realized he used me to hurt my closest friend.

I said, "You gotta get running, kid," motioned my hand towards his watch, "but I need you to do one thing for me."

The Roach didn't do things for people. He was a taker.

I almost felt bad for him, the way I set him up. First I figured out that he supplied Lenny the night a murder was committed. I could do damage with that information. Second I did him a solid and informed him his old friend Lenny might flip on him.

The Roach asked, "What do you need?"

Him asking me what I needed satisfied a quiet vengeance inside me.

"Steel," I said.

"Like. A. Gun?" he said, sounded like he couldn't believe his own words.

"That's what I'm saying."

"You with a gun, Bones? I don't know."

I knew what caused The Roach to hesitate. He and Lenny had seen me at my worst. They had seen me beat guys up and steal from my best friends and fuck their girlfriends and it was all just a thing. I was numb to it all. Then they watched me act like it never happened, like there were no consequences. Back when we came up, I truly was numb to it all.

I grew up, that's for sure. Not surprisingly, the consequences were there waiting for me.

The Roach laughed uncomfortably and said, "You with a gun is pretty fucking scary."

"Aren't I scary without one?"

"So what's the difference, right?" he giggled.

He was nervous now, not me.

"Some shit is getting close to me," I said and pointed at my face, "And I don't know what it'll take to make it go away."

"I don't know, Bones," he shook his head. His ponytail wagged behind him.

"I'll pay. You want, I give it back in a couple of weeks. Keep the money."

"What are you thinking, a hand gun?" he asked.

"I don't know. A nine," I answered unable to add anything else - I didn't know anything about guns.

He kept shaking his head and said, "Bones, I'd say no if I could."

"But you won't," I said back.

The Roach was a hustler to the core. It took a toolbox of skills to make it in that business without a whiff of trouble. Lenny couldn't do it. He had many of the skills, but the only person he enabled was himself. The Roach practically took people by the hand and gently guided them to their darkest places.

Yeah, he'd come through.

"Make it quick," I said, "Ping me."

thirty-three

That morning my boss stood at my desk before my computer booted up.

"Come back to my office," he said.

He took his seat and fished out a business card when I got there. Dangled it between his knuckles.

My office was in Greektown — it was the neighborhood just south of the West Loop where Onyx was located. Only blocks from where I parked my car. I liked the way it felt. I could see value in returning to the scene of the crime; it was like reviewing for a test.

Apparently the test was about to begin.

"The police were here," my boss said, "asking for you."

"They say about what?"

"No," he said, and looked down at the card. He handed it to me and added, "But the card says homicide."

I raised my eyebrows and rocked my head back, "Really? What else did they say?"

"They asked me to check the security and log-in records to see if you were here last night."

"Really?" I said again.

"They want you to go to State Street. Right now."

"Really?" I was right about returning to the scene of the crime. I needed to say something other than *Really*, but I was too shocked.

"Ask for the guy on the card," my boss told me.

Glenn.

"Okay," I said with a wavering voice. "And they didn't say what it was about. Hmmf."

I wanted to give him the opportunity to ask me about it. I could let him know that there was trouble, but the trouble wasn't about me.

"That's it," my boss said.

"Okay then, I'll come back after," I told him, "Catch up."

"You better," he paused awkwardly where he wanted to say something, then said, "Bones."

I took a step towards the door before turning around and asking, "Cops ask for me by name?"

He leaned back in his chair. I could tell he really wanted to laugh, but instead revealed a slight smile and said, "First, middle and last."

I huffed out a quick laugh, "Middle name? Are you kidding me?"

"Every syllable," my boss clarified.

I laughed some more to play it off.

He could be funny sometimes, but he was still a boss.

thirty-four

I sat on Halsted at a traffic light, the one at Jackson. I had just turned off *Illmatic* on my stereo to take the ride to the police station in silence. The quiet would help me prep for my interrogation.

The street activity moved slower in silence. The clouds made the November sky look like ash, so that even mid-morning felt like night.

The neon sign for the Jackson Hotel glowed. The motel was three blocks from my job and I could've looked at it every time I grabbed a gyro for lunch. It wasn't that I chose to ignore the building. I just never looked at it.

My mom lived there once.

After she came back the last time, she lived in an apartment way up north on Kenmare. She stayed in that apartment less than a year before setting her mattress on fire. After the night of the mattress fire I decided never to see her again.

A couple weeks after that decision her Armenian super called to tell me she hadn't paid her rent, and hadn't been around.

I didn't want to do anything for her. I had just started working at the credit reporting agency and was having a great summer — forgot completely about my mom for like four months.

Then one night on my way to a happy hour after work, I took a call from the Pacific Garden Mission on south State Street. My mom had checked in there desperate for a hot meal and a bed.

The woman on the phone told me my mom had been there two nights. The first two nights she attended the required church service at five p.m. Like many other mission-shelters they required you to hear the word of God in order to earn your bed. My mom was a Bridgeport girl — Catholic to the core. But on the third and fourth night she refused the service.

I never asked if she had issues with the denomination being preached at the Pacific Garden Mission, the color of the preacher, or if it was just her independent streak.

The mission was kicking her out. She needed a place to go though, so my mom gave them my phone number. Come pick her up, they told me.

I took a cab over.

My mom was at the curb in front of the Mission when we pulled up. She had a ratty duffle bag on her shoulder and carried a Walgreens plastic bag in her hands – the big square kind of bag with hard plastic handles glued on. She also had a purse, because ladies are not to be caught without a handbag. I was certain her handbag, and the other two bags, were all filled with random newspaper clippings and manic scribblings.

Her clothes weren't particularly beat. Not for someone who spent four months on the street. She probably went on a shopping spree in the donation room when she checked in at the mission.

I stepped out of the cab and took her bags for her. She sat down, and I walked around to the traffic side of the street and opened the door.

As soon as I sat, she said:

'Oh my, you wouldn't believe the number of people that sleep in that place', she said as if she was reading an interesting article in the newspaper. The fact that she long ago abandoned her family and had just gotten kicked out of a homeless shelter never occurred to her.

"Jackson Hotel," I said to the driver, "Jackson and Halsted." The Mission rep had told me they had a vacancy. It was rare to still find flophouses with weekly rates for transients that close to downtown. I wanted to give the taxi driver more instructions to avoid talking to my mom, but his quick U-turn told me he knew the place.

Instead of talking, I stared out the window. It was already dark. People honked as the taxi driver pulled his U-ey. That U-turn chopped two minutes off the ride and earned him an extra two buck tip. The headlights of the surrounding cars beamed on us, momentarily washing our faces of all their color. If only something could wash out the sound too, then I could arrive at the Jackson Hotel in silence.

My mom caught the vibe and tried to keep quiet.

It lasted one block.

Then she burst out with a giggle.

I didn't bite.

She giggled again. She was so excited to see me she wasn't going to let the special moment pass.

She said, 'Oh, your grandfather. He was so proud of you that time you took on the entire football team.'

No. That's all I remembered thinking. No, don't drag me into some delusional memory that never happened. I never played football. My grandpa strangled himself inside the neck of a bottle. He never saw me play sports.

'Oh, you were so strong,' she said.

I wasn't looking at her, but could hear the happiness in her voice. She probably wanted to hold hands or some shit like that. The "strong" comment echoed reality. She always used to say I was built like a tank. That was before she stopped grocery shopping.

She continued, 'You were built like a tank.'

'Mom,' I said.

I wasn't going to take it. It wasn't a matter of the mattress fire on Kenmare or her being homeless or any other thing that made for a last straw. I just didn't want to live in that world anymore.

She sighed out a long, 'Ohhhhhh.'

Of all the incidents, and there were plenty, I remembered the silence of that cab ride. I still thought about it. No doubt, there were more dramatic events between my mom and I. But that cab ride stuck with me. My independence — my house, my job — was all about me. And her creeping into that part of my world wasn't going to happen. If I could've filled the car's cabin up with hatred and suffocated us all with it, I would have.

Seven minutes later our cab pulled up outside the Jackson Hotel.

The Greek guy who owned the place was working check-in that night.

I made a comment about his place turning condo soon.

He looked at me. Apparently he didn't joke about everything like I did.

He told me, 'I have a brother who is schizophrenic. It's a lot of work. He never stayed here, but we had to find him in all kinds of places.'

'How is he now?' I asked.

'Good, we have him in a home. He's stable as long as he's on his medication–'

'I know that,' I cut in. Consistent medication felt like a lottery ticket: so easy to obtain, but that shit never came through.

The elevator operator was on a smoke brake, so the owner worked the handle and took us up. My mom was silent. He and I had a good conversation about the trials of caring for loved ones with mental health issues. The matter-of-fact conversation was an oddity because I rarely met someone who dealt with the same issues as me. My mom was quiet.

The elevator wasn't the only item last updated in the 1950s. The naked mattress in her room had sweat stains that dated back that far. It was the old cotton kind of mattress, without springs in the middle to maintain firmness. The lumpy, uneven and shit stained mattress looked exactly like what it was — one step up from the street. That was the Jackson Hotel.

When he left us there, I set her bags down on the chair.

She laughed, said something about, 'another room, another place,' trying to sound philosophical about her travels.

'I'll be back next Friday after work to pay your rent,' I said, and walked out.

It could've gone differently. She could've been there the next Friday, and maybe I would've taken her out for dinner. But she wasn't. The second week I started checking in on her every couple days. I switched up the times. Six in the morning. Eleven at night. I played with the pattern thinking she had to sleep sometime. I was wrong about that. When my mom was manic she could go a month without truly sleeping.

I visited the Jackson Hotel at such odd times I barely saw anyone at the front desk. The elevator operator was never there, so I worked the handle myself every time.

I operated that manual elevator for four weeks. I never saw the owner again. Finally, I stopped paying her rent.

The night I dropped her off at the Jackson Hotel was the last time I saw her.

thirty-five

I spent ninety minutes in the police station's interrogation room before he walked in and re-introduced himself.

"Detective Glenn."

"I remember you," I replied.

He pointed to his partner, "This is Kostecki," and after I nodded at him, Glenn added, "We need to talk to you."

I could've said, 'No kidding,' but kept quiet. On the far wall of the interview box was a big piece of two-way glass. I hadn't been cuffed.

His partner stood by the door. Glenn asked, "What happened to your face?"

"Fight, Saturday night," I said.

"Those aren't fist marks," Glenn said.

"Took a fall," I answered, "He fell harder."

"Where was this?"

"Spot on Sheffield called Red Rocks," I said, "Check with the bouncer."

The partner took a note. Then they both left.

Then I started thinking about Glenn's job and chain of command, and how the shit rolled down. It started way up top, maybe even at City Hall on this high profile case. By the time it rolled down past Glenn and onto me it was a boulder-sized piece of shit.

I knew they were making me stew in my own juices. They thought solitary confinement for a couple of hours would make me freak out. They expected me to work myself up to a lather by the time they returned.

I came up in solitary confinement. That shit was home to me. There wasn't any lather or juices when they came back. Just me, waiting.

An hour and fifteen minutes later Glenn walked in alone.

"Detective," I said sure to get in the first word.

He shuffled his chair into place and pulled out a pad for notes. His face was mostly jaw. He had bleach white teeth and he didn't quite smile as much as raise his upper lip to show them.

"Your name is Michael Panozzo?" Glenn said.

I nodded.

"And people call you, B, Bo–"

"Bones, that's right it's a childhood thing."

"Interesting."

"To some. And you're Glenn. Kostecki over there?" I asked pointing to the glass.

He nodded.

I asked, "What am I here for?"

Glenn answered, "You confronted JB Foster yesterday and threatened him."

"That was in Kenilworth. This is Chicago," I said. The differences were beyond geographical.

I wondered if Glenn came in solo thinking he, being black, could do a better job on the guy who lived in Bridgeport.

Glenn looked as if his dark green pants had a matching suit coat. He had a light yellow shirt and an orange tie. A pair of brown Brogues brought it all together.

"You're friends with Lenny Supinski." Glenn said. "I want to talk to you about him."

My favorite subject. "Sure."

"You two grew up together?" That's how Glenn started. Glenn wanted the full blow up, all the details of Lenny's life. They had it all by now, no doubt. Still I gave good detail. After I talked about Lenny's small time hustling Glenn asked, "You think that Lenny couldn't make it as a dealer?"

"I think if he could've he would've."

We even chuckled a little over his exploits like the high school pied-piper keg parties and classic failures like free numbies and lines for girls in the back room. Glenn came off as jovial even if he didn't have a full smile or a full laugh.

"Why couldn't Lenny make it?" Glenn asked.

"Ran his game wrong," I answered.

"You seem to know a lot," Glenn said. His compliments and joviality tried to open me up, "You ever deal?"

I smiled. Funny.

"I didn't like the people," I said.

"The people stopped you."

"Pretty much." Right now I clear five hundred bucks a month. Nothing. That's a hobby — my date money. At sixteen, seventeen I could've squirreled away a couple of grand and built it from there. That was huge money for me. I could've got the product and ran a much better game than Lenny — possibly taken out The Roach. But the only freaks and assholes in my life were grandfathered in at birth. I wasn't about to be harassed for product by mad hypes; I didn't want to go to their house, have them at mine, or meet anywhere in between.

"I do what I gotta do," I told them, "but I decided to make money a little cleaner."

"At American Credit," Glenn said, glanced at his notes.

"Reporting," I added for him.

He said, "I find it strange that all of Lenny's co-workers know you."

"I look out for my friends."

"That what it was?"

"Explaining it isn't going to help much, you know," I told him, "My boys are mine. What happens to them, happens to me. We're all responsible for each other like that."

Glenn asked, "Lenny did three stints at 26th and Cali. You responsible for that?"

"Sure."

"You are?" Glenn asked, "Why?"

"He was going off," I said, "and I had to let him go. Some people have to hit rock bottom. Lenny needed to do it a couple times. I was only there when he wised up and started looking for something else."

"So if Lenny was threatened or in trouble," Glenn jumped in. He didn't make it sound like a question, but he slouched his shoulders a bit like he was digging in.

I sat there. Question. Answer. That's the game I played.

"You have any thoughts on that?" Glenn asked.

"On what? Lenny in trouble? Yeah, Lenny's in trouble."

Glenn looked sideways. Then back at me.

"What kind of trouble you think he's in?"

I exhaled, "Well, since you've just held me here for three hours just to talk about Lenny, I'd say he's in *getting-played-for-murder* type trouble. Before today I just thought his bender was *losing-his-job* kind of trouble."

I knew I was much better off giving real information than lies. Not because I feared perjury, but because when shit got negative, I got quiet. So I tried to play it positive and give as much as I could.

Glenn jumped in, "Why'd you go to JB Foster's house?"

"I visited JB Foster," I told him, "Because I'm worried about Lenny."

"What were you hoping to accomplish?"

"I wanted to see if JB thought Lenny did it," I said.

"You just said, you didn't think he was a suspect until today."

"And, well, I'm looking for Lenny."

"Hold it," Glenn held up a hand, "You're looking for Lenny. Why?"

"Why wouldn't I? Going on a bender right now doesn't help a thing. Not with parole. Not with Babi Patras."

"You saw him?" Glenn asked.

"Naw, a friend of ours ran into him last Thursday at this club Onyx. Said Lenny had cash and a case of pharmaceuticals." I checked myself; I had to make sure I was fine bringing The Roach into this. "Didn't sound like Lenny had any other ideas."

"When was this?" Glenn asked.

"Like I said, last Thursday."

"No," Glenn corrected, "When did you talk to this guy about Lenny?"

"This morning," I said, and gave him The Roach's name.

Glenn's face could easily betray him. He had that unblemished light brown skin that would hold off looking old until he was into his sixties, but his upper lip flexed too much. Right then he didn't move. He sat still and thought it through before saying, "We tossed Lenny's apartment and came up with a half ounce of pot."

"So he's going back for a parole violation?" I asked.

He nodded. "We've got a warrant out on him."

I nodded. Then I told him every detail about last Friday. Everything as it happened right until I went to Lenny's house. I told them about my text and added, "And that was it. I expected to see him Saturday and didn't. So I started looking."

"That why you forced yourself into Albert Brongel's apartment?"

"Forced?" I asked. "More like I rang the buzzer and walked up the stairs."

"You posed as Lenny," Glenn said.

"You want to find the man, gotta be the man," I said.

Glenn seemed like he wanted to nod. Instead he stuck his jaw back into his neck. His neck muscles flexed. He finally slipped. A tell. It was coming.

I took a deep breath. It was better to do it then—before he made his play.

Kostecki walked in and set a piece of paper in front of me as I finished my exhale.

In the picture I stood next to the mush-nosed head of security at Onyx. I looked pretty good in the shot. It was too dark to be a great picture, but my posture was perfect, and I definitely looked handsome.

The smushed-nose security guy was the one who flushed Albert Brongel. I made him do it, okay, but Brongel was there and if I could've talked to him inside, then.

Nah, squash that. As soon as I got to Brongel it was over for him. He was just a middle man. The first to be eliminated. No way I could've saved him.

"Tell me about Albert Brongel," Glenn said.

"Lenny mentioned him. They were hanging out a lot. That place Onyx, Monday nights from what Lenny said. So I went up there."

"Albert Brongel was murdered last night."

"I know."

"You were at the scene of a murder fifteen minutes before it happened."

"And asking around about the victim," I reminded them, looked up at Kostecki as he stood.

I had to answer a string of questions about my whereabouts after I left. Where did I park, how did I get home. I steered my answers west, away from the Loop or even Halsted where they could possibly pick up traffic cam footage.

"You ever meet him?" Glenn asked.

"Never, didn't even know what he looked like until this morning's paper," I said.

Glenn came right back in, "What's to say you didn't lure Albert Brongel out and Lenny was waiting in your car for him."

"Nothing can stop you from saying that. But all I can say is I left and went home."

"You searched Albert Brongel's apartment," Glenn said, "You were at the murder scene."

"It doesn't look good," I told them.

"We are going to need to search your house," Glenn said.

Kostecki put a picture in front of me. I had to turn it around. It said something about a judge at the top had the county seal on top. I knew it was a search warrant. Took my time anyway.

"It says suspected involvement in the homicide of Albert Brongel," I read aloud.

"That's correct," Kostecki said.

"Well you got that wrong," I told them. "You think I murdered this guy because I couldn't find my friend?"

It didn't add up. I barely knew shit about the law, but without a gun and without a motive I didn't think they could get to charges.

"You're our little worm," Kostecki said.

"Bring us Lenny," Glenn added, "We've got enough to bring accessory charges against you."

"You couldn't," I said back.

"We will. You might get off, but you'd have to fight the charges from a cell."

"Basically you're telling me you don't know where Lenny is," I said.

They didn't say anything back.

"Good," I said.

"Good?" Glenn said. He bent his neck so his ear almost touched his shoulder. Winced and said, "Good?"

"Yeah, good. Means I'm not crazy for not being able to find him."

"If what you say is true," Glenn's head was straight up again, "The added incentive will help you."

I wondered if Glenn had one of those cop hunches that I helped Lenny vanish. I squashed that thought. Tried to grab a beat from my head. I could hear Nas' voice busting around inside, but only his baritone chops playing at a low level.

Glenn let his arm drop fully flat to the table, "Ready?"

"For what?" I asked.

Glenn pinched the search warrant off the table and swung it between his fingers. The paper tick-tocked back and forth. Each swing brought to mind everything they could uncover at my house: Brongel's murder weapon, diamond earrings, a stack of money, keys to Lenny's house, keys to Lenny's squat, stolen out of state license plates, and my weed.

I didn't want these two in my house. I also couldn't stop them.

"Right now?" I asked.

Glenn nodded over the swinging paper and said, "I'm riding with you."

thirty-six

My phone powered up on the drive back to my house. I slid on my blue tooth. The Ward office would be closed by the time Glenn and his partner were finished.

I needed to correct my stoner moment, and didn't want to wait until tomorrow.

Sunday when I pulled up behind JB on the driveway to his house I stumbled on something. It took me a minute to clear the smoke from my short-term memory. That's why I called it my stoner moment. They happen.

Glenn sat next to me and typed into his iPhone.

When Chris McMahon answered on the other end I said, "It's Bones," gave him a second to make sure I had his attention, "I'm driving back to my house. Got a Detective Glenn riding shotgun. Got a minute?"

"Sure Bones," he said with an obvious air of playing it straight, "Been meaning to call."

"Lenny?" I asked, didn't even glance at Glenn.

"You too, buddy," he said. Chris was a fixer in the ward office — the street-level voice and face of Alderman Hughes.

"Come by when you get off?" I asked.

"I've got a meeting at six."

"Easy breezy," I said, and hung up.

JB Foster took over PSI over twenty years ago. That event is engraved in Chicago business lore. PSI stood for Price Sanitation Incorporated. JB expanded the business legit, made it his own. But since the Price family had issued stock, he couldn't change the name or the stock ticker.

The family he ousted went nationwide with their bankroll: strip malls and commercial real estate. Their buildings in Chicago attained critical mass while their development arm took a cut of every major skyscraper built in the last fifteen years.

Albert Brongel worked for Document Systems or something like that, but the logo I saw on his paystub Sunday morning was no doubt the Price Properties logo. Could the Document place that paid Brongel's check be a division of Price Properties?

Yeah, stoner moment.

thirty-seven

"Need me for anything?" I asked when Glenn and his partner walked into my house.

They came by on their own — no K-9 unit, no metal detector.

"Yeah, stay out of our way," Glenn said.

I walked to my picture window and waited.

I probably shouldn't have, but I texted Dorothy anyway. I decided I should answer some of her questions and not string her out any longer. I asked if she could meet for a quick drink later that night.

Chris McMahon pulled his green Crown Vic to the curb in front of the cop car. Given the abundance of patronage work around here, multiple Crown Vics on the street looked normal.

I quick sent a text to The Roach: Talked to cops. Your name came up FYI. Want to hear from you soon.

"I'll be out front talking to a friend!" I yelled back to Glenn.

Neither cop responded.

"Hey bro, what happened to your face?" McMahon asked when I sat in his car.

I shrugged.

Chris McMahon lived in a parallel universe to mine — one defined by certainty. His pops helped him land an internship in the ward office during college. The job went full time when he graduated. From the time we were in junior high he knew exactly the type of work he'd be doing for the rest of his life. He was married at twenty-six. He'd have a kid by thirty.

Basically Chris was a shining example of what I wasn't. He stayed in one place, let his talents work, and took what came to him. I kept moving, working overtime trying not to get pinned down. Chris's mom ran the city's property tax billing department after twenty years on the job. My mom had twenty years of disability under her belt.

"You alright, Bones?" he asked, and pulled up his eyebrows so that his hairline and ears rose at the same time.

I nodded, happy to not be Michael anymore.

"Lenny doing okay? This is serious," he prodded.

"Lenny's going back up. Violated his parole. And that's the good news."

"That girl was hot. But —"

Girls. Now if there was someone who could commit a crime of lust, I was looking at him.

I tried to picture the cops' progress inside my house. The longer they took, the better. Last thing I wanted was one of them to come walking down my gangway. That meant they'd have been in the basement. In the basement they'd find my stash.

"You working this?" he asked.

"Like for money?" I raised my eyebrows, "C'mon, we're talking Lenny here."

I did a job for Chris. Before he got married last year. I tailed an ex-boyfriend of his wife's. Chris had run across a handful of texts on her phone. Got worried when she went missing for a couple hours one night. He was too worked up to figure it out. And for many of these guys I played the brain, the level head. It was a new adult role for me. The guy I tracked was from Beverly, like Chris' fiance. Well, sometimes I played the body too. I did the job and gave Chris his four hundred buck fee back for a wedding gift.

I kept it as vague as I could and said, "That guy Albert Brongel was Lenny's middleman on some business. Someone caught wind that I was looking for him."

"West Loop, last night?" Chris asked. He wore baggy chinos and a polo underneath his North Face jacket. I had no doubt he'd work his way up to wearing a suit by forty, get out of the ward and into a city job with a pension. That was if he didn't take Hughe's place in the city council. His big blockhead was covered in sweaty black hair from always hustling. His pasty skin highlighted his freckles and his thin red lips.

"He's coming for you," Chris said, jerked his head toward the back of the car.

My heart stopped beating.

Chris tapped his horn lightly to let Detective Glenn know where we were parked.

I couldn't even roll down my window; I was in shock.

Glenn walked up to the passenger side of the car.

Chris hit the passenger side window button. Fresh breeze wiped across my face.

Glenn nodded at Chris like they knew each other.

The cops must have stopped by the ward office to ask about Lenny.

"You have a key to the garage?" Glenn asked. His eyes went back and forth between us. I was too stunned to play it off.

"Uh," I said and arched my back to reach into my pocket. I stopped, sat normally, and said "Yeah. Uh, why don't you just kick the bottom of the door real quick. It'll open."

"We all know that trick," Chris said to him. Nice move, it kept Glenn from asking for my keys. I didn't want to give any more than I had to.

"What about the front of the basement? You have a key to that?"

"It's an illegal apartment," Chris jumped in.

The drunk forklift driver would be home by now.

Chris added, "You need another warrant for that?"

"He's probably home," I told Glenn, "Knock on either door."

Glenn strolled away with the cadence of someone out for a moonlit walk.

"Thanks," I said to McMahon.

"Of course man, whatever. You know you and Lenny were always too damn crazy for me, but we go back."

"I'm talking present day," I said, "JB Foster and Price Properties. They got beef?"

McMahon moved his head back and forth, made a small arc with his chin. Same move his old man did. It allowed them to think it over and turn the arc into a nod or a shake depending on what they decided to reveal.

"Two bodies on Lenny, and this is all I have," I reminded him.

"The kid always hated JB."

That would be Whitman Price. Ten years JB's junior, and finishing up his MBA at Wharton when JB made his play for PSI. Those two competed for models at fashion shows and for the best booths in the clubs. JB's life played out in the business section and gossip pages, while Whitman's family kept their playtime quiet. The differences were boring to me, but people still loved talking about old money versus new.

McMahon moved his chin into an up and down slot, nodding.

"There might be," he said, "Price bid on that city records contract," he said, "Wasn't a good loser."

"Would you be?" I asked him.

He shrugged. He probably never planned on finding out how losing felt.

He nodded his head some more, "Yeah, it was right about this time."

"That Document Solutions or something like that? They have a division that deals in security and storage?"

"Oh yeah. Their security division is the tits, Bones. They already have contracts with the city and state for special events."

"Word?"

"They're like the Midwestern Blackwater."

Glenn walked back up the gangway. My heart stopped again.

McMahon kept talking as we each adjusted a mirror so we could watch him.

McMahon was anxious on my behalf, even if he didn't know what I was hiding.

"Price Properties in the security business?" I said, "First I've heard."

"Their best kept secret. But yeah, their recruiter called me last year about a job."

We paused as Glenn stopped. Instead of climbing the stairs up to the sidewalk, he knocked on the side door.

"Price Properties?" I repeated.

A minute later the apartment's door opened. Glenn started talking and motioning over his shoulder at me.

"The kid, brother," Chris said about Whitman Price, "He's nasty."

"So what? He's pissed JB won the city contract and goes off and kills his girlfriend?"

He winced, and leaned his head back, "Miiiight be a bit obvious. I don't know. That water's way down the river by now."

"You think there's anything to it?" I asked.

McMahon couldn't let the idea go and his face did acrobatics trying to sort it out.

"Anything?" I asked, practically begged for an idea.

"Timing's strange. Wasn't it like a year ago?"

"Does it matter?" I asked.

"Yeah, in all these privatization contracts there's a first anniversary review that allows for the city or municipality to revoke the contract."

"Word?" I said all excited.

Chris' posture straightened up like he was giving me hope.

But I was thinking something else. I asked, "And we're still saddled with that fucking parking meter contract?"

McMahon started to giggle. Sucked in his lower lip and turned his head away from me. Made an overbite onto the same lower lip. He started shaking with the giggles and, shook his head long and deep.

I imagined him on the verge of telling a great big secret about the parking meter contract. It felt like the secret would be so funny we'd both laugh. We'd get so giddy I'd punch him in the arm. He'd hit me back. We'd laugh until our jaws ached.

But it never went that far.

Chris just giggled to himself.

I understood right then and there that the parking meter contract wasn't a joke, it was the punch line.

Chris took whatever knowledge he had and squashed it. When his giggles stopped he looked at me with raised eyebrows and shrugged his shoulders as high as they could go. He wasn't saying shit.

The joke was on us, Chicago. That was all I'd get.

"Okay, you fucking block head," I said, "Save me a day at the library, will ya? Look up that contract and tell me what day it was executed?"

"Text you later," he said.

thirty-eight

"Okay, so it was two guys," I told Dorothy.

"Why didn't you just say two guys in the first place?" she said and threw a soft backhand into my shoulder.

When I texted her as Glenn and his partner searched my house I must have violated some kind of dating protocol. I could tell because we were inside the Goldstar Lounge on Division staring at drinks. We weren't at her apartment. All the hipster music on the jukebox didn't make space for even a bounce of hip-hop.

When Glenn and his partner finished I didn't even walk back into my house. They didn't find my stash, obviously. My house was my sanctuary, but I couldn't stay there after they finished tossing it. What I needed was to blaze a few joints and burn down a brick of incense to get the cop stench out. That'd have to wait. When they walked out, I locked my front door behind them and drove away.

Dorothy's hair was back in a ponytail. The length of her ponytail was perfect. Her face without make-up was sublime. She wore a designed threadbare pink T-shirt, black jeans, grey leg warmers and toe-cleavage ballet flats. She could wear this outfit with her black bra underneath for the rest of our lives and I would not get tired of it.

I rubbed my hands over my eyes, "I don't know, I don't see why it's such a big deal." I hadn't even got to the part I came here to talk about. It was too bad we hadn't had sex yet, because I liked her and hated being on the business end of an unhappy woman.

She said, "Oh, so you pick me up with bruises dotting your face." To her credit she's not mad *mad*. Just trying to wrap her arms around the circumference of my no-talking policy.

Stretch Armstrong doesn't have arms that long.

She continued, "And, I, Dorothy, am supposed to what? Shrug? Ignore it? Ask if you'll take me out for gelato?"

"I like all those options," I said, smiling, "Let's try them all."

"Uh-uh, not happening," she rubbed the length of her left arm lightly.

So I told her. No names. No names of bars or clients or locations. I told her about everything that went down on Saturday night at Red Rocks. We last saw each other on Sunday, so I changed the day in my story to Monday night.

"I didn't go looking for this," I said. I gave enough details to satisfy the requirements of reality and no more. I also told her point-on, "This isn't over. This guy is going to pay. And one time you might see me with bloody knuckles or whatever, I don't know, but I do not talk about this shit. You see my hand swollen, you know what it is. Got it?"

She undid her ponytail, and refastened it while trying to gather a few floating strands of hair.

I loved watching her arms move. That yoga tone drew my eye in and all I wanted was to take her back to her place. Not my place. Not while I was on the cops radar and my house still felt like a breached fortress.

"So you said you wanted to talk?" she asked.

Jesus she would not stop.

Yeah, I wanted to talk. I had to do this otherwise there wouldn't be a next time. Or there possibly wouldn't be a *this* time, tonight at her place.

"You got any weed at home?" I asked.

Even if they came up empty, I couldn't get Glenn and his partner out of my head. I kept imagining them accompanied by a German Shepherd and escorted by a salivating cop.

She took a sip off her Sierra Nevada pint, puckered her face and said, "You're using weed as an excuse to get into my apartment?"

"No, it's just that my stash is gone and…nevermind."

They took my computer. They took it because that's what a scorched earth search looks like. I lifted my seltzer and took a drink. Took an ice cube into my mouth. I set the seltzer down and lifted my cognac, transferred the ice cube.

Dorothy started looking at her nails.

"So," I said. Yeah, the limpest of openings. She was too smart to mock me and say 'So' back.

"You're cool," I told her.

"You're funny," she said.

"I'm Michael," I said, "Michael Panozzo."

"Italian?" she asked.

"Half, the other half's Irish."

"You're mom's the Irish one?"

"She is but we're not talking about my mom, okay?"

thirty-nine

Dorothy slept next to me. An hour ago we finished with our heavy petting, and lay in our underwear. She looked ready for sleep so I faked doz-
ing off so she could relax. Her weed — some flavorless shake — helped
put her out.

I was the opposite — the weed made me feel wired, but not in a paranoid way. Thoughts kept pushing into my head, and shoved out any
drowsiness and any hope that we might wake up together in the morning.

Did hipsters have a thing against digital clocks? I stared hard for a
couple of minutes and tried to make out the time on the dial on her nightstand clock but couldn't. So I started hanging my arm over the side of the
bed and checking my phone at twelve-fifteen. If I didn't sleep, I'd have to
call it a night and slip out — no way I could pace through Dorothy's apartment all night.

Did Lenny have moments like this with Babi Patras? I had no idea.
They had dated, that was it. Lenny played off the ending, and that
could've meant he had just moved on. He might also have been heartbroken. I bet Babi Patras was one of those magical women whose soul se-
duced men with the feeling of aspiration. At this point, I couldn't speculate. It mattered though; I needed to know how far Lenny went to avoid
the truth.

Dorothy had started off our kissing session at her house by placing
a delicate baby kiss on each one of my small bruises. Felt nice. It felt
like the kind of life I wanted to have — where a few kisses could lessen
troubles.

Someone had framed my oldest friend for murder, and tried to do
the same to me. That person was still out there — I didn't know how close.

Checked my phone. One-twenty-five.

One-thirty-two I climbed out of Dorothy's bed slowly. I picked her
phone up from her nightstand next to the clock and brought it to the
kitchen with me. Not once did I think about checking to see if she was
texting with another guy. Nah, I just didn't want to wake her up. I took
her phone with me into the kitchen.

I typed a message saying I was looking at her as I typed and how
beautiful she looked. She did look great. She only wore her panties — kept

them on to keep me honest. The panties didn't match. I'd let it slip. At the same time I patted myself on the back for probably getting her further than she wanted to go tonight.

After her phone chirped twice signaling the receipt of her new text, I put it back on her nightstand and slipped out the door.

One-thirty-seven. I decided to check on my house.

forty

Nobody in the office mentioned my bruise spotted face. My boss yanked his eyebrows down low when I checked in with him, and that was signal enough for everyone to steer clear of me.

At mid-day when I dropped a second stack of reports on his desk I didn't even look at him.

My cube mate brought me back a sandwich for lunch.

Chris McMahon's text came in so I wiped the potato chip grease off my fingers and opened my phone.

The text told me the one-year appeal date was a week away—the day before Thanksgiving. McMahon also wrote, "Check your e-mail," and he added at the end of his text, "Don't mess it up."

"Thank. You." I whispered to myself.

The document he e-mailed was dated next Wednesday, like his text said, the day before Thanksgiving.

I didn't even read it. All I needed to see was the letterhead. Riley & Kleiner. A law firm with a LaSalle Street address printed in one of those simply elegant law firm fonts. They weren't the most prestigious law firm in Chicago. Just the most connected.

The company that won the parking meter contract was a Riley & Kleiner client. The Skyway deal? That one too. The failed Midway airport sale? No need to ask.

I read the cover letter. It summarized an appeal to the city's document storage contract. The documents to be filed in five days aimed to end JB Foster's municipal gravy train and award it to someone else.

I printed the whole thing out and threw it in an envelope.

I held a hundred page document in the envelope and let its weight sag in my hands. I finally had an inside scoop to the havoc going on around me. I felt the weight and knew it was more than information. That envelope would be leverage.

forty-one

Two bodies. I drove home after work fixated on that idea. The gun in my stash had two bodies on it. The shadow wanted to hang both Babi Patras and Albert Brongel on me. I was too new at this to put stuff together as it happened. I needed a minute to digest it all.

I kept thinking, two bodies, in a daze. I parked and walked to the corner store at Thirty-Fifth and Halsted. That place was one slab of bulletproof glass away from being a ghetto shop. I grabbed a case of Miller Lite cans. The cardboard box was moist with humidity inside the smelly store.

I thought I was being watched when I left the beer spot.

I didn't spot a tail. I hadn't dealt with this before, couldn't tell you what a PD tail looked like. I had no idea if they were skilled enough to put someone on me without me noticing.

My house was still a mess from yesterday's search. My bed was littered with the contents of my dresser. My kitchen was torn apart. The bathroom was a wreck. Luckily I still had a stereo, because the dicks took my computer with all my music on it.

Even inside my house it felt like I was being watched. I knew I was really getting paranoid when I started thinking about the US Constitution. That article about illegal search and seizures: it aimed to prevent us from living in a military state. I started to think about colonial times, and shit like that.

I had to do this small thing.

The back door to the illegal basement apartment was right next to my furnace. My tenant was listening to sports on AM1000 too loud. This day fell within the calendar year so the guys on the radio were probably talking about the Bears.

I knocked four loud raps on his door.

My tenant needed two minutes of hacking and wheezing before he could answer the door.

"Sorry, man," I said and held the case of beer up for him, "about yester-day with the cops."

"I need a little notice about this shit," he said scratching his hair, "They can't just come barging in here and searching my things."

His things, when he moved in, consisted of a tube TV and a couple boxes of clothing that proved to be full of faded jeans and freebie T-shirts. He also carried a blue plastic milk crate with a table-top rotating fan sticking out.

"I feel the same way," I said, "They caught me by surprise. Friend of mine is in trouble."

He grabbed the case of beer from me. He made like he was getting a better grip and propped it on his knee. I should've bought the twelve-pack. They were cold. He fished his fingers through the handle and in-side to test the cans.

"That's not cool, man," he said and I couldn't tell if he was talking about yesterday's search or the beer.

"I know, I know," I said.

Then I got out of there.

forty-two

It was one in the morning. I had spent the last hour with Dorothy apologiz-ing about leaving last night. I got it, I told her, no woman wanted to wake up naked and alone. She accepted the apology, and told me to go home.

Too bad, because that night I was tired enough and was positive I could've fallen asleep at her house. Also, I didn't want to go home. I still hadn't cleared out the debris from the search.

It would've been easy to jump on the expressway to get home. At this hour I only needed to slide in among the big rigs crossing the city, dip in between their hulking masses and ride the current to the South Side.

I didn't want to hurry back to my mess of a house, so I stayed local.

I turned on *Illmatic* and forwarded to track six, "Halftime." The bass line kicked off the song as I rode over the expressway.

A set of headlights popped up behind me just as Nas' roiling lyrics kicked in.

Chicago had a few diagonal streets that cut through the grid. I rode Elston into the heart of the city. The street cut through a low-slung corridor for business that operated out of loft spaces. The new, brighter streetlights lit up my path as if it were daylight.

I was too distracted by that car to listen to the music.

The tail drew gradually in until it rolled up behind me for the red light at Grand Avenue by the Buddha Bar. It was a blacked-out Crown Vic with a guardrail on its front bumper.

I thought it was the cops so I just acted like I didn't notice them.

I headed towards the loft district on the west end of downtown and I made all the lights.

The Crown Vic held my tail so I minded my speed and signals. I turned east and then south and was about to cruise past the train stations.

The cops still hadn't made a move. I was on the CPD radar, no doubt. If the car behind me called in my plates, dispatch would've come back with instructions. I couldn't think of a reason why they hadn't hit their flashers to pull me over. A little harassment would've made their night pass quicker.

I decided to test the tail.

At the corner of Madison I turned right.

At the next corner, I pulsed the brakes at the red light and turned right again.

The blacked out Crown Vic rolled through right behind me.

I yanked another right to get back on track. The tail followed.

That wasn't the PD.

Just when I was ready to throttle the engine, I caught the red light.

I stopped and adjusted my rearview, trying to make out the driver's face. He pulled up off center behind me so that the driver's seat sat in my blind spot and I couldn't make him without craning my neck. I couldn't shake the idea that he was a cop, even if the passenger seat was empty. In the mirror I could only see the side of the driver's head. I could see his ear sticking out from under a baseball cap. The cap had a grey bill and a dark upper. That was it. I couldn't even see his chin.

I pumped my breaks to see if the pulsing red lights could add a texture to the darkness, make it easier on my eyes.

Nothing. White guy with an ear.

Maybe it was JB Foster's guy from Sunday morning. Maybe JB's *shit stain* warning meant he would be the one trying to put them there.

First I thought, 'Go ahead and try me.'

Then I thought, 'Well, if he's got a gun, I'm fucked.'

My head bobbed even though I had stopped hearing the music minutes ago. I glanced at the stereo to see the last seconds of "Halftime" click down as the song faded out.

I gunned it when the light turned green. He gunned it too.

I changed lanes, got a look at the side of the car. All black with generic black mag wheels. The pock marks on the car's side gave it a Mad Max look.

Caught another light. Instead of waiting I turned left onto the one way.

He turned too.

I didn't feel like I could do anything until I got away from the Loop. I always equated getting clear from the infrastructure downtown to freedom.

I stupidly played cat and mouse all through downtown as I headed south down Canal Street toward the bus station.

The turns I made, he made. The speed I kept, he kept. The action-reaction part made it feel like a driving game. For a second I got caught up in the strategy, until I realized that I wasn't interested in driving games.

The guy could also be the shadow — the force that materialized when I talked with Albert Brongel two nights ago. That night I didn't even get a look at his ear. Whoever it was had expected me to stay knocked out long enough for the cops to find me holding a murder weapon.

I worked over my two theories as I headed under the viaduct before reaching the bus station. JB Foster's muscle, or the shadow man.

Now what?

I suddenly didn't want what I was waiting for — the long empty blocks of Canal Street heading straight south into Bridgeport. I kept thinking gun. I kept thinking bullets.

I stopped at the red light next to the bus station. On green it'd be nothing but wide-open streets. Canal Street would be vacant at that hour.

I stared into the glowing traffic light. The bulb behind the red glass was pulsing with heat. It flickered with uncertainty. I blinked and realized it was just me projecting. The hairs on the back of my ears and on down my neck raised up.

I blew the light. I jammed the gas pedal to engage the passing gear. I turned on my brights. I turned on my hazards. I rolled down my windows as I took that first stretch past the post office and pushed my car like I was racing a quarter mile. But it wasn't a quarter mile. It was a straight shot a mile long into Bridgeport.

I didn't have any other plan but draw attention to us both. Only speed could do that now, so I drove as fast as the car could carry me.

The blacked-out Crown Vic blew the light too.

I stupidly held out hope that he was a cop until I blew that red light. His cop flashers didn't ignite. My drag-racing antics were treated just like all the turns and starts and stops I made over the last ten minutes — the driver did exactly as I did.

The Roosevelt Road intersection was coming. It was a busy street in daylight. I rubbernecked my head around as much as I could to check on traffic. There were just a couple cars. We had the light but the crosswalk counter was at four.

One car, a red Scion hatchback with tinted windows, gained speed as it headed to the intersection.

I checked the counter on the crosswalk and saw it flash as it counted down to zero.

I started honking my horn and waived my left arm out the window to nudge the red hatchback through the intersection before I hit it.

The traffic light tried to play me a favor and turn green. Except the Scion didn't stop. It sped up.

I yanked the wheel and screamed and tried to steer around it. I saw the break lights on the red hatchback glowing and thought, no breaks, no, keep driving.

I didn't feel an impact. My car came under control by the time I reached the other side of the intersection, so I checked my mirror.

The black Crown Vic clipped the Scion. I saw the red glow of the break-lights go dark when the car started spinning.

The red hatchback spun sideways. The Crown Vic barely washed out before the driver righted it again and shot through the intersection.

The road ahead of me was basically a ramp. Canal Street elevated sharply to meet a set of train tracks. Cars driving at normal speed often bottomed out on the run up.

Beyond the railroad tracks the road crossed a drawbridge where the River we drove along cut under Canal Street.

My six-cylinder Camry wasn't much of a drag car. It wasn't much of anything except the perfect whip for my habits. Until tonight.

The Crown Vic jumped through the intersection at Roosevelt. I hoped a cop car was parked in the big parking lot to our right.

The black car's engine screamed as it pulled up behind me. No cops. Once we got past the parking lot to our right there'd be practically nothing until Bridgeport. Just some small warehouses that supplied Chinatown.

"Cops and pens!" I screamed as the Crown Vic pulled up on me. I wanted to look at the driver. But sixty-five on a city street didn't leave me any room for error.

Pop-pop. Gunshots.

He hit my car. Fuck. I couldn't tell where. My focus was on the wheel and the gas and making sure whatever move I wanted to pull wouldn't wash the car out and leave me at a standstill.

I swerved deeply and slammed the brakes to throw him off target. He slowed with me. I gunned the car again — whipped the wheel to jump over to his driver's side.

He blocked me in place.

I decided to turn off Canal, but didn't want to project my next move. I wanted him to think I was jetting straight back to the safety of my neighborhood.

The tracks were coming. I pressed the gas so hard it could've spot welded to the floorboard. The passing gear engaged.

I looked in the mirror, looked ahead. Looked back again.

Each time I looked in the mirror the Vic got closer, like it had a rope attached to my bumper and was reeling me in.

I looked ahead. Tracks.

The blacktop rose sharply. The incline up to the train tracks started with a lip before escalating quickly. My car squatted when it hit the lip. The force of the big machine transitioning from straight and flat to up a ramp caused my tires to slam up in the wheel wells. The compressed suspension felt like the car was crouching.

I hit the top of the ramp and screamed over the train tracks "Ahhh-hh!" hoping my car took flight.

I hoped because that meant the Crown Vic would too.

I wanted the street to take him by surprise.

I pictured my tires and suspension dangling in the air — like a set of kitten's legs when you held it under the belly.

Then my car slammed into the ground, my wheels compressed the struts and slammed up in the wheel wells again.

I lost control. The tires pulled and grabbed for traction in any direction they could get. That made my steering wheel shimmy. Like some frantic fucking morse code up through the steering column.

The Crown Vic drove faster and weighed more so he took the jump harder. Bounced higher, swerved deeper.

The shakes in my car's tires dampened slightly. I looked ahead to the intersection at Eighteenth Street. I wanted to turn right down Eighteenth and hop onto the expressway four blocks away. If I could execute the turn without projecting my move, I might throw him off course for ten or fifteen seconds. In that time I could sprint the four blocks and cut up the on-ramp.

My car was shaking less, but shaking. I gripped the steering wheel and slightly turned it. I tried to visualize the tires calming down as I commanded through the wheel.

The tires didn't respond. My car had settled, but not enough to turn hard. I couldn't risk a move like that. The longer I kept moving, the better.

In the middle of the intersection at Eighteenth and Canal he started firing again.

My car was a big target, no doubt. The way we bounced around after landing he'd be lucky to hit anything. I couldn't deny one thing — he was gaining.

As the road approached the drawbridge I caught sight of the sign for Lawrence's Fisheries. It was a seafood shack nestled next to the drawbridge along the river. The location might give the impression that a fresh daily catch waited inside. Not from that river. Not from anywhere around here. I'm sure the fish was frozen and trucked in from parts unknown. The fisheries stayed open late and catered to truckers and security guards wagging full key chains attached to their belts. They often stood loosely around the counter jawing about the Bears and Bulls. The menu was simple, either deep-fried fish or shrimp in a basket over a bed of fries. They had three cars minimum in the parking lot, always.

Gregory Rossi

I pulled the wheel slightly left.

It made for an awkward swerve. In order to control the car I needed to squeeze my hands tight enough around the steering wheel to displace the sweat on my palms. I swerved back right. I was slightly ahead of him now and losing more ground.

He didn't swerve with me; he remained straight in order to get his shot off.

Driving the stretch of street between the train tracks and the drawbridge didn't give me a good option. If I drove straight it would give him an easier shot. If I swerved his shot would be tougher, but he'd gain ground faster.

I swerved again. If I timed it, I could cut the wheel hard right just after I crossed the bridge and fish tail directly into the Fisheries parking lot.

The Crown Vic didn't like the look of my weaving.

His engine screamed behind me.

Sixty yards from the bridge he came up faster than I expected. I was veering left, and needed to jerk the wheel back right. Just as I started to yank the wheel—

The Crown Vic rammed me.

My car wobbled out from the nudge. Luckily he didn't hit me at a solid angle.

I jerked the wheel back right.

Lost a lot of speed.

He gained on me as if I had simply given up.

Just before I reached the bridge he caught the other side of my car with a solid hit.

I cranked the wheel left again. Even with my speed dropping it was too much to control.

I jerked the wheel right, then started to turn it left again when I hit the bridge.

The metal grating of the bridge had been buffed from decades of car traffic. Instead of being oxidized like the rest of the girders, the metal grating was polished to a bright silver. The car skidded on the slippery smooth rails across the bridge's expanse. My wheels jumped when they hit the lip on the other side where the metal transitioned back to pavement. The car started bouncing.

I gripped the wheel. It was the only control I had left.

He rammed me one more time.

My car tires tried to stick to the road. Their whole form was dedicated to that one thing. Gravity tried to help with the task and I thought the tires were going to hold for a second. I slammed the brakes and tried to turn into the spin. Except I wasn't spinning, I was tipping. It felt like a thousand tiny rubber arms reached out the bottom tread of the two driver's side tires. The little rubber arms tried to grip the oil-stained black top below. The tiny arms I imagined reached for a corner, a minuscule crack — anything for a grip.

Not a chance.

The wheels on my side came off the ground. A ton of metal whipped onto its side and slammed to the road. My car punished the ground below it and the crumbling metal of the body and the engine rocking on its mounts sounded like an explosion.

The car planted on the passenger side and rocked gently. The undercarriage exposed like a pale belly.

The crash rocked my bell. My head gonged from the aftershock. But there was clarity between the deep gongs rocking my inside.

I looked out the passenger window and saw the ground. The driver's side window looked up into the night.

I don't know why, but I turned the car off. As if turning the ignition off could stop the gas tank from exploding.

I held my keys in one hand. The next thing to do was unclick my seat belt. That was it. One move, and I had a chance. No move, no chance. I couldn't think about the Crown Vic's driver. He could be right outside my car about to poke his gun in the window above me and start firing.

The only thing I thought about was getting out.

I shuffled my hip up. Everything was sideways so it wasn't easy. I didn't know yet how bad my hip hurt. I lifted it up and slammed my hand into the buckle and popped the button as hard as I could.

It worked.

Next I had to get out the open window. I had opened the window back up by the bus stop when I started the drag race. In the moment I thought I might try and wave down a cop. It was a dumb move back there - as if a cop would yawn at two cars drag racing at sixty-five on a side street unless they saw my hand.

Before I moved my body, my hands found a grip around the doorframe above me. No window, no shards of glass. No cut on my hand.

I kicked my legs from under the steering wheel and crouched inside the car's cabin.

Then all I needed was to hop out.

First I popped onto the side of the dashboard and driver's seat. They were upright since the car was teetering on its side. After I hopped into that position I stood up, with everything above my knees standing outside of the car.

Then I sat down on the roof. I extracted my legs so they didn't catch onto anything in the doorframe. I extended my legs over my windshield and slid down onto the pavement.

I ran around to the belly side of my car.

I could only see the back of his head.

He was running away from me, back to the Crown Vic.

I heard someone yell from the front porch of the Lawrence Fisheries off to my left.

We had an audience.

I didn't bother to look over, didn't want to.

I could hear the voice yell, "You alright?!"

If I decided to turn and run toward home the witnesses could've seen my face, no doubt.

Except I always had that natural instinct to run into darkness, away from visibility.

I waved my hand in the direction of the Fisherie's front porch, as if to say I was okay. Then I ran in the opposite direction, north.

To the witnesses at the Fisherie it seemed like I was chasing the Crown Vic.

In a way I was.

The driver ran into the open car door. I still couldn't make his face.

He put the car in gear and swung around. All I wanted was his license plate. That was it. He wanted to give me something else.

He stopped with the car's passenger side facing me. The window was down. He was looking right at me. It would've been the perfect angle to check his face, except he held a gun in front of him.

"Hey hey!" I heard close behind me, "You okay?"

I couldn't look back. I wanted to. I wanted to turn and yell for the idiot to go back to his shrimp basket. But I couldn't turn, not with a bead on my brain.

I decided to dive low. I figured his aim through the car window had enough range to track me side to side. But not up or down.

I fell down onto my hands, stayed elevated on my toes like a bug so I could move without getting into a full crawl.

The shots came as I fell.

Pop pop.

He missed me, but not my gas tank. The explosion lit up the night.

I looked back and saw a skinny guy in a white jacket flying through the air. At my angle on the roadside I wasn't in the direct path of the explosion. Felt the heat and the explosion in my chest and ears. But the skinny guy was right in front of the car's undercarriage.

I hopped up and started running towards the Crown Vic thinking, license plate, c'mon.

Oklahoma. That's all I saw. An Oklahoma plate.

By that point in our chase I didn't need the license plate though. I knew who it was.

I ran up the street with my arms raised as if I wanted the Crown Vic to stop. I didn't. I raised my arms in a quick celebration because I still had a chance to get away.

The Crown Vic sped up Canal to Eighteenth and bolted left to the expressway. He'd be up the steep incline of that on-ramp and gone in fifteen seconds.

He was made though. Without a face, without anything, he was still made.

Not because he was the only guy capable of running me down. Nah, any operator with enough muscle could pull a group of thugs and a fast enough car together for that job. But I also knew it was him, just because of that.

He worked alone. And he thought he could handle me by himself. That would be the mindset of an ex-military type. The kind of guy who counted on flawless execution. The way he drove. The perfectly off-center stop back at the red light so I couldn't make his face. The way he ran back to his car. The way he fired the gun. Precise, controlled.

It was pure instinct on my part, but I knew it was JB Foster's security guard.

I got him first on Sunday when he parked behind me, and I earned my conversation with JB.

He tried for payback tonight.

I didn't have time to gloat. I still had to get home without getting picked up.

forty-three

I caught a cab and made the driver pull up two blocks from my house.

I felt fine on the car ride. The pain hadn't registered through the adrenaline yet.

Then I tried climbing out. When I planted both feet on the ground, my hip was locked — seized up during the ride. I used my arms to pull and lift myself out of the car. Then I needed to hop out of the way so I could close the cab door.

I tapped on the hood of the cab, so he drove away. I stood paralyzed not wanting to put my foot up on the curb.

The right side of my body, the side the car slammed on, was in shock. The shock showed itself in different tones. My shoulder thump thump thumped with a prickly deep electric vibration. The outside of my hip was pulsing in long gongs that never thinned out into a high note. And the bell in my head still rang.

I wrenched my hip free from its socket. Scraped my feet along the sidewalk. Then down the alley behind my house.

Taking my keys from the car was my second lucky move for the night. I needed them to enter from my alley. And instead of kicking the back door to my garage open, I slid the key in silently. I opened the door six inches or so and snaked my arm in. Fingered for the button. Got it. The big garage door scrolled open. The light shone through my glass block windows into the small patch of grass in my back yard.

I didn't want to attract attention, but I couldn't control it either.

Inside my house I kept all the lights off. First a quick shower and mirror check.

The only marks on my face were the gravel bruises from Monday. The week had stretched long enough that they felt permanent. I swallowed five Advils and cupped some water from the bathroom sink to wash them down.

I pulled down the blinds in my bedroom and turned the light on.

Threw all the shit on my bed back into my dresser.

Laid down at two-fifteen.

Deep breath. Deep breath. I imagined taking hits off a bowl, tried capturing that relaxed feeling that ushered me to sleep most nights. The effort felt good, but I didn't relax.

Put a pillow over my head.

My eyes were closed for a half-hour.

At two-forty-five the doorbell rang.

That's what I was waiting for.

I let it ring again. Couldn't tell from bed but hoped the police strobes weren't lighting up my street. My nosy neighbors could sense that type of action deep into R.E.M.

The third ring was a rapid-fire dingalingaling.

Living room light on. Slow trudge to the door. Porch light on. Opened the wood door.

Detective Glenn. I opened up to let him in.

Something flew at me, banged into my chest.

"Hey man, ow," I said squinting, my eyes not adjusted yet, "The fuck?"

"Let's go," Glenn said.

Looked down. My license plate fell and clanged on the tiles at my feet.

I checked over his shoulder. No squad. No partner.

Funny. I drag raced through downtown in one of the most heavily policed cities in the country. My car exploded. I ran through the same streets and took a cab home. Didn't see a single cop.

But one shows up at my door, over an hour later.

"What?" I rubbed my bare chest. I only had a pair of shorts on.

"To the station." Glenn said, he wore a simple black turtleneck, faded blue jeans and tan Timbo hoofs.

Extended my arm and waved my fingers in gimme fashion.

"Got paper?" I asked.

"Paper? We have your car," he said.

"Whaddya mean?" I replied.

"You rolled your car on Canal Street, there's witnesses saw you running away."

"Me?" I tried not to play too dumb, "Car's in my garage."

"License plate RLL 637?" he said and shot his eyes over to the floor.

"That's mine," I said pointing at the plate, "But it's in the garage," I raised my eyebrows, not too high.

"Show me," he demanded.

"Minute," I said and trudged back into my house. The walk slightly thawed my joints and got me acclimated to the pain. After I slipped on pants and a shirt, I walked barefoot out the front door and escorted Detective Glenn down through my gangway.

The cold cement felt great on my feet. I hoped the chill would travel up my legs and numb the throb in my bones.

I kicked open the back door to my garage.

"My car," I said.

"You're not surprised."

"What should I do, jump up and down? My fucking car is missing. I. I. I. I don't know."

I led Detective Glenn inside my house. We stopped at the kitchen table. My car keys were on top of the information packet Chris McMahon sent over. That envelope was key, but if Glenn whiffed its contents I'd be hauled in right now. He only needed one more suspicious thing to yank me off the streets.

I picked up the keys and dangled them before his eyes.

We walked into my living room. I sunk into a chair. He stayed standing.

"Chased, rolled and shot at. Bystander was caught in the explosion. He suffered a concussion and minor burns."

"Exploded?" I asked again, "I don't know what to tell you."

The interior of my house looked significantly smaller whenever I had people over.

"You're lying," Glenn said.

The throbs hadn't died down, but my stomach was empty so the Advil had an all access pass.

"Okay," I said good to keep my answers short. My breaths were clipped anyway.

"Where were you earlier?"

"Here. I was here," Added a pause like I didn't know what else to say. "My car was here. Was."

"I'll take you to it."

"Hey man, no," I said, ", I'm not going anywhere with you. You're setting my boy up."

"Who's setting who up?" Glenn asked.

"You, you want Lenny to take the fall."

I raised my arms to rub my eyes. I snuck in a wince while my hands covered my face. Then I smothered it with my palms before I dropped my arms down again.

"I'll take you to see your car," he said changed his tone so it sounded like he was doing me a favor, "It doesn't have anything to do with your friend Lenny."

"A personal escort from a homicide detective?" I pondered, "Doesn't have anything to do with my friend getting framed for murder?"

He paused for a second.

"Your plate is on the watch list," Glenn said.

"Yeah, because of Lenny," I pointed out, "This isn't about my car."

He couldn't bullshit around the car anymore, so I told him straight up:

"Someone set Lenny up," I said, figured I had to make the point if he refused to see it for himself.

"Right, right Michael. Lenny tell you that?"

"Bones," I said, "Just call me Bones, man. And he did tell me that before he disappeared. I believed him. Said someone gave him twenty-five grand for access to JB's loft."

"How'd he get access?"

"You probably know that. Extra key. Lenny swiped it."

"Who paid him the money?" Glenn asked.

I was too tired to move my body. All expression ran through the squiggly lines on my forehead. "Albert Brongel, that's why I went looking for him."

Detective Glenn didn't say anything.

"Let's say you think Lenny killed Albert Brongel too. Why?" I asked.

"Drinking buddies. Brongel knew everything Lenny had said. Knew how jealous he was of JB. He told Albert Brongel that he loved Babi Patras so much if he couldn't have her, then nobody could."

"Oh, please," I said, "if there ever was a terrible line it was, *if I can't have her then nobody can.*"

"Then why is Lenny hiding?" Glenn asked.

We went round and around again. He jabbed and I jibbed back. I made it be known that I wouldn't tire of his questioning and that my story would never change.

Detective Glenn all but admitted that they had a witness who could testify for Albert Brongel's version of the story. I needed to know who that was. I thought about asking Glenn straight up, but feared the witness would wind up on Lenny's body count too.

That was the only new part. The rest was a square dance.

We walked all over the same ground again, wound up in the same place.

Glenn asked, again, "And that was the last time you saw him?"

"The last time."

Scratched his scalp, tilted his head and looked at me.

"Let's go. I'll take you to the station, fill out your police report."

On my stolen car. Nah, I wasn't going to ride to the police station with a cop.

I asked, "You said it was totaled? Won't drive again?"

"Don't bullshit me, Bones, you can play dumb but I don't have to believe it."

"If what you say is true, Detective Glenn," I said and managed to sit up in my chair a little, "Then I'm never driving that car again. I'm tired. It can wait until morning."

He walked towards my front door.

I lifted myself up to follow him.

"Got insurance?" he asked and turned around with his upper lip in a snarl.

"On my car?" I said, "It's the law."

"No, on you," he said through his bleached teeth, "Accident like that is tough on your body."

forty-four

"Hello?" I answered my phone just after eight in the morning, coffee in hand.

It was Thursday morning. I had one more day to go until I could see Lenny again.

"Michael Panozzo?"

"Yeah."

"This is Jerome Evon, Director at Albany House in Evanston."

A tingle racked my spine that masked the pain in my shoulder, hips and neck.

In the fifteen minutes I'd been up I kept moving the joints hoping to work out the pain. It hadn't worked. I did have health insurance. Not through my shitty-ass job, but an emergency room type policy I took out myself. So I did the self-diagnosis thing. Bone bruises, I had decided, right about the time the phone rang.

Jerome Evon continued, "We're the resident house where your mother, Carol-"

"I know who you are."

His voice was soft. Not quiet soft, but lacked edges, lacked friction. I pictured him with glasses and a round paunch. I assumed Jerome Evon's rounded-out, edgeless voice was a finely honed tool. Managing a facility stacked to the rafters with crazy people required a voice like that. Managing low wage nurse aides and custodians dealing with a half-way house stacked to the rafters with crazy people also required a voice like that.

"We received notice from the State about your mother's Medicaid. It seems her status is under review."

My mom's voice broke through the background, "Let me talk to him!" she shouted, "Let me talk to him!"

What was happening in my body was a joke. That joke you tell as a second grader. Like your friend comes up to you, *oh, man, I cut my finger. Look it hurts so bad.* And you tell him, *cut off your hand and your finger won't hurt anymore.* That joke was the funniest thing for a seven-year-old kid. My mom's voice was as funny as that joke. Still it made me forget about the pain for a minute.

Jerome Evon said to my mom, "Carol, when I'm finished you can talk to him."

I said, "I don't want to talk to her."

"Now just a minute, Michael," he said to me, "This notice tells me that in the event of a status change your mother will no longer be eligible for Medicaid as of the end of this month."

Ten days.

I asked, "She have some kind of breakthrough in her treatment?"

He answered.

I didn't listen. No way she was moving into my house in ten days. Not twenty days. Not ever. Caught the tail end of his answer:

"Now if she were to stay here at Albany House," he finished, "monthly costs run at four thousand dollars."

"You get a call or a letter?" I asked.

"It's a letter from the state," I pictured him holding it up. It looked strange to him, no doubt. He was sitting next to a woman who had been deported from foreign countries. She had jumped from mental ward to mental ward to transient housing to homelessness and finally to a half-way house. And that was just since I turned eighteen. Her brain was un-medicated for much of the last fifteen years and the wiring up there amounted to a jumble of split ends.

"Michael," she shouted over Jerome Evon, "You have to take care of—"

"WHO WROTE THE LETTER?" I shouted into the phone, didn't want to hear another syllable from her.

"Carol, Would you just. Here—" he set down the phone without saying anything to me. "Now you have to." His voice got quieter from my end of the phone. "Jessie, Jessie, take her please. Carol, I will talk to you when I finish."

"I want to talk to my son," I heard her say.

Her speaking voice was unrestrained as usual. Even as a kid, I remember how in conversation she spoke without inhibition, without wondering if anyone cared or believed what she said. The volume. The diction. All of it completely void of self-awareness.

One thing was new. Her voice carried panic. It was the first time I can remember her speaking in that tone. Everything, the whole time growing up was a thick layer of bullshit. As if she thought words could rosie-up our lives. As if her saying, "Everything will be alright," could make anything all right.

Nothing but lies as far as I knew.

My jaw clenched. Heard the shuffle of the phone being picked up.

"Sorry about that," Jerome Evon said, "She's excited."

No shit. Why did he tell her about the letter?

"You said it was a letter," I asked, "Tell me who to contact."

I grabbed a pen and paper, wrote down the contact information.

"Now it may help—" he said.

I listened intently. I thought here's a guy who navigates the bureaucracy like a baby on a bottle. I listened like he was going to drop some bureauocratic wisdom in my lap.

Instead he said, "If you spoke to your mother for one–"

"I'll call you back."

Click.

forty-five

I paced a trench into my kitchen linoleum until the library opened at nine.

I stood in front of the library door for five minutes. Then I bolted inside ahead of a couple Chinese women and a Bridgeport mom with wet hair, no coat, and a Tasmanian Devil T-shirt that read, "Life's a Bitch."

One of the most popular songs off *Illmatic* was "Life's a Bitch." That CD was now char-broiled inside my car.

I logged on to the library's computer and rented a car – six hundred bucks for a week.

I navigated over to Stub Hub and overpaid for some tickets for Sunday night's Eryka Badu concert. Getting gutted by the Stub Hub machine was easier than a face-to-face scalper.

Before I logged off, I e-mailed work and called in sick. I liked to be straight up with my boss, but telling him my car was stolen on the heels of getting interrogated by the police department wouldn't work.

The quotas were fierce at my job. If I missed another unplanned day, I'd likely get fired.

forty-six

My phone rang on the walk to the police station. I thought it was The Roach calling about the gun.

"Yeah, this Bones?" The voice asked.

I guessed by the sound of the voice he was a black guy in his mid to late twenties.

"Who's this?" I asked.

"Forget about names," he said, "You want to find Lenny?"

It took a minute to register his statement as a proposition, because I was the only person who knew Lenny's location.

I answered, "I might."

"You do," he said. The guy's delivery sounds like he's riffing off rehearsed lines. His voice confirms my suspicions that he's working from a script when he added, "We can take you to him tonight."

Again the talk made the pain receded from the front of my consciousness as I walked the four blocks to the cop shop.

He didn't wait long for an answer before he said, "I've got a car for you to follow. It'll take you to him."

I couldn't figure out why someone would set this up. It wasn't JB Foster's guy. He'd find me without making a trackable phone call. The shadow? Was it the shadow from the night Albert Brongel got killed?

"What car?" I asked.

"The car doesn't matter," the guy said, "What's at the end of the ride does."

"Who are you?"

"That also doesn't matter," he said, "I'm just the messenger," it sounded like another canned line — I imagined the guy's boss standing in front of him, watching him execute on the phone.

"Lenny who?" I asked to throw him off.

He pauses, unable to riff back immediately. "Your friend."

"There's more than one Lenny out there, kid," I told him, "Give me a last name."

The background hum surrounding the guy's voice disappeared. I could tell he held his hand over the phone. When he lifted his hand, the hum came back and he said "Supinski."

"Yo, messenger, sure you don't want to put your boss on the phone so we can speak directly?" I said with a straight voice. I had done everything but call him scrub.

It was his turn not to answer.

"Ok, here's how this might work," I told him, "You give me the plates, the owner of the car's name and address. Then you wait and see if I show up."

"You want what?" he asked.

I told him again. I hurried into the police station and sat down on the bench by the door. I raised one finger to the Desk Sergeant. I opened my bag to fish out my pen and slid out the last page from the stack of papers inside the envelope.

The voice on the other end finished conferring with his superior and came back.

"You ready?" the messenger asked.

"Yep."

"License plate," he said and I took dictation as he rattled off the vitals: license plate, truck make and model, owner's name and address.

"Got it?" he asked.

I didn't bother reading the vitals back to him while I sat in the police station.

"Got it," I said and made like I was going to get off the phone all cordial like, "So yeah, I'll be there. See how this thing goes off, see what you have to say about my boy."

"Okay," the messenger said. He kept the conversation to business so didn't add any cheery salutation.

"Alright, then, talk to you later," I said and hung up.

The Desk Sergeant looked up at me as I laughed. She was probably running through her mental list of misdemeanor offenses to see if it was illegal to have a kid who looked like me laughing like that inside a police station.

My phone rang again. The number was blocked.

I raised my eyebrows to the sergeant and said, "Incompetents," pointed at the phone, "My car was stolen. I'll step up in a minute."

"Bones," I answered.

"Eleven o'clock tonight," the messenger said.

"Got it. Where?"

"Text you at ten," he said.

I hung up glad someone had it worse than me this morning. All I had to do was rot at the police station for a minute. The messenger probably just had the phone yanked out of his hand, and then got hit upside the head with it for fucking up the phone call.

I looked up. The Desk Sergeant was gone.

forty-seven

"Ms. Griffin, can you be more specific," I said over the phone, "About what has changed in my mom's status?"

On the other end, I heard a woman named Sue Griffin shuffle papers. Sounded like a stunt. Like there weren't any papers with my mom's name on them.

"I don't have the file here," she said.

The frustration in her voice didn't seem directed at me, so I tried to be patient.

I worked out of a Kinko's on Clybourne – Chicago's great stretch of strip malls. The store was near the car rental shop. I finally got my stolen car report at the station.

"Ms. Griffin, my mom last worked over sixteen-years ago. In that time she hasn't had a stable address for more than a year. At times she had no address to speak of. She has no skills, and although she doesn't have drool on her face she can't be responsible for herself."

She didn't say anything.

"I'd like for you to tell me what caused her status change to be under review."

I sat in a cube at the back of Kinko's. Kept my mouth tucked into my shoulder. The rent-a-computer section of the store was empty, but I still tucked my mouth down because I didn't want anyone to whiff my business.

"Like I said-" she told me and paused while she looked through her computer.

"I know what you said, and I believe you're trying to be helpful. Can you tell me what the normal process is for someone getting off disability?" I wanted to know if there was an appeal process.

"Well," she said with her soft voice. I figured she was a social worker. Always liked those kind of girls, always thought they couldn't hurt me. "First there is a status change notice."

Obviously. The status change notice made this phone call happen.

"Does the recommendation come from her case worker? Is there a review process for a second opinion?"

"I have to tell you, Mr. Fox."

"Panozzo," I corrected. She obviously hadn't tuned in when I first introduced myself, "My mom's last name is Fox. You can call me Michael."

She said, "I've never seen a person taken off disability."

That threw me. Lost my nice phone voice and everything.

"You new?" I asked.

She caught the edge of my voice and returned it, "Excuse me?"

Upsetting her would get me nowhere, so I spoke slowly to find my
rhythm again, "How long have you worked there?"

"Five years," she answered.

"And you haven't seen this, not once?"

"Never," she said, happy to be definitive.

"Ever hear of anything like this?" I asked.

"Not on disability," she said.

Of course not, I figured the stuff was like an STD—once you had it,
the shit was yours to keep.

"Can you give me the caseworker's number so I can follow up on this?"

"Nooo," her voice showed signs of wear and came out with a soft rasp,
"We can't provide caseworker contact information."

Made sense. Caseworkers spent all day on the streets. They needed
to make progress from case-to-case-to-case. Any appeals or questions
would go through an office.

"But," she said and lifted her voice.

The changes in tone and pitch flitted in my ear.

She continued, "I don't think the caseworker is going to yield new information on this matter." When she finished saying that sentence I
could hear her breath draw in as if she wanted to take it back.

I spoke. It felt like my voice traveled into my phone, up through the
cell booster on some rooftop nearby, skipped to the next booster and
another, and however that shit got translated to a land line, it landed
and jumped up through the receiver Sue Griffin held in her hand. I imagined I could feel her warm hand on the receiver.

I felt like my head popped out her end of the phone and whatever I
asked she would tell me. Even if the questions could lead to trouble.

"You weren't supposed to tell me that were you?" I could've been
looking right at her.

"No," was all she said.

She didn't say, no, I wasn't. Just, no. She had crossed the line telling me that. Doing so in two letters made it easier for her.

I could handle a case working foot soldier. They operated street-level, like me. They understood the catastrophic effects mental illness could have on a family. No force would be necessary on my part, just a meaningful talk. I could start with one street-level conversation and work my way up.

Except Sue Griffin had basically told me that the order to change my mom's status didn't start with the street level caseworker. It came down from on high.

forty-eight

At the copy shop I made an extra of the documents Chris McMahon sent me. I double-checked the date — yes it was still dated the Wednesday before Thanksgiving.

I had finally read the document on the subway ride up here. Most of the document was legalese. The summary page proved to be all I needed to know.

Document Services — the name on Albert Brongel's paystub — was appealing the city's decision to award JB Foster the document maintenance contract.

The city had a structural debt problem. That's why they started selling things off. I tell everybody all the time, it was open season in Chicago, and even the streets were getting sold. At first I sounded like a paranoid fool to people. I'd talk about how the smartest business minds in the country were angling for deals like JB Foster's.

All the biggest banks created the company that bought every parking meter in Chicago. The same set of investors bought The Skyway. The Midway Airport deal fell through, but they'd come back bigger, with more money and tempt the city into another bad deal.

We lived in an epically ironic age. Nah, it had nothing to do with writers and filmmakers making flimsy documents that couldn't hold up to the struggles of my life. Our epically ironic world came down to one simple thing. The rich guys didn't want to spend a penny in taxes, but they'd spend a half-billion lobbying to get a regular cut of the government's revenue stream. I felt the heft of those documents in my hand, and realized people were willing to kill for that kind of cash.

I didn't know how or why yet. But I was sure Babi Patras' murder had something to do with these documents.

I bolted out the copy shop door, dialing Vicente Duarte's number.

"Vicente," I said after he answered. I was walking to the car rental shop, "This is Bones, the guy who found the earrings."

I thought that I did his mom a favor by recovering the earrings. The long silence on his end of the phone told me he saw things differently.

"Hold that thought," I said, I didn't want him to waste his breath. "I need to meet your mom. Right now. Then we're finished."

forty-nine

I told JB Foster that I'd wait in the lobby.

JB told me they didn't have a lobby, it was just the doorman behind a desk. They took the couches away for a sculpture, he said, so all you could do was stand around.

Sounded like a lobby to me, I told him.

Looked like a lobby too.

I leaned against the wall so I could see how JB pulled up. *Take a cab,* I had told him, *make him pull up right in front of the door.* That plan wouldn't stop him from getting a guy around the back door to meet us upstairs. I couldn't control that.

I waited four minutes before a green and cream checker cab pulled up.

I didn't want JB Foster nervous about a scene in front of the doorman, so I lifted up the envelope with the appeal inside and waved it when he walked in the door.

"Mr. Foster, got the papers right here," I said.

I caught his pace and we stepped to the elevator.

He walked in first.

I stood in the opening before the elevator doors closed.

"There's more," I said, holding the envelope out so he could see it but not take it, "Anyone lays a finger on me and you never see what else I have."

Inside the elevator JB glanced at me sideways and said, "Waste my time and the cops'll lock you up on harassment and suspicion of assisted homicide."

"I see you talked to your lawyer on the way over," I said. The doors open and as he stepped out ahead of me I added, "Good move."

I tugged the brim of my White Sox hat to my eyebrows as I walked in to the penthouse.

The apartment was a murder scene just one week ago. This wasn't the place to focus on that. It had happened. I wasn't going to get anything from the place after Yolanda Duarte scrubbed out her penance earlier this week.

"Okay, tell me about last night," I said, as soon as the door closed, "Everything you thought about doing, everything you know you did. And anything else you can think of."

"This about your car?" he asked.

"Just start talking," I said, pushed my hat up a nudge.

He pulled his Blackberry from his inside breast pocket and put it on the island. It was lit from an incoming call, but not buzzing.

JB stood across the fat island on the side by the appliances. I stood between the bar stools. Yards of black granite spread out like a void between us. Maybe JB needed a moment; maybe he felt something he couldn't yet recognize while staring across the vast blackness.

He would be right to guess that I was already in the void. I acclimated quickly and felt my way through it with increasing speed. But I wasn't there to drag him down. I told myself: slow. Easy. Let this play out.

He asked, "Yolanda, the cleaning lady. How did you get her to do that?"

After her son hung up, I checked out my rental car. First I headed west and ate a big meal—two steak tacos and two chicken tostadas. Her son called me back in the middle of my meal. After I finished eating I stopped in Dusty Grooves and picked up another copy of *Illmatic*. I couldn't imagine not owning that joint; walked out with the Tenth Anniversary edition, the one with the extra disc of remixes.

I met Yolanda, the cleaning woman, on the street down in Printer's Row. She wore sweats, sneakers and a faded periwinkle polo shirt under a black puffy coat. Her lips moved quickly when I pulled up. Prayers, I decided.

Yolanda placed the call to JB's office. It was the one-week anniversary of Babi Patras' murder and her status as the one who found the body got her passed through to JB within minutes. I didn't need to tell her to speak urgently, she just did. The only coaching she got from me was to say the call was important. As soon as JB got on the phone, she handed it over to me and I did the rest.

"Let's just say," I told JB Foster over the black slab of granite, "My resources are different than yours, but just as effective."

"I know guys like you," he said across the island, "just like you."

Guys from the old neighborhood? Is that who he thought about when he said that? I had figured all along Lenny worked himself into his job as JB's driver because of his South Side cred.

"Don't pretend here," he said, "You're way out of your league."

That's probably what the guy thought last night too.

I didn't let it bother me, figured he needed to vent.

"Right now, Mr. Foster, we are in the same arena," I held out my arm and pointed my finger down, swirled a big circle around the island, "So it's time to play. Like I said, tell me everything about last night. This," I spread out all five fingers from my right hand and placed my fingertips gently on the stack of papers in front of me, "depends on it."

He walked the expanse of the kitchen and over to the dining room table. The Great Room of his penthouse loft contained a living space, dining room, and kitchen with superfluous square footage to boot. The view through his windows was the original—not a black and white replica like the one that hung on Albert Brongel's bedroom wall.

JB walked back into the kitchen, said, "Water?" Opened up the big side-by side fridge.

"Sure."

He pulled out two waters. Then he talked. JB took a slow, steady walk through last night again. I kept him on a leash and executed delicate yanks on his line whenever he started to wander. But he got back home and I believed he didn't know about Canal Street until this morning.

That's what I needed to start.

"Lenny didn't do it. I'm going to beat that drum until you get it," I said, "But that's not why I'm here."

Unscrewed the bottle of water and took a sip. My body was ready to give out, so I tightened up my posture, locked in my hips and moved as little as possible. Had to tell myself the Advil was fighting a losing battle, not me.

I pulled the top two pages out of the envelope. I took the first page of the appeal, faced it toward him. Then I took the second page and flipped it over. Put that sideways on top of it, so all he saw was the letterhead and the date, the rest was whited-out by my make-shift cover.

"Fair play, take a peek. Look at the date. This is what you get when we're finished."

He took a step forward so he could lean over the black island.

"Touch my hand and yours is broken," I added.

He looked up through his eyebrows, asked, "A quid pro quo?"

Condescension wasn't going to throw me off. I'd just use it as fuel on his face if needed. "Whatever," I said, added an eye roll, "I'm getting what I want, you can call your side whatever fancy name you wish."

JB looked at the page. Nodded.

"Your guy. Your driver, the ex-special forces guy. What's his name?"

"Vince Hendricks."

"Meet him before?" I asked.

"Yes, the city contracts his security firm for all public events deemed to be a national security risk."

"That's a lot of events."

He shrugged.

"You hired him after Babi's murder."

"I needed a driver, not my own personal talk radio." His phone buzzed, this time he hit a button to silence it.

He knew something. It was obvious in the way he walked through his story about last night with all the slack in the leash. Already I could tell his attitude had changed since Sunday. Something else was on his mind and I called him today at the right time. It helped that I waived an answer in front of his face.

"You got the head of the firm to be your driver?"

"Only a week. His other guy takes over on Monday."

"Interesting date," I said, nodded down at the paper. When I lifted my eyes from it I said, "Talk. Office, home. service record. All the way down to the stripes on his underpants."

JB gave a good shit-eating smile. Pure sarcasm.

"Glad you liked that," I said and stuck my chin out at him, "All of it.

Known associates. Cell phone. Now."

Vince Hendricks arrived in Chicago four years ago. His ties to Price Properties began years before that, in Oklahoma. The Prices' real estate arm operated a chain of tax-free warehouse corridors near airports around the country. They were basically grand warehouse developments that allowed businesses to delay tax payments due to some loophole. With Hendricks they started a security division originally meant to protect the warehouses. I didn't tell JB I knew that. After 9-11 the Price family eventually spun the security division off into it's own private company.

JB talked for twenty minutes straight.

The picture he painted matched the snippet I heard from Chris McMahon. Hendricks and the Price Family were pushing to be a Midwestern Blackwater Ops. Blackwater already had stateside operations, but their pipeline to government money flew from the Chesapeake. The Price Family had been a fixture in Chicago long enough to know that a Great Lakes pipeline pumped the same green paper.

"Price family still associated with the operation?" I asked.

"Private companies don't have to disclose that, but he must be."

"Agreed," I said, "And their logo rips off the official Price Properties logo."

"Could be a hold over from the start of the business," JB replied.

He stole a glance when his phone lit up. While his eye was there, it buzzed.

"Hold on," he said and held up a palm.

I let my voice drag out in annoyance and said, "Put it down."

"My lawyer," he snipped back, "wanted me to check in after we started, tell him I was safe."

I locked on him as his Blackberry buttons clicked. His shoulders looked rounded, comfortable like, like when you watched someone at a club send a message. It didn't look like he was ordering up muscle.

"Ok, you know something," I said as he set the phone down, "Otherwise there's no way you give me this amount of time. Does it have anything to do with this?" I pointed to the stack of paper.

JB didn't know what the paper contained. But it was business. I never lost sight of wanting to know if the papers under my hand somehow involved Babi and Lenny.

JB started after a practiced pause, "Three weeks ago my security manager quit without notice."

"Hendricks hire him?" I asked.

JB shook his head, "Disappeared. We've looked, couldn't find him."

"Airplane tickets?"

"Mexico, but no hotel room in his name, no credit card charges on his card.

"Who told you this?"

"I deal with a private firm, a very good one," he said, "Like I said three weeks ago. I asked *them* to look into it. Hendricks wasn't in the picture. Besides it's not his kind of work anyway."

"Yeah," I said, "The government doesn't pick up the tab on that shit. So, how'd Hendricks come to work for you then?"

He shook his head at that.

I guessed, "Whitman Price?"

He nodded. Stared at me like we shared a new realization.

"How? You guys aren't friends."

"Far from it. But I'm on a handful of boards around town, and I serve with more than one member of the Price family on each of those."

"Oh, so they were all magnanimous and offered the services of their close associate."

He shrugged, "Something like that."

"Exactly like that."

He said, "Listen Michael, is it Mike?"

"It's Bones."

"Ok, ok," he rubbed his hands back through his hair, "What does this have to do with Lenny?"

"Something."

"Lenny is out of my hands. I can't help you. And I'm uncomfortable talking about my business with you."

I was about to say we hadn't talked about his business yet. But we had. His security head was now in play.

"You'll be happy you did," I said, "Who is your head of security?"

"Dan Daly."

"Anything else about his disappearance I should know?"

"He's been found."

I guessed again, "The superior services of Vince Hendricks?"

"Exactly," JB shook his head, took a pull off his water. He blew out a breath. "I tried to get my money back from the PI firm. They billed me for four grand. So I called them on it. I don't like being ripped off. Not this week. Not ever."

That was it. JB met me because he felt like a fool. Someone duped him and he couldn't figure it out. He stood there and I swear he looked real, not this plastic man in a suit. With his guard down, I peeked a man distracted by deep grief. I thought he told the truth when we talked, but I didn't fully believe him until now.

JB loved her — the thought randomly popped in my head.

He continued, "I asked Vince what information he had my regular PI firm didn't. He wouldn't show me his reports, claiming it would violate Homeland Security protocol."

At this point in our talk, I should've told him about last night. About Vince Hendricks in a Crown Vic with Oklahoma plates. My car. My body. Another life at risk.

But, last night wasn't done on JB's order. Although he had skin in this game, I didn't think he knew what move to play next. His lawyers most likely told him to wait and see.

"Last piece, then I'm done," I said, "When you bought the family out, by all accounts they accepted the arrangement."

"*Acquiesced* is the word that likes to be thrown around," JB added.

"Lot of words like to be thrown around," I said, "But what happened? Screaming? Shouting? We'll-bury-you type threats?"

"Smart family, the Prices. I learned from the best. They weren't victims. They wanted to be bought out. Promoting me showed them that they had no passion for the sanitation business," JB slid his Blackberry to the side, "And Whitman for all his faults, he turned his trust-fund into a formidable real estate portfolio while he was still in B school."

"Oh, so they just signed the papers with a smile?" I asked.

Half smiled, "Not exactly."

JB Foster was back there. The partial-smile stayed on his face and it looked like he was reliving his own come up. South Holland kid proved himself to the world. Achieved boldface status for his name.

I didn't have any other questions. I really just threw that last one out there. Like hey, I've been following your shit my whole life and just wanted a little back story.

He looked up at me. Steadied himself all sincere like. "They went cold. I thought the offer would never go through."

"Because it was wrong for them," I offered — it was all I knew.

"Nah, the offer was right for all of us. But when I got the idea, it took me over a year to bring it all together. And I was dating their daughter. Nobody ever talked about that. For unrelated reasons, relationship issues, I couldn't date her anymore."

His phone buzzed yet again, tried to inch itself back up the counter into his eye-line.

"Hardest thing I've ever done," he said.

"Money over love?" I asked.

"More complicated than that. Strange that it came to this. Her name was Jax. I've thought about her a lot this week. When Babi and I started dating last year, I thought about it then a lot too."

"She still around?"

He just looked at me. A quid pro quo didn't apply to matters of the heart.

"Give me your number," I said before I walked away.

He did.

I typed it into my phone and hit the call button. Couple seconds later his phone lit up.

He stepped to the side to glance at his phone, then back at me, "I already have your number."

"And now you have this," I said and put the documents back into the envelope. I paused before sliding it over to him, "With this you owe me."

"I thought this meeting was a favor," he replied.

"This meeting determined whether I would do you a solid," I answered, "Information about Vince Hendricks that I already knew doesn't make for a fair exchange."

"Okay," he said, "What do you want?"

I slid the envelope across the black counter.

He caught it under his flat palm as if we played air hockey on the most expensive table ever.

"Not now, we'll talk when this is finished," I told him. Then I added, "I'd fire Vince Hendricks effective immediately, if I were you."

He pulled the papers out, ignoring my comment. Started to read.

I turned and walked to the door.

"Wait."
Looked over my shoulder at him.
"You said there was more," he said.
"Lied. But that's more than enough."

PART II: **IT AIN'T HARD TO TELL**

fifty

'It's your life. Or Lenny's. You decide,' Gesso had said.

I mouthed Gesso's line to myself, 'My life or Lenny's.'

Looked through the gun's sight at her.

"Gotta bust, Bones," she said.

"My life," I said aloud, "Or Lenny's."

She didn't need to reinforce her threat; I did it for her.

"The choice," I told her as I lowered the gun, "Is mine to make, huh? And that threat's supposed to put me in a corner? Huh. All you did was voice the scenario running through my head all week. You're, like, stating the obvious, Ms. White Light."

We first heard of her when Lenny got his high school hustle going. Lately, The Roach was under the impression she went underground. I learned much later — when I started hanging around painters and writers — what the name meant. Gesso, the product, was the white wash primer artists used to prep a new canvas for action. Or more to the point, the white wash primer they used to paint over old artwork so they could start anew.

Gesso, the woman, personified white out. The blank canvas. Or more accurately, the white light. As in, the white light at the end of tunnel. The last thing you saw. Gesso.

"You still have a few things to learn," she said and started the truck. Her head ducked down, looking for something. Then she began to adjust her mirrors. "Look, you might get away with something simple like claiming your car was stolen. But the cops are hot on you. They think you have Lenny."

"You have intel on the police work, huh," I said and instantly had an idea. "Okay, how about this? The cops have a witness. Someone — don't know if it's a guy or a girl — can testify that Lenny told Albert Brongel he was going to kill Babi." I didn't bother to review the names what they meant. I assumed Gesso knew. "It's not a direct tie. Brongel was the direct tie. But it sounds damning."

"That's not going to help you," Gesso said, and clarified, "Lenny, yes. But you and I are talking about something else."

"You want me to play your game, Gesso?" I said and looked her dead in the eye. It was the first time I said her name and I wanted to clock her reaction.

Nothing.

I added, "Get me that witness's name."

"Tomorrow lunch," she said, "I'll give you a call."

Seeing how it was past eleven at night that would be a remarkable turn around.

"I've got to work tomorrow," I said.

"The credit business never sleeps does it," she tacked on flippantly.

She wanted me to feel like she knew everything about me. She wanted me to be scared about losing my job. She could know my shoe size for all I cared. There was no way she could leverage my crappy no-benefits job against me. Besides, I already planted the seed today — I was taking a new gig.

"After I get the intel," I said and slid my car into reverse, "I'll hear you out."

The F-150 pulled out. The open parking space revealed my mom's old building. She lived here right before she went homeless, and got kicked out of the Pacific Garden Mission.

I couldn't resist the memory. Her standing in front of that building in her big underwear and bra wearing the bathrobe her hairy Armenian super had brought down for her. She had smoked in bed and set her mattress on fire. The fire department was wrapping up that night by the time I got there.

The F-150's brake lights dimmed as Gesso pulled away. Up at the corner the F-150's blinker was flashing in advance of Gesso's turn toward Lake Shore Drive. I pressed the memory of my mom back down. Focused on Gesso's blinker as I blazed through two stale yellows to catch up with her and the F-150. I made the tail heading south.

fifty-one

The tail lasted almost two full listens of *Illmatic*. Hegwish was a haul. The neighborhood always felt more Northwest Indiana than Chicago to me. Adults there shopped over the border in Hammond and the kids clubbed in Cal City.

My body was pain free and tugging toward sleep. Still, I was glad I followed Gesso.

She parked the F-150 in a driveway — the address matched the data I ran earlier in the evening. The F-150 had a payday loan on it from Liberty Finance. I looked around at the other cars on the block. One stood out from the rest — a white Range Rover. I took down the license plate and left before Gesso finished with the F-150's owner.

fifty-two

I knew a couple of idiots who received payday loans from Liberty. I heard them at parties talking about the hottie that worked there. These neighborhood guys used every stupid name short of calling the clerk a nigger — brown sugar, black mamba — and even gave her a fake name that started with a Q. I would listen to them talking about her and think, *man you're talking about getting a payday loan in public. Where women can hear you. Shameless.*

It could've been a set of coincidences lining up. It could've been no coincidence at all. But I was going to find out.

Friday morning I slept in. Skipping work again meant I had effectively quit my job.

At eleven in the morning I drove to the Maxwell Street Depot at Thirty-First and Canal. I was starving. No matter what time of day, that intersection reeked. Around the clock stacks of pork chops sat on the grill. You couldn't actually see the pork chops because they stewed for hours under a pile of chopped onions. The onion smell formed a bubble twenty yards deep around the joint.

The Maxwell Street Depot wasn't fashionable food-truck food. It was the cheapest grocery store pork-chop on a dollar store hamburger bun. But they stewed so long you could usually eat part of the bone. I ordered two pork-chop sandwiches, mustard only.

I ate and looked at the strip mall across the street. There was the requisite tanning salon, and a cigar store, and a travel agency. And at the far left side was Liberty Finances' Bridgeport outpost.

I finished my chops, walked across the street, and went inside.

The clerk at the counter of the payday loan joint was an attractive young black woman. Not as hot as Gesso, but she stood out in whatever neighborhood she came from, no doubt.

She had the *Sun-Times* on the counter. She closed the paper and put it on the desk below.

A small flat screen was mounted in a corner. Oprah's face covered the entire screen as she delivered a monologue.

"Can I help you?" she asked. She had a sweet voice and spoke with a smile.

I asked the cutie a bunch of remedial questions. I made myself out to be someone desperate but doing my due diligence. She was great at customer service.

Her big brown eyes carried sweetness. I could see her easily charming the neighborhood rats.

Ultimately, I took a business card with her manager's name on it. I told her I'd be back at four-thirty.

I left and walked to the back of the building.

I stood in the alley behind Liberty Finance blinking my eyes. A white Range Rover. Same license plate as last night. Same car.

I was shocked the intel came easy to me. I figured it was because it had nothing to do with helping Lenny. Secondly, I couldn't believe Gesso — the ultimate street legend — managed a payday loan office.

fifty-three

It took me three hours on Friday afternoon to get a line on her. Five phone calls and an office visit later I found someone to run the license plate for me. The white Range Rover was registered to a woman named

Morgan Simmons. She lived in a high rise in Hyde Park by the University of Chicago.

None of it made sense. Gesso legit? It didn't match the threat on my life, or the intel she was getting from the cops. The only thing it matched was the branch manager's name on the Liberty Finance business card.

fifty-four

At four-thirty I walked into my kitchen, and set down my phone. It buzzed while I was in the bathroom.

While I took my shirt off, it buzzed again.

There were two texts.

Scotty Smuda wrote: Hawkeyes.

And a blocked number wrote: 29 street viaduct, 5:30 pm.

Even with Gesso's threat on my head, Scotty Smuda's text was much more interesting. It was Friday afternoon. I definitely didn't need him to text me his location.

Without thinking, I went and turned on my TV.

My oldest friend was holed up in a squat. I had lost my car and my computer in the past week. Damaged my body enough that I was conscious of each move I made. Except I didn't walk to the living room, I floated. It felt like all the nerves along my neck and down my spine were tied to little helium-filled balloons that carried me to the TV. I turned it on. WGN was on commercial.

They came out of the commercial into the weather report. On a normal news day the weather could take up a ten-minute segment. Tonight it was a quick ninety-second blurb before they went to commercial again. I feared the worst — urgent news waited on the other side of the break.

My phone buzzed again from the kitchen. Another text.

Then another buzz from my phone. This time it was a phone call because the buzz didn't stop. All the buzzes set off alarms in my head. My eyes glazed over from speculation as WGN ran a promo for tonight's programming — the last commercial before heading back to the news.

I didn't want to miss the news so I stayed on the couch. The constant vibration caused my phone to shimmy along the table. After four straight minutes of buzzing it apparently slid off and and smashed onto the floor. I hoped the linoleum provided a cushion.

I didn't look into the kitchen though.

I stared at the TV.

Lenny Supinski stared back at me.

Lenny Supinski wanted for the murder of Babi Patras and Albert Brongel. My oldest friend was now a hot stepping fugitive. My next thought: I could go down with him. The serious news stressed the anchor out a bit. The evidence wasn't explicitly laid out, but I could see their case. Former boyfriend. Introduced Babi to JB. Unrequited love. Criminal history. Violated his parole in conjunction with the investigation. My stomach was in knots.

I needed a breather so I went to the kitchen and picked up my phone. Four missed calls and a dozen texts. On the neighborhood phone tree all paths leading to Lenny came through me. All along I knew his prison release dates and the dates his parole ended. Knew when his piss tests were. All that.

Scotty Smuda's text was first. Six down the list was the same message, this time from Frankie: Meeting SS at Hawkeyes.

Yeah, got it.

Scotty owned Lenny's squat in Canaryville. He gave me keys after I met him at Hawkeyes last Friday. If Lenny got nabbed at the squat, then Scotty might face charges for harboring a fugitive.

I couldn't let that happen.

I opened my basement stash box and pulled out the keys to the apartment.

Threw my White Sox hat back on and bolted out the door.

I needed to attend to Scotty. But first I had to delay Gesso.

fifty-five

The white Range Rover was still parked behind Liberty Finance. She hadn't left for our meeting yet.

I found a napkin and a Sharpie in my glove box.

I wrote on the napkin: 7p/29v.

There was no way to know if it'd work.

I didn't make Gesso as the forgiving type. I didn't expect her to give me a second chance at this meeting. But she'd be watching the news too. The news greatly effected her "Your life or Lenny's" threat. And besides–

I stopped trying to analyze.

Scotty had called. I had to answer.

I jumped from my car and put the note under the white Range Rover's windshield wiper. I wanted to make sure the napkin'd get her attention.

I hip-checked the Range Rover's front fender and walked away.

Gesso's car alarm ricocheted in the alley behind the strip mall.

The alarms in my head hadn't stopped since Lenny's mug shot came up on my TV. Lenny was wanted for murder.

fifty-six

"Tonight, Scotty, I'm moving him tonight."

"It's on the news, Bones," Scotty said, nodding his chin up toward the TV.

Frankie stood there and watched us.

"You're not on the news," I said, "That's the important thing here. You're fine."

"Yeah, but," Scotty shook his head long and slow, "If he gets caught for this, they'll start charging everyone involved." he looked up at the TV again. Scotty read both papers every day. Scotty listened to the news every day. He was the most informed contractor I'd ever talked to. He capped it off by adding, "Do you know how much attention this case is attracting? The story might go national."

"Do I know?" I asked then answered, "More than most." To offer up proof, I held up my clunky rental car keys. "Chased down Canal Street on Wednesday. Rolled my car. Rolled it. Got shot at."

He and Frankie both shook their heads.

"Yeah," I put the keys in my back pocket and hit a firm nod with my chin and said, "I know."

"Let me ease your worries like this, Scotty."

I reached up both arms, squeezed Scotty's shoulder with one hand,

and Frankie's with the other.

"I don't trust anyone, Scotty. I don't trust anyone but you and Frankie," I squeezed both shoulders and let my hand drop. "I'm not going to let anything happen over the next twelve hours, twelve days, twelve years. Never. I would never do a thing to make you think that you couldn't trust me back. I fucking got this."

They both took swigs off their beers. We don't talk about trust and shit normally, so it wasn't like Frankie or Scotty were gonna whip up a big bro moment.

"That's alright. Don't say anything back, you pussy," I smiled, "I got this. I had it. It was never out of my hands."

"Lenny's not in your hands," Scotty said.

"If he was he'd be back in county now, possibly with a shiv in his side. Hence the squat you little bitch, which," I pulled out his key from a front pocket, "Here's the key back. None of this will be able to touch you come morning."

"No," he said right back, "Tonight. It's over tonight."

"Alright," I said and we shook hands, "I'll text you later."

fifty-seven

I stood in the shadows of the Twenty-Ninth Street Viaduct at 6:58 comfortable under it's cover.

Bridgeport viaducts regulated my life. Coming home or going out always involved passing under a set of railroad tracks or a highway. Viaducts swallowed light. They were dark even in the daytime. For me, that darkness marked the passage of one event to the next. Like the silence on an LP between songs, viaducts marked the beginning *and* the end.

Bridgeport's main spine of viaducts ran under the railroad tracks heading straight south from downtown. Many of the side-street viaducts were still paved in cobblestone. None of them smelled like piss. There was a viaduct for every east-west street from Twenty-Sixth to Thirty-Ninth. There were north bound viaducts too. And more than a few diagonals along Archer.

Gesso pulled up in her white Range Rover.

I opened the passenger door and checked her hands. No weapon.

I had the gun with me again. A day later, and still no idea how to use it. I put one hand in my coat pocket and climbed in.

She looked at my pocket. She knew. Thing made me self-conscious anyway so I took my hand out.

Gesso wore a shiny green polyester tracksuit with a green bandana over her hair. The tracksuit had yellow stripes down the side. If she had a dress code like last night, I bet her shoes were green All Stars. I didn't bother looking down by the pedals. She had green eye shadow on too. She looked great behind the wheel. Her Range Rover had those fresh brown leather seats that looked like a field of cattle stitched together.

She pulled off the curb.

"We're not going anywhere, are we?" I asked.

"We're going away from here. People know me in this neighborhood. Your ballcap doesn't hide your face enough."

"I'm not hiding," I said.

"Really?" she said and gave me a glance like she thought otherwise.

"Don't tell me you're a loan officer, Gesso," I said unable to believe her legit lifestyle, "That would be the let down of all let downs."

"Never mind what I do," she said, "I take care of my people."

She cut north, up towards Chinatown. I wasn't going to raise a stink, or the gun, unless she headed south.

I had an hour to spare after meeting Scotty at Hawkeyes, so I jetted home to do research on Liberty Finance. They were a regional outfit, owned by two guys from the western suburbs. On their website I saw pictures of them with the second ranked state senator. They were on the front steps of the Statehouse in Springfield.

We were driving up Canal in the right lane, ready to head toward Chinatown.

"Turn left here," I said, "I know a spot."

"There's only one place?" she mocked.

"Humor me," I shot back, "Left."

She switched lanes and jumped left.

I let the silence ride for a few blocks until we crossed Halsted. Then I directed her into the In Between portion of Bridgeport — a two block section isolated from the rest of the neighborhood. It sat between the expressway and the South Branch of the Chicago River. Most of the In Between was residential, then along the river there were a few warehouses that'd be empty tonight.

I had her pull into the parking lot of a construction equipment company.

She drove to the back of the lot along the river. The car faced downtown and the glittering lights of the skyline.

"Interesting," I said out of nowhere, "the game you're playing."

"Oh, I'm playing a game now," she said.

"Yeah, let's call it *low finance*," I answered.

She undid her seatbelt and cocked her hips so she half faced me in the car, and said, "Low finance. Has a ring to it."

"Yeah," I huffed out a fake laugh, "The ring of a cash register."

"I'm guessing you changed your line of work, but not your employer. Your employment, eh hem, contract wouldn't allow it. So you went from providing one valuable service," that being the role of the heavy, the white light, "to another."

I piqued her curiosity, because she finally asked a question, "How so?"

First, I told her, there was no way she managed payday loan offices and occupied her day scheduling low wage loan clerks and shuffling heavily regulated papers. No way she concerned herself with the laws of lending, for a stable paycheck.

"Not quite," she corrected, "I take care of my people. For the clerks like the one you talked to earlier today," the cutie with the blue oxford, "Working for me is a fortunate position."

No doubt, I told her, but a fringe benefit to Gesso at best.

I was never interested in dealing; I never wanted to push product onto people. One thing that fascinated me, and the one thing I talked to The Roach about, was how to account for all the extra money. Where did he hide it and then clean it to make it legit.

There wasn't any concrete data behind my theory. But as I researched for that hour I came up with an interesting scheme. There was a way to launder money through loans. If you reversed the cash flow — pay out clean money up front in the form of a loan — it amounted to a unique way to beat heavy money laundering fees. It would only work if you used a legitimate financial institution.

I put my theory out there for Gesso.

She replied, "You should take comfort in that old saying: ignorance is bliss."

"Bullshit line if I ever heard one," I said.

She propped a foot up on her brown leather seat. The white rubber sole of her green All Star looked brand new — like she knew she wasn't getting her pristine leather seat dirty. She said, "In this case ignorance equals bliss. You speak of things you should not know."

"But there you have it," I said, "Now, you got the witness' name? The one who can testify against Lenny?"

"Better than that," she said and slid a small packet of paper out from her visor, handed it to me, and added, "Jon Jardine."

I stared at the picture. He could have been anyone. Handsome fellow dressed in all black. Except as my eyes gravitated to his nose I realized he wasn't just anyone.

"The security guy at Onyx?" I asked more to myself.

"That's him," she confirmed.

I looked through the papers attached to the picture: a copy of his driver's license and press releases printed off the web about his life running security for high profile clubs.

"Who else knows about him?" I asked. The packet of paper was pretty flimsy. But the name was important.

She gave a slight lick to her lips, showed only the tip of her tongue.

I looked out the windshield. The massive smoke stack of the coal-fueled Fisk Plant across the river dominated our view. White entrails billowed out the smoke stack.

"Lenny," Gesso finally said. I didn't like hearing her say his name. "He could cause problems."

Sore neck be damned, I rolled my head back.

"Ahhhhh, ha ha," I groaned, "That's good."

I didn't answer her.

"He's been in touch with your friend, Roach," she added.

My head came up off the headrest.

"This week?"

"This week," she answered.

That meant Lenny didn't follow my order and not leave his squat. I started thinking through the situation, but Gesso jumped in. Filled in the necessary details.

"Lenny made demands," Gesso added, "Wants help disappearing."

"Anyone know where Lenny called from?" I asked.

I looked across the seats at her. She paused. Gesso could've been a music video girl. This car. The way her body filled out the tracksuit. Her hair. The warm glow from the dashboard lights on her immaculate skin.

She turned to me. I had to remind myself that her serene face equaled fear on the streets of the South Side.

"Yeah, someone knows where the calls came from," she said plainly, "You."

I wanted to ask if she had tickets to see Erykah Badu Sunday night like I did. I got stupid like that and wanted to impress at the worst time. I held back.

"I am not the guy," I said.

"Albert Brongel," Gesso said and added, "Canal Street. You don't just stumble into multiple run-ins with the cops. That just doesn't happen. You know why, Bones?"

"If I asked myself *why* about any of this, I wouldn't be here right now."

"You better start asking," Gesso snapped back, "Because you've got decisions to make. Your life, or Lenny's."

"Again. What exactly does that mean?" I asked.

If I followed the logic, then Lenny dug himself in a deeper hole by threatening The Roach. If Lenny flipped on The Roach, then Gesso's bosses were concerned The Roach would flip on them. Really The Roach would have to flip on a middle-manager first, who might in turn flip on Gesso's bosses. Either way the shit was on Gesso's radar.

"It means you're going to tell me where Lenny is," Gesso said.

"And deliver him to his, his," I was about to say *executioner* but switched after I stuttered and said, "Execution."

"He made too many mistakes," Gesso said, "Even if the police find him. Do you think he'll be safe inside?"

She was right. If Gesso's bosses wanted Lenny, then he couldn't hide in jail.

I had no idea how my life could substitute for Lenny's. The trade had to be simple, but still I was thinking about Lenny. His picture on the TV. His phone call to The Roach.

I had a few hours before I wanted to go get him.

"Monday," Gesso said.

"Wha?" I asked.

"You have until Monday. That's what I'm here to tell you."

I looked over and gave her my warmest smile. "You could've texted me that. You're here to give me this," I said and held up the docket on Jon Jardine.

She stared back.

"So, uh," I acted shy as I fumbled for my phone. I opened it and poised my fingers over the keypad, "How about giving me that math so I can be in touch?"

She slid her foot down to the floor, straightened the pants on her track suit, and reached to put the Range Rover in gear.

"That's good, Gesso," I told her, "Being ignored. This week I could use a little more of that," and put my phone away.

She'd be in touch.

I knew that.

fifty-eight

Lenny. It was over for him and I. The only reason I planned on taking him from the squat now, was to protect Scotty Smuda. The only reason. If what Gesso said was true, and I didn't doubt it, we were finished.

That meant good-bye Lenny. I needed to keep this promise to myself.

I wasn't surprised. I didn't trust Lenny. The only difference between him and the rest of the world is that I gave him breaks. Until now.

I was going to put Lenny's fate squarely in his own hands. This was going to be my parting gift to him.

I drove by the Walgreens on my way home and picked up two packs of Marb Reds and a box of hypodermic needles.

At home I put a pot of water on to boil. Emptied the plastic bag on the counter and rolled the edges into a makeshift bucket.

Left the burner on and took a shower.

When I climbed out the water in the saucepan was simmering. I turned the gas up and it started to boil.

I never used that pan anyway. Picked it up at a yard sale when I moved in. Couple pans in the box were decent, but this Teflon coated sauce pan never made sense.

Opened one pack of Marb Reds. Put the cellophane wrapper and the foil tongue from the cigarette pack in the plastic bag.

Ripped the cigarette box open and put all twenty smokes into my left hand. Held them evenly.

Then I ripped off the filters and shook the ends of the cigarettes over the plastic bag until the loose tobacco sprinkled out.

Held my hand over the pan and kneaded the cigarettes so the entire handful — paper and tobacco — sprinkled into the water.

Turned the burner down so it wouldn't boil over.

I swear if I looked in the pan I'd see Lenny's face. He was the only thought in my head. I could kill him, I thought. Hell, it looked like I was getting prepared to do just that.

While it boiled, I jumped downstairs and grabbed the rest of Lenny's money and his car keys. Brought them upstairs and put 'em in an old freebie duffle bag.

Every couple of minutes I stepped over and stirred the mix as it boiled down.

Those were just my actions. The entire time I worked and waited I thought one thing. Over. This was it for Lenny. I promised myself, and I was going to keep that promise.

Forty minutes after it started the pot was ready.

The tobacco shreds were dark and hard inside the water. I couldn't tell what happened to the rolling papers they were wrapped in. Must have disintegrated. The four inches of water had boiled down to a half-inch.

Found a clamshell eyeglass case in my desk that I no longer used.

Opened up the case and set it on the counter.

I pulled out the needles.

Turned the gas off so the pan could cool for a minute. Dipped the needles into the mix and drew the plunger. I filled three spikes.

After filling each needle, I replaced the needle caps and set all three gently in the clamshell case. Closed it. They fit snugly inside.

I tossed the clamshell into the duffel bag.

Took out three more plastic bags from under my sink and nested the one from the drugstore inside them.

The garbage bag was now full of the Marb Red filters and the entire box of unused needles.

Dumped the pan's contents in the toilet, and put the pan in the garbage bag. Heat from the pan melted the innermost bags, and the plastic shrink-wrapped itself against the pan's side.

Closed my nose to the stink from the burning plastic.

Opened up the kitchen window. Set the pan and bags on the window ledge to cool in the late November air.

fifty-nine

I stood in the dark gangway across the street from Lenny's squat. It was a little after eleven Friday night. I had been there for an hour watching his building. There was no activity.

My car was parked two blocks away. The duffel with his money and car keys was in the trunk. The spikes inside the clamshell eyeglass case were in there too.

The building where Lenny stayed looked just like the one my grandparents lived in when I came up. A couple blocks behind me were the Stockyards where my grandpa worked as a young man.

As I looked at the building, I kept staring into the darkened gangway leading to Lenny's unit in the back. At first I tried to pierce the shadows and see if Lenny lurked in there, waiting for me. Or waited for someone else.

When I was a kid we always walked the gangway to get to my grandparent's apartment. They lived on the top floor. I can remember how their gangway was cool even in the thick of summer since the sun never reached between the buildings. At the back of the building we'd climb up the slanted wooden back porch to the top floor.

I had stayed there once as a kid. I was nine and my mom hadn't completely gone off the deep end yet. She still wound up in the hospital once a year. She still wasn't around, like ever. But she had a boyfriend then. They had planned a vacation.

It was the only time I stayed with my grandparents. Usually they stayed with me when my mom checked into the mental ward.

During that week my grandma took care of me.

I got to run in all the candy stores and not feel the need to steal. I made my grandma sit at the counter at the Bridgeport Restaurant. She let me do whatever I wanted that week.

Candy. Hot dogs. Child-level fireworks. That week my grandma bought me my first White Sox hat. Up and down Halsted like I'd never been a million times before.

And at the end of each adventure, I'd walk with my grandma down that cool gangway in mid-July. Then I always sprinted to the top of the back stairs because I was the fastest and the strongest and nobody could get up there like I could and still not be tired. I'd watch her come up behind me. She didn't take particularly long. She was like sixty, not that old.

The memories got deeper, the longer I stared into the gangway leading to Lenny's squat.

In my memory I know all those good things are there. The candy and the White Sox hat and eating cherries out of the cherry bin at the grocery store. But all I think about is the back porch.

Up and down all week long. How many times? Not enough.

The memories are sweet. I think of that single week as my entire childhood. It was the only time I felt completely taken care of.

The following year, I was away at sleep away camp when my grandma died. I'm sure she planned it that way.

When I returned home from camp, my mom and grandpa picked me up from the bus station.

'Where's grandma?' I asked.

Orky, my grandpa, was sober.

'She's not here. She passed away,' he said. He didn't smell. His voice was grovely as ever and the flesh under his chin wagged.

'Passed away?' I asked.

My mom took over, 'She died. She fell down the stairs in the building.'

'The back stairs?'

'No the ones leading to the Ryan's.

My grandpa didn't add to the story.

'She broke her neck and died,' my mom finished.

That wasn't true.

My grandma had committed suicide. She walked out onto the back porch one evening. Maybe after dinner or something stupid like that. Took care of Orky one final time. Then what? Lifted a leg up? Could she do that in her house-dress with her sixty-one year old legs? I don't know. Whatever. She rolled over the damn railing. Fell over the banister into the gangway. Three tall stories, then splat.

Took a year for the blood-stain to come off the gangway's sidewalk.

When I came back from that memory, it was the only memory that mattered.

I shifted my weight in the dark gangway across the street from Lenny's squat.

I wished I could've resisted the memory. As I stood there, it came in waves with the details piling on one after the next. My first White Sox cap. Hot dogs. Butterscotch candies. My insides surged. Then I felt the most amazing feeling: anger. Over and over. The word repeated in my head. Sitting there in that gangway, seventeen years later I was mad about being lied to about my grandma's death.

I had been mad all along, no doubt. But for all those years I was a fish and the anger was water. It just was; I never had to know it was there. Then I felt it, and the word came to my head. Anger. On repeat.

It was sublime. I felt anger. More importantly, I felt something.

It was the first time I put a label on a feeling.

Anger was the first emotion I truly felt, and completely understood.

That feeling propelled me out of the shadows, and across the street to Lenny.

sixty

I hopped across the street.

Walked right down the gangway.

I just walked. And watched.

First thing I did was to look for light. No light shone out of the side window from Lenny's squat. If the kitchen light was on it would light up the gangway.

Next, as I approached the back of the building I looked to the garage. If Lenny had the squat's bedroom light on, that light'd shine on the back wall of the garage.

First I needed to catch light. Then I'd look for moving shadows.

The garage wall was dark like everything else.

Turned the corner at the end of the gangway and took the four wooden steps up to Lenny's door.

The door to Lenny's hung open.

The lights were off inside.

I didn't step through the threshold. I stood still and listened. Smelled. No smoke. Wherever Lenny was there was smoke. Poked my nose in the doorway. The apartment smelled stale as all get up, but no fresh cigarette smoke. Didn't hear no throat-clearing grovel. No flick of a lighter or scratch of a match.

Lenny was gone.

sixty-one

I turned around walked out.

Vince Hendricks popped into my head.

I thought about the news. Maybe WGN was showing Lenny on his perp walk with Detective Glenn behind him holding onto his plastic cuffs like reins.

I had no idea. Well, I did know one thing.

Whatever the situation, the odds of me helping Lenny approached zero.

I walked back out the gangway, and climbed the stairs back up to the sidewalk in front of the building.

Damn if those Canaryville streets aren't the most comfortable kind of dark and quiet you could find. My medicated body still felt great. I wasn't sluggish. But I didn't want to start going round and round again. Thinking over and over and over through the same thoughts, the same scenarios, facts, situations, people, timing, schedules, connections.

I stood on the sidewalk and rolled my neck around nice and slow. When I finished and the crackle of my neck quieted down, I heard footsteps.

They sounded from a couple houses up the sidewalk. The hairs on my neck didn't even flinch. I liked that. I stood there listening to their rhythm. Caught the rhythm as if the steps disturbing my peaceful pause

were expected. As if the minute while I stood there enjoying the darkness was just another song break.

Someone was coming for me.

The sound clacked on the sidewalk up to my right. I decided to stop
this game of hide and seek — let whoever it was come to me.

Caught the beat of the steps, heard them getting closer. Treated the
situation as if I were a DJ mixing music. Thing about matching beats
when you're trying to mix two songs together is that you can't be in two
places at once. You can hear the next beat coming and you can feel it.
But you can't go get it.

The steps got louder. I refused to look.

That's the way it was on the decks. Even when you know what song
you're switching to next you can't just jump to it. You've got to stay home.
Stay with your beat. Make the next track come to you. Twist and turn
that wax until the beat hovered, until it was ready to click into place.

The footsteps were there, and I needed to just let them come to me.
I couldn't walk to them, or walk with them. I could only be here. And
that's where I stayed.

Before anyone could reach out and touch me, I faced the steps.

Detective Glenn.

sixty-two

Without a warrant they couldn't cuff me, I think.

They treated our trip to the station like a courtesy ride. If it was a
formal arrest, I thought, they'd have called in a squad so they could put
me in the back cage.

They patted me down to make sure I wasn't packing.

I'd gladly go with them if it meant they didn't want access to my car.

Their car was parked a block back — too far to see from my perch
across the street earlier.

Glenn's partner drove. Glenn took me to the rear passenger door and
did his thugiest job of squeezing me in. Manhandled me into the door.
He lifted his elbow just as my head was ducking into the car. Jacked my
head into the roof of the car.

"Just for the record, this is bullshit," I said when we all sat inside, "You think I know where Lenny is, and yet I show up at the same building you guys are watching. Don't you think I'd be trying to stay away from you?"

The car pulled off the curb and drove past Lenny's squat.

"I think you knew where he was all along," Detective Glenn said back to me, "And now you don't."

I didn't reply.

The car turned left at the bottom of the block. Swung another left to head back up to Pershing.

"I'm sure you have a story to match with what you just told us," Glenn tacked on, "Doesn't mean I believe you. I know you knew Lenny was there."

"Oh. Okay," I said, "That keeps it clean. I can't argue against your hunch."

Glenn's partner pulled a right onto Pershing and headed east toward the police station. The two detectives murmured in low voices.

I didn't listen.

I needed to stay on the street.

I didn't have a lawyer. Over the years none of Lenny's counselors had impressed me enough to keep their contact information. The Roach kept his work below the radar, never even whiffed a cop in his apartment until Lenny disappeared.

I needed someone with skin in the game, and my options were few. I didn't think any charges would stick. Letting Glenn try meant spending a couple days in lock-up, and no way in hell was I doing that. Besides, Scotty said he wanted his involvement finished. Tonight. He had done a favor for Lenny with the squat. Now I needed one myself.

I moved my head back and forth between Glenn and his partner like I followed their conversation.

I couldn't arch my back to get my phone out. It was wedged in the bottom of my front pocket. If I arched my back, I'd grab their attention. Instead I started pinching the phone from the bottom and squeezed it up to the top of my pocket like it was the last drop of toothpaste in the tube.

After it slid out, I held the phone down below my knee.

I dialed Scotty Smuda.

Cleared my throat while I dialed. It was a lame distraction, but their chatter did the job well enough.

It sounded like they were talking charges — grounds for holding me.

I glanced at the phone while it dialed out. Watched the screen until it connected on the other end and started counting time.

When I thought I heard Scotty's voice I pulled the phone up to my ear.

"Hey!" Detective Glenn yelled.

"Scotty bro," I said.

Glenn swiped at my arm.

"They picked me up," I spoke as fast as I could. "Nobody was at that apartment you asked me to go check out."

"Off the phone!" Glenn said, reached for me again.

I leaned my head and elbow backwards until I could see up and out the rear window while my elbow touched the ceiling.

Glenn couldn't reach the phone. He swiped at my legs.

"What?" Scotty said on the other end.

Glenn's partner started yelling, "OFF! OFF! OFF!"

I told Scotty, "Two detectives are hauling me in. Can you send a lawyer?"

"Pull over!" Glenn yelled. His butt raised high up in the air. He was getting ready to pounce.

"I, I," Scotty said, drifted off into silence. He probably thought about his dad. As connected as his pops was, he couldn't get the old spark plug involved in this.

I said as fast as I could, "Tell the lawyer to not mention it to your pops. OK?"

As the car jerked to the side of the road Glenn flew over the seat. Landed his body fully on mine. His forearm braced across my head. He had the rest of his body on top of me too, so all I could do was twist my wrist awkwardly up and offer up my phone.

With the phone away from my mouth I screamed, "Just call him, call the lawyer!"

Glenn snagged it out of my hand.

Then Glenn pivoted his body so that he landed perfectly in the rear passenger seat. I hoped that thirty seconds on the phone was enough, because the detectives were in complete control now.

My twisting out of reach had me crumpled up behind the driver's side.

Detective Glenn kicked my feet away from his legs.

When I recovered and finally sat up, it looked like Glenn had been there for a year. Had his little snarl on his face. Held his gun in his lap.

Pointed right at me.

"You can't move fast enough," Glenn said, "To avoid this whole clip." he didn't even divert his eyes from mine or wag the thing to show it to me.

The car jumped back into traffic.

Glenn raised his eyebrows.

The car approached the Dan Ryan Expressway. Glenn broke the seal on his lips, about to say something.

The car's blinker went on. They were switching lanes to take the left onto the expressway. We could jump on and jump off a few exits later and save minutes on getting me to the station.

If they didn't go left onto the expressway, they should go straight up to State Street. We could ride that all the way up to HQ.

Instead the car swooped right.

We cut down the expressway ramp. We were headed south. Away from downtown. Away from headquarters.

"Where now? Homan Square?"

"You're never going to see that lawyer," Glenn said, "We're going to drive all night."

"Until what?" I asked.

"Until I get something to take back to the office," he answered, "Namely, Lenny."

"We got the gas card too," Glenn's partner chimed in.

"We can drive until you piss your pants. Until you pass out," Glenn said. He twisted fully sideways in his seat. Both of his eyes and his gun were fixed on me.

It sounded like they were ready to drive until Tuesday. I on the other hand didn't want it to last another hour. I needed to get out of that car. I needed to start now.

Detective Glenn's face said he'd be satisfied just ending it right then, with ten to fifteen tightly grouped bullets.

That's why I needed to talk my way out. There was no other option.

"How come the earrings never got released to the press?" I asked, "Such a useless piece of evidence that leaking it wouldn't hurt a thing."

No response.

"Let's just confirm something," I continued, "You don't know about the earrings. Babi wore them the night she was killed and they were never found. They never appeared in the paper. And as far as I know they never appeared in an evidence report."

Glenn shot back, "What do you know about evidence reports?"

"I know Jon Jardine is the witness you're using against Lenny. You never told me that."

Neither of them answered.

We were well past the Skyway exit. We picked up enough speed so that when we hit that big buckle in the road around seventy-ninth street I banged my knee on the back of the driver's seat.

The Dan Ryan Expressway nestled twenty feet below the level of the local streets.

Deep breath, "Anything on Vince Hendricks?"

They ignored me. I decided to just speak in statements.

"Vince Hendricks. You guys know who he is. Glenn," I said, "did you know JB Foster got a new driver the day after Babi was murdered."

I asked, "Do you know who that driver was?"

My head cleared enough to hear a throbbing bass drum. I thought it was just me — my bell had been rung too many times this past week. Then a gigantic white Cutlass Supreme streamed beside us. Caught the rhythm like I owned it and let it stay in my head as I watched the Cutlass push ahead.

"That's right, gentlemen, you have guessed correctly," I said in a game show voice, "You keep up with me and you'll have what you want in no time. Vince Hendricks. I even have a document at my house that proves Vince Hendricks is going to appeal JB's city contract first thing Wednesday morning."

Glenn's partner started laughing as he drove, "Oh, G," to Detective Glenn, "I'm going to pull this car into the next lane." he tried but a big eighteen wheeler droned up next to us. "Oh, that truck's next to me," Glenn's partner added, "I think I'll file an appeal to get that truck to move." he then wiggled the wheel and cackled at his own joke.

Glenn bared his teeth. He didn't seem like he had a guffaw in his repertoire.

Then, silence.

"Let me now ask something. Is any of this less circumstantial than what you have on Lenny? Coincidence that Vince Hendricks has tried to take me out? Convenient that he became JB's personal bodyguard for the week prior? I have the legal documents that say otherwise, gentlemen," and corrected myself, "I mean detectives."

"What's Hendricks going to get from killing Babi Patras?" Glenn asked.

"Hendricks. No, lets be fair. Hendricks — or one of his guys — enters Foster's loft to either plant some evidence or steal paperwork. Probably take something. Something that helps them make JB Foster look vulnerable. Maybe nothing big or even worth noticing to JB. But after what happens a week later — whatever's going to happen in the lead up to filing the appeal — the city will no longer trust JB's company. Which by the way is a company JB bought from the Price family. Oh, and by the way Whitman Price is Vince Hendricks' boss."

Suddenly, the sounds coming out of their talkies changed from the random sounds of a store-bought police scanner to direct requests.

Squawk, "Car 865, Kostecki, over. Car 865 Glenn, over."

They both dialed their talkies down.

We exited the freeway. Over was right.

Scotty must have called his lawyer. I hoped he'd done it out of friendship. I didn't care if he did it out of fear.

The longer we rode with the lawyer on the clock, the hotter it got for the detectives.

They started meandering through the greater South Side. Despite being in a squad, I loved the tour. A couple times I started to chant, "Jurisdiction! Jurisdiction!" as we readied to cross an invisible border. But Glenn's partner always turned in time.

After I ran out of details I wanted to reveal, I just talked about the neighborhoods we drove through.

Ninety-minutes later, they pointed back north and drove through the University of Chicago and to Lake Shore Drive.

Glenn's partner turned off the Drive at Thirty-First Street. It was the same overpass I took when I jogged to the lakefront. Soon we'd reach State Street. When they turned north it would be over for me. Time to give up.

All I could hope was that they didn't have enough on me to hold me indefinitely.

"What do you say, detectives?" I said, sitting up.

The State Street light was next.

"I got papers for you at my house. When we're there, I'll call the good counselor off. You head home, and it's all forgotten by morning. No grievance filed, nothing. We are talking about Scotty Smuda's family attorney here."

I didn't need to explain what that meant. Every city employee with a clue knew that last name.

Glenn's partner blew the red light at State Street. Went straight.

"Yeah," I said, "I know you guys did your homework."

"Shut up already," Detective Glenn said, laid his gun down on his thigh.

I curled a lip at him, "But I do the legwork."

sixty-three

I flopped the legal documents onto the table and puffed up over my big catch. Detective Glenn and his partner looked at the stack of paper. Their car was double-parked out front.

"The evidence," I said, happy the gun and earrings were in the rental down in Canaryville.

Glenn's partner called the desk sergeant as they started to read the documents. He handed his phone to me while the sergeant wrangled Scotty Smuda's lawyer. They continued reading while I told the lawyer to back off. It wasn't the Smuda's family lawyer, just some young kid from the firm. Probably my age. In our brief conversation I could tell he was disappointed. I told him to bill me whatever he wanted. Thanked him for his work.

"What's to say Vince Hendricks and Whitman Price weren't planning on filing an appeal all along," Glenn asked.

"Why wait?" I said and extended my arm to the document, "Just file if they're going to file. They're waiting for a reason. You ask JB Foster and he says Vince Hendricks isn't working for him as of Monday. It's coming to a head."

I talked through my hunch with them. Hendricks would move in Monday or Tuesday. Then on Wednesday they could blind-side JB when they filed the appeal.

"I get the feeling I'm going to need some help," I told Glenn and his partner. I didn't have anything concrete, but felt the need to recruit.

"Good luck with that," Glenn said.

"What about you guys?" I suggested, I just didn't know what I was suggesting, "It'll be a lead–"

"You're crazy, kid," Glenn said, "Not a chance. Zero."

His partner didn't enter the conversation.

"Whatever," I tried to shrug them off, as if I ran the best event in town, "Something's going to happen. It's up to you if you want to be there."

Detective Glenn never bit. His partner let the hook dangle on his lips though. He seemed to wait for that nod from Glenn as much as I did.

The nod never came.

They left with the paperwork. They could've left with my stereo and I would've escorted them out with a fat ass smile on my face.

sixty-four

Saturday morning I walked down to Canaryville to grab my rental car. On the way, I stopped back into Lenny's squat.

The door still hung open. I walked in.

Flicked the lights on. In the bedroom I could smell the sheets. They were saturated with stale sweat. Four Coke cans stood on the floor next to the sleeping bag. Each can topped with a sprinkling of cigarette ashes. There looked to be another pack's worth of cigarette ashes sprinkled around the cans on the drab gray carpet. The ashes near the cans proved that Lenny at least tried to keep the squat respectful. I picked up the cans. Rubbed the ashes into the carpet.

Six cardboard slabs from frozen pizzas were stacked on the kitchen counter by the rest of the empty Coke cans. Those cans too were topped with ashes. A plastic grocery bag sat on the counter too. Lenny apparently placed the bag with the intention of filling it up. Except most of the frozen burrito wrappers, empty bags of chips and dirty paper towels lay on the counter.

In the sink there was a plate with a fork on top of it and one empty glass coated with greasy fingerprints. Brown and burnt crumbs littered the counter.

The bathroom was empty. Empty. I hadn't checked last week, but I saw the shower didn't even have a shower curtain. There wasn't even a towel hanging to dry. No toothbrush. It was the only room that look completely cleaned out.

I cleaned the place as best I could. I didn't wash anything. Put the drinking glass and everything else I could find in the garbage. Stripped the smelly sheets and dropped them in the garbage too.

sixty-five

"Service was the hallmark of Whitman Price one and two," the speaker was saying, "Their empire grew through dedicated service to their constituents." I didn't know who she was, but she was the spunkiest member of the four-person panel discussion I was watching.

After cleaning Lenny's squat and picking up my car, I went out for breakfast. Hunger screamed in my ears. I ate and read both papers. Turns out today was basically Price Family day at the Chicago Historical Society. Then tonight was a huge gala in their honor.

The Historical Society started the day off with a symposium about the Price Family legacy in Chicago.

"Greed seemingly never came into their business plan until the current generation," the woman said. She looked to be in her fifties. Wore a silk blouse under a grey wool sweater. She had a pair of tortoise shell reading glasses teetering on the end of her nose.

There were four people on the panel. The guy who sat on the far end wore a brown suede jacket. He stuck his hand out to interject, "A proper analysis of the business conditions in the particular eras would also indicate each Whitman was a product of his time. They've adapted so as to not get left behind. There is no argument that the Price family is a family of businessmen."

I had arrived late. In my rush to sit down and avoid disapproving gazes I sat on the program, so I didn't have the panelists's names in front of me as I listened.

"Men," the woman pointed back. I was surprised her glasses didn't wiggle with her gesture, "Even if you can make anyone here believe that men are motivated by any factor except greed, you win the point on that. That's a big IF, Dick."

Richard P. Hutchison. Next to the table where everyone sat was a big blown up copy of a book cover. The cover was crowded with images of buildings and large letters in gilded type. The cover suggested empire. The book's author, Richard Hutchison, was the dude with the suede jacket.

The woman wagged her finger some more and kept after him, "But there's no denying the Price family is absolutely archaic when it comes to women." she pulled her elbow off the table and sat up straight, "None of them run divisions of their company, none of them are spokespeople for any of their charities," she was ticking them off on her finger, "No women run a business of their own despite their considerable acumen and pedigree before marrying into the family. And. And one of them is untouchable. Or worse, Dick, unmentionable."

The woman speaking seemed familiar, except I couldn't place her.

I instantly recognized that she was talking about someone exiled from the Price Family. It was easy for me to see that, my family was defined more by exile than family.

Besides me, the crowd was full of white-hairs. The kind of people who still paid attention to history and cared about families who capital- ized the F. Still believed in all that monoculture bullshit. Made sense that I was one of two young people here. The other was an extremely hot woman about my age. She wore fashionable horse-riding pants and knee-high boots. She also had a grey wool sweater just like–

I suddenly leaned over to the old woman next to me and asked, "Is that Carly Marino?" about the woman dominating the discussion while balancing her glasses on the end of her nose.

The old lady nodded.

Carly Marino was one of Chicago's most respected talking heads.

The other two panelists apparently didn't want to disagree with the most credible network anchor in town. As long as the talk was conten- tious those two remained silent.

The chatter among the four of them got lively a few minutes later. They had moved on to an architectural critique of the Price buildings around Chicago. The Price's always claimed they only tore down old eye- sores. Their PR line was effectively that they weren't interlopers like Donald Trump. The Prices' touted their work as progress.

I didn't know. I just didn't like the fact that Trump knocked down the old *Sun-Times* Building. I was probably the only one who felt that. Chicago as a city was an architect's dream. But I thought Chicago needed an ugly building — a broken nose like the old *Sun-Times* Building if you will — in order to look beautiful.

The symposium was cool. I stepped out regularly to interesting talks and gallery events. The ones I attended usually centered around street culture. I liked these events. But after listening for fifteen minutes I felt like the thoughts in my head were more interesting than the panel's. So I tuned them out. I had started, finally, thinking about Whitman Price.

Price had gamed the system, just like any hustler. Chris McMahon had spoken with a note of warning in his voice about the Prices and Vince Hendricks. They had built an army. Whitman Price was getting rich on tax dollars while the police wasted their entire budget on a farce of a drug war.

Recognizing "Jazzy" Jake Jaszinski jarred me from my thoughts. He stood ten feet beyond the left arm of the hottie in the front row.

Jazzy's curly hair was immediately recognizable. Carly Marino's husband.

When the talk ended Carly Marino walked straight to Jazzy Jake. The other three panelists lingered by the table and fielded questions from the white hairs in the crowd.

Before Carly could reach Jake, the hottie from the front row intercepted her.

"Carly," she finished her step and clicked her heels together, stood bolt upright. She started talking but I couldn't hear her over the buzz of conversation. I stepped over and stood in the wings, kept an eye on Carly like I was a fan and wanted to talk to her.

The hottie was saying, "an unfair representation of the family's attitudes."

"Sophie," Carly Marino said, "It's not my place to tell you whom to marry. But, that doesn't change my opinion. For all their charities and all they do for the city." Carly was being diplomatic. She had to know the Prices were stealing from the city. "They treat one of their own like a leper, have her hidden in a nice velvet lined cage. Out of site, out of mind. Jax Price was my best friend. Now I'm her only family. They have ignored that woman, Sophie."

When Carly started to walk away, the hottie turned. She was Sophie

Constantini. Whitman Price's fiancé. I recognized her from the papers.

Carly paused as Jazzy Jake helped her into her coat. She took her purse back.

I walked out ahead of them. The main hall buzzed with a troupe of workers setting for tonight's gala.

I stood out front.

Carly and Jake walked out in heated chatter; it didn't even look like they noticed stepping into the chilly November air.

Jake lifted his head briefly to look for a cab.

I stepped to them.

"Ms. Marino, can I ask you something? I don't really want to impose, but it's important to me. Maybe not to you, but I'd appreciate the minute."

I had Jake's attention, so I gave him a big smile. He did his best to cover cool cultural stuff around the city. He worked in an environment hostile to culture, no doubt. My look gave him props.

"I'm shocked to hear you are still in contact with Jax Price," I said, "My old man was high school friends with JB Foster and the way he talks about JB and Jax has always intrigued me. I wondered where she was."

"That's by design, young man," Carly said. She was a class act, didn't blink at my White Sox cap.

I didn't bother with my name.

"So she's still alive?"

"God, yes she's still alive. The Price family has her quarantined, but she has a life. She has friends where she lives. And a job."

"Maybe that's why my dad always got quiet when talking about her," I said, "My mom has mental health issues, too."

"She still loves JB. But he hasn't seen her in years. Used to be he'd drive out to St. Charles occasionally. But that stopped a couple of years ago."

I didn't have anything else to say, and I felt bad for holding her up. Said something about appreciating her comments and was about to let them step to the curb.

"Do you have a card, Ms. Marino?" I asked, "I have something totally unrelated. But I have information about a battle between Whit Price and JB Foster. It's going on right now and I can get you information by the end of the weekend."

Carly looked at me.

"Hey, it's just a card. Worst thing is you never respond to my e-mail."

She looked at Jake.

"I'm not wasting your time," I told her, "If you have a problem with Whitman Price, then you're going to have a lot to be thankful for next week."

sixty-six

Standing inside my opened car door, I peeped Sophie Constantini walking toward the Historical Society's parking lot.

I decided not to sit down.

She walked straight to the black Mercedes C 230 parked next to me.

"Hi, Sophie," I said, "We haven't met but I knew Babi Patras. I'm more of a friend with her brother. But you guy's were friends right?"

She was lost in thought. Her eyes only diverted at the last minute, and looked at me.

"Even in there," Sophie motioned back to the Historical Society, "I was thinking about Babi in there."

"Interesting panel," I said.

She added, "Carly has it all wrong."

I added, "She obviously took it personal, huh. Tough comments."

"Babi and I were talking about starting a restaurant," Sophie told me. It sounded like her auto-response all week when people asked her about Babi. "We formalized a plan the night she was murdered."

I just let her talk.

She went on, "I left JB's loft that night walking on air. We were both so excited. We became great friends, but that meeting was purely business. We worked out a partnership. The next day at work, I already started putting together the contract. Then I heard the news."

"I know, I know," I said, "Jim and the family are devastated too."

Didn't bother with a fake sendoff. I just started to sit in my car.

"I'm sorry, what's your name?" Sophie asked when I bent down.

I gave her a fake name, smiled at her. I wanted to see if she would flirt a little.

"I didn't see you at the funeral," she said. She evidently didn't flirt with tweekers.

"Oh, I hit the wake early on Monday. I was at the church. But I don't do burials and the luncheon. They're not my kind of after-party."

sixty-seven

"So," I said, nodding in the direction of Jon Jardine's two flat screens, "This is security the old fashioned way."

I found him in the back office at Onyx. His laptop sat on his desk nestled inside piles of paperwork. The two flat screens on the wall above him showed images from at least eight security cameras.

"How'd you get in here?" Jon Jardine asked.

"Through the font door," I answered.

I had buzzed the Onyx front door on my way home from the Historical Society. A bar back let me inside.

Gesso had given me Jardine's home address, but I thought it better to catch him at work. His co-workers might keep him from being overly aggressive.

The information Gesso gave me told an interesting story. The press release for Onyx's opening included a paragraph on Jon Jardine's history working clubs around Chicago. It looked like he switched clubs every two to three years—whenever the newest, hottest club opened. He trained Golden Glove boxers and he himself trained in MMA.

Jon Jardine stopped reviewing a spreadsheet. Payroll, I guessed.

A skinny woman with a bleach streak cutting through her pitch-black hair sat at another desk. She looked up at me. I assumed she was Onyx's bar manager.

I gave her a quick smile, returned my gaze to Jardine.

"Five minutes," I said, "All I'm asking."

Made it seem like he'd be doing me a favor. I wanted to talk to him away from the bar manager.

He changed screens on his computer. Punched a couple of buttons, picked up his phone as he stood.

I led the way to the VIP section. A bartender was setting up behind the front bar. He rocked John Legend's second album and man did that guy sound heartbroken even when he sang about love.

I walked to a booth and sat down. The location would be fitting. We'd be swimming in Babi Patras's and Albert Brongel's ghosts. They had both been in these booths before. I know I was comforted by the thought. Didn't think he would be.

John Legend wailed loud enough so the other people working throughout the bar wouldn't hear us.

"The Albert Brongel thing scare you?" I asked.

He didn't say anything. Shimmied to get his phone out of his pocket and started hitting buttons.

I continued, "Interesting me coming in here on the same night Albert gets murdered."

Jardine lifted up his phone, so I was staring at the Apple logo on the back. The flash lit up. I didn't flinch.

"Isn't that overkill?" I asked, "You have the security cameras rolling, right? That's why you clacked all the buttons on your computer before you left your desk."

Just like the other night, he still didn't say anything. Figured he'd been a defendant and a witness in enough club-related court cases to know better.

That was fine, I could do this on my own.

"You lied to the police. Albert Brongel never said one word about Lenny being jealous of Babi." I repeated, "You lied to the police."

He looked at his phone.

I knew what that was about.

"You lied to the police and you're working with Vince Hendricks," I said.

Made sense to me. Jon Jardine saw himself as more than a matriculated doorman. He'd have to leave the club scene eventually. Since a job with Hendricks was his out, there was no way he'd officially step up for Lenny.

I talked like I was on record, "I saw Vince Hendricks leave the club right after Albert Brongel Monday night."

Jardine's eyes set on me. Yet I could tell by the way his eyes lacked focus that he only half listened. He looked like he had something else on his mind.

I didn't mind. All I wanted to do was issue my threat and get what I came for.

"Do yourself a favor before this gets too prickly," I said, "Put your phone down, open up the audio recorder."

He set the phone down.

I thought about taking it from him. I would've yanked it from just about anyone else. Except this guy could fight. His nose told me all along I couldn't hurt him. I knew guys like him, some repressed shit inside them got off on punches to the face. But it wasn't his nose I worried about. It was his forehead. Thing was shaped like the angled edge of an anvil. I could picture our grappling coming to a submission-hold standstill. Then he'd start pounding that forehead into my nose. Crush a cheekbone. Batter an eye socket.

I couldn't take his phone, so I spoke into it.

"I repeat, I saw Vince Hendricks leave the club right after Albert Brongel on Monday night. Did you give that testimony to the police? Or was he conveniently forgotten in the run down?"

Still nothing. His dispassionate stare oozed from around his smushed nose.

"Did you provide security footage of Lenny's bender the night Babi Patras was murdered to the police? Or did you conveniently keep that for yourself?"

Movement. The flesh around his eyes squeezed with interest.

"While showing the police footage of me in the club on Monday night, did you care to mention Vince Hendricks? Show him exiting the club on Brongel's heels?"

His jaw fell out of its lockset.

I said, "Dude, turn the fucking recording device off. I'll keep talking you right into suspected obstruction charges."

Nothing.

"This is your last chance," I said because I knew I was running out of shit to say, "I'm going to ask you something nice and easy. Just turn the device off."

"What could you possibly do?" he asked back.

Good move on his part. He wanted to get my physical threat on record. Liked it. Two could play at that game.

"Nothing at all, Jon," I said while pulling my own phone out, kept talking as nice as I could, "We're just talking."

Typed a text message but didn't enter a phone number.

I showed him the screen, "Goodbye kneecaps. MMA a memory."

"You're threatening to shoot out my knee caps?"

"Not at all Jon, just asking a favor as a friend of Lenny's."

Typed again, showed it to him. "Might be six months, one year."

He smacked my phone to the ground.

I looked at my phone on the ground, then back up at him.

"Wrong play," I said. Made like I was getting up to get mine.

Jacked his phone out of his hand. It slid across the room and came to a stop by the steps.

He jumped from his seat, reaching for my legs.

I slid further into the booth. No way I wanted him at my legs. He started pulling the booth's table out of the way. His instincts were precise. I grabbed the table from my side. Put my hands on the edge and rammed it toward him. The table caught him mid-thigh. An opening. I hammered my legs and pushed him back. He tried to skip his way around the side. Kept trying to push back too. I had the momentum. Did my own little pushing slide-step to keep my body opposite his as we pushed the table between us.

I rammed full bore.

His hands slipped, tried to adjust.

Luckily he probably never scuffled like this before. Otherwise he'd have an angle. His body wasn't losing the battle; it was in constant adjustment. The table slid easily across the carpet. Until it didn't. The base caught in the carpet and the momentum tipped one side up. I rammed harder.

Table went belly up. Jardine tried to parry it off like it was a flurry of kicks.

Wasn't working. I switched my grip and torqued the table up. Flipped it, caught him on that anvil of a forehead. His arms were still executing defensive moves one after the other.

He finally got a grip, and started to move the table aside.

My advantage was about to end.

I had to go left leg because the angle of the table. I felt like a football player doing the blocking sled and coming off it in a kick. I had pushed him back back back, until the table snagged and flipped up. Then as he threw the table top aside, I kicked.

Jammed him in the nuts.

When he keeled, I busted. Grabbed my phone on my first running step. Grabbed his phone with my next. Sprinted toward the door.

The hapless bar-back was walking around to peep the ruckus.

I bolted past his ineffectual yells.

I had parked in the same spot as Monday. Five blocks away on a non-through street. No sirens pushed me there this time. Just my legs and the swivel of my hips as I navigated the Saturday traffic on Randolph.

I zigged toward Halsted, then came back around to throw him off.

His phone was already buzzing in my hand.

I missed the first call.

Sitting in my car, huffing, the second call came in. The number on the screen was tied to the picture of his office mate. Same jet black hair. No bleach streak.

"This Jardine?" I asked with a big smile.

"You're dead."

"Jardine, thanks for calling," I said cheerily.

He puffed big time. Pictured him a couple blocks away, free arm swooping a big gesture trying whip up energy for his distant threats.

"Dead," he repeated.

"No really, thanks. Now that I've got you on the phone, I'm going to need your PIN number."

He made his voice all deep and raspy, "I'm going to rip your fucking throat out!"

"He-hem," I cleared it for him. Started my car and pulled away.

"Give me fifteen minutes, okay Jardine? I don't need the police crawling up my ass-crack again. Fifteen minutes and you can have your phone back."

I'm sure he made the effort to chase me. A block later without finding me, he then jetted back to the club and burrowed the bar manager's phone. For some reason I pictured him wearing a gorilla mask. He held the bar manager's phone and walked under the El tracks on Lake Street as he yelled, "GIVE ME MY PHONE BACK NOW OR I WILL SPLIT YOUR RIBCAGE APART AND RIP BOTH SIDES OFF," his voice as deep and rageful as he could make it.

"Okay Jon," I said through my laughter, "Think like this. I know you're having a hard time. But you get your phone back in fifteen minutes. That's a lot closer to right now, than me dropping your upwardly-mobile, poor-service piece of shit in the river."

He didn't say anything.

"Thought so," I said, "PIN. Now."

Before I hung up, I made sure I had access to his phone book. I also put the phone on Airplane mode so he couldn't do that lo-jack thing to me.

I drove south, over the Eisenhower Expressway to the empty streets around Cook County Hospital. Started with the number he called from. I entered the woman bar manager's number in my phone. Scrolling back up through the names, I couldn't believe it, but he had Brian Urlacher's name in there. Wrote it down. Make a good prank one night. Stopped in the R's to see if Derrick Rose was in there. Thankful he wasn't. D-Rose didn't mess with chumps. Almost got caught up searching out current White Sox and Bulls players. Caught myself. Just nudged the phonebook up to the P's and found my mark. Whitman Price. Got his number.

Sat there for a minute to scroll through Jardine's texts.

Nothing from Whitman Price.

Spotted a text conversation with VH. Wondered if VH in this instance stood for Vince Hendricks.

"Friends," I said to myself, "That's nice."

"See you then. There." Was the last text from Jon Jardine to Vince Hendricks. I needed to calibrate my reading, as I scrolled backwards in their conversation from bottom up.

The thread told an interesting story. Vince Hendricks wanted original footage from the Onyx Security cameras. As I suspected, Jon Jardine wanted to work with Hendricks. They had made a deal.

Hendricks didn't reveal details in his messages. But on Monday night they had a job scheduled for one in the morning.

sixty-eight

Before I started driving again, I forwarded the text thread to myself. Then I accessed the pictures on Jon Jardine's phone and deleted my portrait. Finally I accessed the voice memo feature and deleted the file time-stamped a half hour ago.

When I finished I drove back over the expressway to the West Loop. I should've turned it off. Could've broken the phone out of jail and kept the device myself. That's what I thought about doing as soon as I got out of Onyx.

But. Jon Jardine had to make his appointment on Monday. He couldn't miss another text from Vince Hendricks. If he did, then Hendricks' plan would change. Whatever the plan was. But if Jardine lost his phone or admitted to Hendricks that I peeped the thread, Hendricks'd change his big operation and Jon Jardine'd be out. I didn't know much. But I wasn't about to know less. So I decided to return the phone.

I parked in the street with my hazards on.

Ripped a piece of paper off my note pad and wrote Jardine's name down.

I walked inside The Wishbone. Wishbone was a prettied up soul food restaurant in the West Loop a few blocks from Onyx. I rocked this joint on dates occasionally. Never did much for me. The menu had some flavor to it, but not as much as it should. Suited my dates well, though.

A gorgeous caramel-skinned woman stood behind the podium.

"My friend is dining with a group later, and I need to get him his phone," I said through a warm smile.

Her practiced red-hot smile welcomed the gesture on my part.

"I'm the nice one," I told her, as I handed it over, slip of paper on top, "He's kind of a jerk."

She laughed like we were sharing an inside joke. Her laugh and smile would drop straight as soon as I turned away. Just like mine.

Next, I drove toward the China Club lofts. When I was a block away from JB's building I called the bar manager at Onyx.

The phone picked up.

I was greeted by silence.

Jon Jardine was back to his old self.

"Wishbone," I told him, "with the hostess."

sixty-nine

I texted JB Foster: *Need to show you something. Now.*

I waited. I was ready to jump up to the North Shore, catch him at his big house if I needed to.

He texted back: *Unavailable.*

I can get you back her earrings, I texted.

I started reading the string of texts between Jon Jardine and Vince Hendricks again.

It took a second for JB to respond.

At the loft, he texted.

It hurt him to write that, I was certain. People like JB Foster measured their success by the absence of people like me in their lives.

I accepted my spot here. But I had designs on another role.

The doorman at the China Club Lofts made me wait ten minutes.

I rode the elevator to the top floor. The doors opened to reveal a woman I tried not to think of as tits on sticks.

Tall with the kind of curves a comic book illustrator practiced. Nothing fake. Genetic lottery type stuff. The waves in her magazine-worthy hair caught the light like a chandelier. No apparent make-up. Looked to be about my age, and way out of my league. She didn't look to be in anyone's league. She wore a great pair of jeans. Hooked around her elbow was both her purse and one of those big knit scarves that came in a continual loop.

She said, "Yes, that's right," into her phone and bumped into me as I exited the elevator.

"Excuse me," I said.

We danced around each other.

Her eyes lit up in a mischievous smile.

She didn't say a word, just pursed her lips.

I walked to JB's front door thinking she looked more Friday night than Saturday afternoon.

He let me inside and I walked to the island with a knowing bop to my head. But I wasn't about to bring it up.

"I have no more patience for you," JB said. Again he stood on the appliance side of the island.

He wore heavy cotton sweat pants, with slippers, and a cashmere sweater.

"Not asking for patience," I said and took my place on the stool at the edge of the black expanse.

"Listen," I said to him, "You're going to want to see this," and pulled out my phone.

"Whatever, Michael," he said, back to Michael again. "Isn't anything you have on that phone beside the point now?" held his hand out to my phone and made a stop sign.

"Why?" I asked, "You talking about the warrant?"

JB lifted his palms up, gesture said, *what else.*

"Doesn't change a thing," I said.

"It means they have their man," JB said.

"A man," I corrected, "They have a warrant for a man. Who happens to be the wrong man. Why else would Vince Hendricks shoot at me? Because something points to him, and that thing is Lenny."

"Look, you've helped me a great deal with the copy of the appeal," JB said and keyed something into his phone, "My lawyers are taking it from here."

"What are the lawyers going to be doing Monday night besides charging you triple time?" I asked.

JB freshened up his coffee.

I could've used one too, but he didn't offer.

"Look, I've thought some more about this," JB said, "I don't see how anyone but Lenny could've done this. Nobody would come here looking for sensitive documents or information. This is basically a crash pad," he said and swung an arm out wide. JB set the coffee mug down and continued, "I don't take my work home," set his mug on the black granite causing a hollow ring to chime through the loft, "Haven't carried a brief case in over ten years. I do all my work in the office regardless of how long it takes."

"The point?" I asked.

"You're saying this was corporate espionage. Except there's nothing here," again his arms wide and channeling a real estate broker's gesture.

"What if they wanted to plant something?"

"I'd have found it and cleaned it up," JB answered.

"What if they wanted to kill Babi to distract you?" I asked.

"There was nothing to distract me from."

"Someone wanted to get to you," I said.

"Sure," JB replied, "How about the jealous guy who was just demoted to glorified airport runs?"

"You're finally doing some decent reasoning on this," I said, "But you're way off base."

"Because?"

"Because Monday night comes before Wednesday morning," I said.

"What's that supposed to mean?"

JB had the air of moving on and tackling business — things that were impossible before the PD issued Lenny's warrant. His face was more relaxed than it had been in our previous two meetings. He still stood bolt upright, legs spread like he commanded a boardroom audience. But he was riffing now, not worried about covering his ass or his stock price.

"You gotta get real, JB," I said.

"And you're going to tell me how," he paused and mocked, "To. Get. Real."

"No," I said sick of his attitude, "I'm going to show you why."

I pulled out my phone.

I showed JB the opening of the text thread between Vince Hendricks and Jon Jardine.

I explained Jon Jardine and his bogus police statement. I told him about how Jardine has put up a roadblock to all my inquiries regarding the club on the night of Babi's murder and the night of Albert Brongel's murder.

JB nodded politely, but unattached. He pointed a finger at my phone when he thought the timing was perfect to show interest.

There was nothing worse than being humored.

"I want to make a deal," I said to him.

"We're at the deal point of our talk here?" he said, chuckled.

"Since you've stopped listening, I'll step to it."

"Presumptuous, eh Michael?"

I corrected, "It's Bones, and you're going to have to get it right."

"Why's that?" he asked, "We're finished."

"That's what you think," I said, "On Wednesday we'll just be getting started."

He asked, "What's that supposed to mean?"

I said, "That's my deal."

"What do I get out of this deal?" he asked. The humor in his voice made me want to smash his face.

"I save your ass," I told him, "This ain't over by a yard."

"This really is funny," JB said, rubbed both hands back through his hair and then picked up his coffee cup, "Ok, what do you think you'll get from me?"

"Two things," I said.

"You want two things," he quipped back, "in return for doing me one favor?"

"It's no small favor."

"Fine," he said, pursed his lips up tight, "Humor me, what are they?"

"These PI's, the ones you hired to find Dan Daly your former security guy. They good?"

"The best."

"Second best if you went and hired Vince Hendricks after them."

"Point," JB floated a hand in my direction, "They're the best available without Homeland Security clearance. "

I told him, "I need you to hire them."

JB was already shaking his head.

"No, listen," I said, "First part of the deal is this. You hire them to work alongside me on Monday night. If Monday night is a bust, I'll pay you for their time. If it's not, you pay them yourself."

"Keep me going here, what's the second part of the deal?" JB put his coffee down, and said, "You said there were two, two parts to this?" Held up two fingers. The nail on his middle finger had a black bruise on it.

"That's right," I said.

"You're funny you know," he said. "Should be a comedian or something like that."

I couldn't tell if he was humoring me or dismissing me.

"Since you're on a roll," he made a rolling motion with the index finger on his free hand, "keep me going, what's the second part of the deal?"

"Tell you in a minute. First let's talk about you. Then I tell you the final term."

Held his hands up in the air again. It's his mock giving-in gesture.

"Your show, Michael."

"It's Bones. Again. Tell me about your contract with the city. Not the financial terms. What kind of warehouses do you run and do you have them secure."

"Already taken care of. I put an additional guard on each warehouse as of yesterday evening."

"Which makes?"

"What?" he asked.

"How many guards on each warehouse? How many warehouses? What are the contents of each? Your best move on this is going to be consolidating your guys, not spreading them around."

"What does this have to do with you?"

"Nothing here ever had anything to do with me. I'm a nobody. This is about Lenny, and it's about you."

"I've got three warehouses," JB began.

I told him, "You're going to be talking for a minute. Want to sit down?"

seventy

It was almost dark by the time I got back to Bridgeport. The Saturday before Thanksgiving I spotted more than a few neighbors unloading groceries for Thursday's meal.

I went in and laid down for a nap without even turning a light on.

It looked like nobody was home.

When I woke up I couldn't tell what time it was. I'd left a magazine over the face of my clock radio. I knew I had slept at least ninety-minutes.

I laid there in the absolute quiet. I resisted moving because once I started, I'd wreck the quiet. Saturday nights in my peaceful house was bliss. One of my favorite times during the week. Usually I'd hustle all day and come home to take a nap around five or six. I'd sleep a couple hours then lay in bed and read until eight or nine. Then I'd get up, bump music, make coffee, smoke up and dance. Then shower and shave. And dance. And smoke a little more before heading out for the night.

Coming from chaos, those moments when I lay in bed reading in that peace and quiet, it felt major.

Then the moment broke. There was a creak up my back stairs. My house was old enough that there were certain spots you couldn't sneak around. I always noticed squeaks in the floor and friction in the doors. I never made a noise when I was a kid. First I didn't want to arouse my mom — it was best to avoid her. Second, I was always sneaking out for a midnight walk, and when I sneaked, I snuck silent.

Another creak.

I peeled the blanket off of me slowly.

I still hadn't cleaned everything up after Detective Glenn and his partner tossed my house. My nightstand was a mess.

The drawer hung open. Inside it was a six-inch Dekalb Cornseed buck-knife. Heavy handle with an ear of flying corn etched into it. A friend from college gave it to me when I went back to his family farm one weekend. Sweet blade.

I chicken winged my arm around and lifted the knife out as quietly as I could. Cupped the handle in my palm to dull the sound of the click when I swung the heavy blade out.

It snapped into place.

Held the knife backhanded.

Another creak, this one closer still.

I couldn't move. Paralyzed myself because any creak from the bed would ring like an alarm. Their search of my house would bring them right to me.

Vince Hendricks. That's who popped into my mind. He refused to lose. I admired that. He was coming to clean up his mess.

Three more minutes of waiting and the creaks got closer. I heard them progress through my kitchen. Then down the short hall. A creak echoed into the bathroom because the door was open. Then nothing. The short span from the hallway into my living room was solid. When girls slept over I lay in bed and listened when they walked to the bathroom. They'd get silently out of bed. My bedroom floor didn't budge. Then three or four creaks as they stepped through the living room. And silence as they walked the short hallway into the bathroom.

My bedroom door was wide open. In the dark, I could see a shadow gather in my doorway. The darkness that gathered wasn't as big as I expected from Hendrick's frame.

But they hadn't gotten into my house by ringing the doorbell. It was Hendricks or one of his guys.

He took one step into the bedroom.

I took a deep breath.

The second step took him past the open door.

I propelled my body up first with my elbows. When my torso was off the bed, I planted a foot and slammed him into the dresser and fell on top of him as we hit the ground. I let my full weight crush onto his body.

I couldn't make out whether there was a gun or not.

It wasn't Vince Hendricks. Too short and too light.

I wrestled the guy and jammed my right arm, the one that held the knife, against his head. I managed to twist his neck and was ready to pull my hand and slash the knife across his face and rake the side of his head. I thought about slicing all the way until I cut under his ear.

"Bones! It's me!"

Wasn't Vince Hendricks. Wasn't even a guy.

"Gesso?" I said and pointed the heavy blade right into her eye.

seventy-one

"I came to talk about Lenny," Gesso said quickly. Her smokey voice more undertone than tone.

I sprayed spit as I said, "Send a fucking text."

My knife quivered with enough tension that if I let go it would still hover above her eye. If either of us slipped she'd have to find an array of eye-patches to match her All-Stars.

"Get that knife out of my face," she demanded.

"My house," I said and waggled the blade up and down so that it never left the diameter of her eyeball.

Dug my knee into her inner thigh. Dug an elbow into her ribs. My arms pinned hers down.

She didn't move.

"Your friend, Lenny, he's still missing."

It wasn't a question, so I didn't answer.

She added, "I came by to make sure you were clean."

"You'd have nothing to do with me if I was clean," I said and sucked more spit back in.

She added, "My employers they're pushing me to bring you in."

"No business of mine." I couldn't tell what was up with my saliva glands. Things were gushing and I sprayed more every time I spoke. When I wasn't talking I just sucked in the wetness and swallowed.

Sucked all the saliva in like I intended it to be the last time, "You haven't said a credible thing. This knife is awfully close."

"So close you can taste it," Gesso said and bit her lower lip. Lit her eyes up all playful like. She paused. Then her entire face went cold. "They're ready to move on to The Roach if you don't come around."

I almost laughed imagining that bargain. "They're going to offer The Roach to choose between his life or Lenny's, too?" I laughed.

Gesso shook her head back and forth, "Not The Roach's life for Lenny's. The Roach and Lenny for you. They're ready to close Roach's shop."

"I thought I had until Monday?" I asked.

"You do, but they wanted to raise the stakes on you. Let you know what you're in for."

"What is it? They want me to deliver Lenny to them?"

She nodded long and deep and her nose looked like it almost grazed the shiny blade.

"And if I can't find him. What do I have that they don't?" I asked.

"If you're thinking money," Gesso corrected me, "They've got so much it causes them problems."

"And the laundry is your chore," I said.

"The army is always looking for soldiers, Bones," she said and she wasn't talking about Uncle Sam.

She wanted to move. I could feel the makings of a wiggle down in her bones at the same moment she suppressed it. Figured she wouldn't ask to be let up again, probably liked the idea of playing her hand from the defensive position for once. Maybe she expected it to throw me off. Maybe she could play a victim's hand under my grip, make me feel sympathetic for a subdued woman.

I stayed on her, said, "Never played that game, and I'm not starting now."

"Way they work, Bones, they're trying to make it so you don't have a choice," she said.

"My servitude gets Lenny his life, that what you're saying?"

She nodded again, kept her eye on the blade.

"They think I'd do that for Lenny?" I asked.

"Haven't you already?" she replied.

What Gesso didn't know. What nobody knew. Was that I was done with Lenny. I had his bag packed and the needles ready. I just needed to find him.

It still bugged me that she knew something about Wednesday night on Canal Street though. I know I hadn't told anyone. Vince Hendricks certainly wouldn't have told anyone that I got away. Maybe Whitman Price knew, maybe. Gesso connected to him? Did Price have a connection to her money laundering business?

"You hid him, didn't you, Bones?" she asked.

Didn't answer.

She continued, "Scott Smuda is one of your buddies. You make a quick phone call," her voice all radio DJ smooth. "Nice, easy favor to ask of an old friend. Nobody knows but you and him. And nobody is getting to Scott Smuda. Nobody."

Just the mention of Scotty made me want to jam the knife in her eye socket until it scraped the back of her skull. Do Not. Fuck. With my friends.

My mouth was still moist as I thought of everyone involved. Then for a second my mom flashed into my head. My mind snapped through it all in a few clicks. Where she lived. The phone call I got from the boss over there. My talk with the social worker. On top of all this, I had to think about my mom being on the streets again.

Leveraging the people closest to me was one of the oldest tricks in the book. That didn't surprise me.

What surprised me was that I still hadn't decided if Lenny was a murderer.

Gesso hadn't told me anything new, really.

My mind raced. Manic wasn't the word. It all came rushing up at once — including Lenny's current location. My body maintained control over Gesso.

Speculation over Lenny had ran through my day. While I talked with JB and Jardine the back of my consciousness fiddled with it like a loose thread. The thread tickled at the back of my throat. I wanted to bite and pull on it, but couldn't get a grip.

Basically, it felt like I was trying to get my own attention.

Right there, pancaking Gesso to the floor, the thread pulled loose. One second nothing but a tickle. The next I just knew that nobody took Lenny from his squat. He relocated on his own, and someone helped him do it.

When I toured his squat this morning I noticed the bathroom was clear. No toothbrush. No shaving kit. Those items'd be useless if Vince Hendricks picked him up. If Hendricks got to him, he couldn't brush his teeth through the gag in his mouth. He couldn't shave with his hands bound. No, Lenny was hiding on his own.

My mind came back and leveled with Gesso, "This is going nowhere. It's like you're slinging spitballs at the wall," I huffed and saved up some breath, "And yet you broke into my house."

I did not stop myself from spraying spit on her as I thought about her breaking into my house. I opened up the nozzle and said, finally, "Get to the point."

I flexed my body, all my limbs one at a time. Pressured the points. Let her know I didn't slip.

"I need help," Gesso said. Her voice had that stripped down tone of truth.

Didn't bother with a smart-ass comment.

"I want out," she continued, "I can't do it alone. So I want you to figure out the best way to do it. Lenny could never have done this by himself. From all I heard, Lenny is a joke. If you can make him invisible, I want some of that."

"And your little bargain here," I wagged the knife again, in the event her eyes had adjusted to its stillness, "Fact or fiction?"

"Oh, that's real. No loose ends. These guys run a business," she said.

"It's more than that," I corrected her.

"Okay, now," she said and got my attention with her pause, "Think I have a chance at retirement or even reaching old age with this work? Knowing what I know, doing what I did?"

"Out of Chicago?" I asked.

"Has to be."

"I been a lot of places," I had a good collection of license plates to show for it, "But I got no game anywhere else."

"You can get me out," she said flatly, "Anyone else they have covered. I do it myself and there's a paper trail or someone who recognizes me."

"They know who I am," I corrected.

"So did the PD and still got jack."

Hard to gesture or anything in that position. All I could do was keep the pressure on. Show resistance.

I thought about her argument. Her bosses had unlimited resources. Foot soldiers in every corner of the city. Wasn't a stretch to think they had an inmate in every cellblock in the state. A plant in the PD, Motor Vehicles, and any other major department. Even if Lenny cleared the murder rap, he was still going up on his parole violation. He might not even clear central booking before I got a phone call with this message all over again: Lenny's life for my services.

What Gesso told me didn't mean her bosses were looking for a soldier. They were looking for a warrior.

"Cost you more than money," I said.

"What else?" she shot back.

"Work for me, Monday night."

Money and a favor — those were my terms. I should have thought about it longer, but my mind couldn't take in any more variables. I decided off the cuff that if I got help on Monday night, then we could start talking about her.

"Let's start with getting that knife out of my face," she said.

I drew the knife up four inches. I was flattened against her long enough to know she didn't pack a weapon on the front of her body. I got up on my knees.

"Turn over," I said.

She gave me a look first. Then she turned over. I frisked her legs first, down to her black All-Stars — squeezed her shins and around the front of her feet. Arms, pits, neck, ribs. Didn't apologize when I felt her ass and between her legs.

"Just making sure," I said.

I stood up.

"Turn back over, get up slowly," I said pointing the knife at her.

When she turned over, I reached my free hand out to help her up.

seventy-two

I sat in my garage with the door open and looked beyond my alley. I didn't have neighbors across from me, just a parking lot.

My eyes glazed over as I stared blankly beyond the parking lot at the headlights of passing cars on Halsted.

I thought about being Lenny's first call last Friday. That was the key to finding him. If I didn't answer or didn't help, I asked myself, who would he turn to next?

At least last week there were other options. Those options disappeared after yesterday.

To find Lenny, I just needed to deal with those other options.

Lenny was closer to his friends than to his brother, like me. The list was short.

Halsted traffic crisscrossed before my eyes.

The lights showed me the way.

I pictured the grid of streets. Pictured cars rolling up to stop signs. Miles away I imagined cars as they idled over speed bumps on quiet warehouse roads. Traffic piled up at red lights. The streets and highways crept slightly faster than usual at this hour on a Saturday night. The big rigs would be there too. They streamed in and out of the Stockyards and other warehouses around here every hour of the day.

The lights on the street ahead put me in a trance. My thoughts stayed down by the Stockyards. Canaryville, where Lenny's first squat was, was adjacent to the Stockyards along Halsted.

I wondered if there was any chance Lenny returned to Scotty Smuda's.

Then I let that thought go.

The cheap motels out in Cicero were an option for Lenny. But not without a ride.

I doubted any of his other options would think to go there. Unless it was me — I was the only one who would risk the drive.

My thoughts jumped back to Canaryville.

Lenny couldn't have gone far. Certainly didn't go east toward the Dan Ryan Expressway. Across the expressway was the old Robert Taylor Homes. No place for Lenny. He didn't go north toward Bridgeport into the heart of the city. He didn't go south toward Englewood. West of his squat was the Stockyards. He wouldn't go to the Stockyards.

Back-of-the-Yards.

Made sense. No city bus. No cab. All he could risk was a walk and hope nobody looked too hard on his way. People around here were good for looks, but they always kept to themselves.

I only knew two people with places there. One was a smelly old cat lady from church. The other place was The Roach's stash house.

The dashboard lights cast a warm glow over my face when I started the rental.

seventy-three

Lenny lay on top of a bare mattress. He squirmed in slow motion, as if his body was in pain. Except he wasn't in pain. Not by the look of the pharmaceuticals on the table next to him.

The white powder on the table-top had to be heroin — otherwise Lenny would be up and pacing out a bump-off against himself.

I stood and watched him from the doorway.

His half-lidded eyes recognized me. He contorted slightly faster after he looked away. Full consciousness was deep in his veins getting man-handled and dragged around by the heroin.

Heaven for Lenny that night was a dirty mattress in a rotted-out basement. Sometimes heaven for Lenny was his coffee table and the TV. A club. A boat party on Lake Michigan. Damn, probably County lockup, too. Heaven was wherever Lenny sat, or stood, or lay with a bountiful score in front of him.

I stepped up to the bed. Before I threw the duffel bag onto the floor I pulled out the clamshell case. Poked Lenny in the ribs with it.

"I hope you're not puncturing your spacesuit, Lenny?"

I'm great at futile effort. Warned Lenny plenty over the years about his habits. Explained that his habit was the reason he lost all his customers to The Roach. Even warned him about heroin.

Bones, don't worry bro, his voice would be rasping up like a motherfuck, *I never puncture my spacesuit.*

Because in Lenny's mind snorting H was, you know, the healthy option.

I was glad I brought the tools. One thing I grabbed before leaving my garage was a socket wrench set. Used it to remove the security bars on the basement windows of The Roach's stash house. I didn't know which apartment in the building The Roach rented, I just figured I'd start at the bottom and work my way up.

There was an illegal basement apartment — just like a zillion others through the South Side — that had a shitty rotted-out kitchen and a bedroom. It was a step down from Lenny's last hideout.

Looking at the table next to him I thought, Lenny didn't spend much time here.

Lenny held two, maybe three weeks worth of shit. Two baggies full of white powder. A baggie full of pills. There looked to be three types of pills in the bags and I didn't bother to guess what for.

Not a single weed leaf or discarded stem. Lenny's supply had nothing to do with recreation.

The mattress was a full size. He lay next to the table. I took the other side of the bed. Sat with my back up against the wall. Crossed my feet out in front of me.

Lenny lay writhing next to me.

Lay my arm on top of his shoulder — just rested my elbow there while my hand lay in my own lap.

There was no pillow on the bed. No sheets. He just lay there wiggling with the H flow in his veins. He seemed to be coming out of it, not going in.

I wasn't going to stay long.

I sat next to him. As he lay there I just kept my elbow over his shoulder for a couple minutes. Until I could feel some warmth transfer from my body to his clammy flesh.

In my mind, once I laid eyes on him the game was over.

I wasn't going to waste a minute.

Started to talk.

"Lenny," I said, "Bro. Your mom made the best beef Stroganoff, like, ever. I mean, you know, in like sixth grade, I never heard of that shit before. But man, I remember staying at your house one Saturday from morning until night not wanting to go home. I don't remember if I ate lunch with you guys or not. I just remember it getting dark and still not wanting to go back to my house.

"Sometimes it was like your mom made it special for me. I always wondered about that. Remember that time you got pissed off at me? Threw the idea in my face that our friendship was based on Beef Stroganoff. Kinda hurt, dude. I don't think I talked to you for a year after that. But looking back on it now I think you were jealous because I had this special thing that I shared with your mom and you were jealous. Beef Stroganoff and deviled eggs.

"Of course you remember that shit. How I'd come by every Thanksgiving and Christmas morning. Your mom always made deviled eggs on holidays. Them shits were my holiday, you know. I'd wake up and come by your house before noon. You're mom would be stormin up the kitchen. She'd have a platter of deviled eggs all ready for when the rest of your family arrived. And I'd eat those things until she told me to stop.

"Remember that shit Lenny?"

He started smacking his dry-ass lips with his purple leather tongue.

"Then around noon, twelve-thirty I'd go back home and rot.

I got up and filled a glass of water.

Set the dirty glass beside him.

Came back around to my side of the bed. Sat with my back against the wall again. Put my arm fully around him that time.

"Dude. I don't know if I ever told you this. I used to sneak into your house when you guys weren't home. If you were visiting your grandma and I just wanted to be somewhere other than my room, then I'd just let myself in. Use the keys stuck under the gutter. Times like that I never ate anything in your house. Never stole anything.

"Yeah, yeah, I stole some shit from you a couple of times. Those Ray Bans. And that hoodie. No doubt. I always think about that shit, like, I'll pay you back someday. You know.

"But I didn't steal that shit when I let myself into your house. Sometimes I'd watch TV. Cable TV. Few times I just sat there. Getting into a real home made me feel, less, I don't know. Anxious?"

Lenny made an animal sound.

Nudged him hard with my elbow.

"I'd slap your face but don't think it'd help," I told him, "Here, drink some water."

I got up and walked around to his side of the bed. Picked up the glass and poured some water into his mouth. He choked on that shit. Spit it back up and onto his shirt.

I hoped the coolness would help wake him.

"Another try?" Held it up before him.

He nodded. Took a proper drink.

Put the glass down, took my spot again. Sat on the bed next to Lenny Supinski. Wanted for murder. Wanted for a parole violation and failure to report on a warrant. Lenny Supinski. Fucked up on H. Reached my arm to his far shoulder again, pulled him in tight.

Lenny took drugs to escape. His knee jerk reaction as an addict. I honestly think he could've dealt with it better if it was just one drug. Alcohol. Or coke.

For Lenny it was just drugs. Whatever he could get his hands on.

As kids we tried sniffing glue together. We smoked anything that looked like weed. Sniffed sugar, salt, tobacco, snuff and other shit up our nose. We took some pills from his mom we thought were diet pills. Those were just the drugs we tried that didn't work.

"Did the Murphy sisters do shrooms with us that night?" I asked, "When we were talking to each other through the bedroom walls at your parents' house? I don't remember."

Bobbed my head. As usual music surfaced in silence. Nas' track "One Love," the one written like a letter to his homey in prison. The xylophone started dinging in my ears. Then the fat beat. And it hung there in my brain—the fat beat and the xylophone noodling. Nas' voice spit pure on that track—full of raw emotion colored with nostalgia. The xylophone rang perfect with drippy remembrance. Shit came out my brain like it was a speaker. Funny, "One Love," was the first track you talked about when introducing a newbie to *Illmatic*. The song so reminded me of Lenny, I had avoided it all week.

There was no denying that the song fit the mood sitting there next to him.

Lenny was locked up. Except Lenny could walk out any time. He just needed to stop snorting. His bars were little white lines that dangled before him. All Lenny had to do was wipe his hand before his face and sweep them onto the floor. Shit was damn near impossible when you're an addict.

I equated it with being crazy. My mom could control her craziness if she would only stay on her meds consistently. Lenny could clean himself up if he didn't self-medicate. My mom needed to put her brain in a box—stop with all the governmental conspiracy, Princess Di, scratching bullshit notes on scraps of paper. Lenny needed to break out of his box—step into a different reality.

Thinking about them two. It was like I was the coin, and they each took a side.

Lenny started to sit up. Raised his forehead all comic like, as if crinkling the skin just below his hairline would lift up his eyelids. Started pushing his arms a little, like he wanted to sit up next to me.

I got up again and walked around to his side of the bed. Lifted him up by the pits.

Guy was shivering.

"There," I said.

I got hot so I took off my long sleeve T.

Another forty minutes and he'd talk again. Problem was I wouldn't be here. When I decided to say goodbye, it was goodbye.

Took my place next to him. Pulled him close so his head rested on my shoulder.

My mind went blank. White. Nothing for minutes.

Lenny's greasy head smelled like shit. His body smelled worse. Twelve days in and the stubble on his face came through his acne scars patchy and uneven.

Laid my free arm out before us. Looked at my tats for a sec.

I had a stick figure scarab beetle inside my elbow.

"Remember that one?" I asked him and pointed at it, "The Roach all geeked out like it had something to do with him. We were at The Roach's house blowing graphic bongs that night. And you asked what tattoo I had in honor of you? Remember that shit? Of course you do.

"I told you I had a sphincter tattooed to my asshole."

Lenny's chest heaved up a chuckle.

"Frankie was there that night too," I reminded him, "laughed so hard he puked on the floor."

Lenny wriggled and sat up a little further. Looked at me, but he was still too weary to talk.

He started to reach for the table next to him. No way he would snort shit on my time. Not even the coke for a pick-me-up.

Watched him grab for the pack of Marb Reds. I approved.

He lit the smoke, nodded as best he could. His whole upper body shivered out the nod. He couldn't control the fine movements of his muscles yet.

"The Roach. You called him? Threatened to tell the cops about this place if he didn't put you up? Got comp'td with enough shit to OD yourself."

Lenny looked at me hard. Chest heaved. Chin went up. It was a shrug.

"Thought so," I said, "You're still breathing, Lenny, try harder."

"Bones," Lenny said.

That was it.

"Lenny, I fucking care about you because I love you. You're not like a brother. You are my brother. But this ain't gonna ride. If you knew who was looking for you, you'd clean your act up and jump in or out. I came to give you the out."

Let it sit so it sounded serious.

"I can't help you anymore."

Even before he disappeared from the squat, I had decided over the past week that I couldn't help Lenny anymore. Sure, I could take him to some motel in Cicero. That was about it. Then what would I do? Take him out of town? And where would I drop him when he got out of town? Would I wait in some windswept town with dead cornfields in the middle of winter, wait for the bus to come? Then would I leave? Or would I follow the bus for a bit — longer than a bit — before I finally turned away?

Yesterday I realized that while I was working for him — getting shot at and beat up — he fucking betrayed me. He betrayed my work on his behalf.

No. This was about goodbye.

Lenny wouldn't be truly free until I said goodbye.

I wanted to give him his freedom ahead of schedule.

I opened the clamshell next to me. Took out two of the needles. They still had caps on the end so no accidental stabbing.

"Liquid fire there, Lenny. Fifty milligrams of concentrated nicotine. Marb Red, of course. Takes about eight milligrams in the blood stream to cause a severe heart attack. I trust you'll be able to find a good vein. Even though you said you never punctured your spacesuit I didn't believe you. It was one of those white lies you told me, like you would your mom if she asked.

"Three." I said. Paused to let it sink in, but not too long. "Or," I said lightly, "Your car is parked on the same street over by McKinley Park. Keys in the bag. Even wrote the address down for you. Your choice."

Shook the clean spikes in the case. "These three right here," I told him, "or what's beyond that door."

Closed up the clamshell and threw it onto his lap.

"I'm still taking care of the murder charges," I told him, "I'm doing that as much for me as I am for you. You need to do the rest. Clean up, get your head on straight. If you decide you want a chance, that's your only chance. That and what I left in the bag for you."

I paused before adding, "Otherwise your best bet is right there," and pointed at the clamshell.

Stretched my free hand further across his lap with my palm open. Wriggled my fingers.

Lenny put his hand on mine and we shook.

Tears jumped in my eyes. Held his hand firm and shook.

"Goodbye, Lenny."

I let go and wriggled his hand loose.

Got up and walked around to his side of the bed. Bent over and gave him a hug. Kissed his smelly hair.

Turned and walked to the door.

"Bones," Lenny said. The tar in his veins reverbed deep. Blood in his lungs was rich with chemicals. The chemical-saturated blood cells couldn't carry much oxygen from his lungs to the rest of his body. Created an odd pressure inside him. His voice showed it.

I turned back to him.

His head was on a deep nod. Eyes working overtime. He gasped before speaking.

"Go."

seventy-four

Whitman Price's biggest gala of the year was his Historical Society Fundraiser. By the looks of the set-up from earlier today, history sold at a premium.

Historical Society. Two words never felt more distant from me. The classic architecture of the building felt alien. I imagined the crowd inside. I'd never fit in with that crowd. But that wasn't what bothered me.

Confronting Whitman Price at his party while protected by the city's elites played wrong.

That's why I stayed in my car and watched from the parking lot. I snagged a handicap spot close to the Historical Society's entrance. Had my White Sox cap on. Chilled out listening to *Illmatic* until they walked out: Sophie Constantini and Whitman Price. The columns of the Historical Society lit up perfectly. A Silver Fox in his trim tux and his supple beauty in her gown descended the stairs. A driver stood beside a silver Benz and opened the back door for them.

I started my car.

The entrance to the parking lot ran parallel to the drop-off circle in front.

The Benz glided up drive and turned right onto Clark Street.

I watched them go north on Clark through the intersection. Cranked my whip into traffic. Jetted around a Navigator to catch the burnt orange traffic light before it turned to red.

The freshly waxed silver Benz was an easy mark. Like one of the Historical Society's klieg lights tracked its moves. Four turns? Six? Dunno, it was a mindless tail. Soon enough they stopped at a restaurant.

Took me fifteen minutes to park. I walked back to the restaurant and peeked my head in, smiling meekly at the hostess. It was a casual place, and yes they were there.

The table next to Whitman Price was turning over. One bus boy just cleared the plates while another waited to wipe down the table. Solid service in these places.

Before a napkin was set, I was in a chair.

I said, "Sup guys," and wagged the bill of my hat at them.

"Him," Sophie Constantini said, "That's the guy from earlier today."

Whitman Price looked at her and said, "Looks like the stalker type." He played it like he didn't know me. I bet otherwise.

"Let's not play the name game, Whitman," I said leaned my chin into my palm. Elbow rested on the table. "You know me. I'm sure your surrogate made sure of that." I smiled my warmest smile. "I'm pretty bored with messengers though, so let's have a little chat. Okay." I said it like it was a question. It wasn't a question.

The bus boy walked straight to the hostess.

"May I?" I asked Sophie as I gestured to her chair. I thought it would be better than having Whitman Price shoo her away. She was hot, and I wanted to save her some dignity. She'd need it after the news got out about her fiancé's antics.

When she stood up, I slid in across from Price.

"Whit, you don't follow the police blotters much do you?" I asked.

He didn't bother to look puzzled.

"You haven't gotten any reports about, say," I spoke completely straight — no eye movements, no gestures, "Stolen cars getting crashed on Canal Street?"

"Dude, my cars have drivers," he said.

I found it cute how even these rich kids talked street these days. Except I knew their streets were freshly paved and trimmed in lush vegetation.

He probably thought he looked charming sitting in that casual restaurant in a tux. Thought it lent him a salt-of-the-earth air.

His white hair was perfectly coiffed. Face shaved so clean it looked like it was waxed. His eyes were turned down at the corners because he was not happy to see me.

"You're surprised I'm still here, aren't you?" I asked. "Your soldier boy didn't get me. Hasn't got me. Won't be getting me."

His back faced the door. So all he could do was dart his eyes to the windows. He was looking for back-up. They darted back to me just as quick.

"Maybe Hendricks didn't tell you about our, um, run-in Wednesday night. I'd be surprised though. Because I'm sure after he murdered Albert Brongel you kept a tight leash on him," I spoke quickly. I assumed he could follow along because he already knew the story. "I'm sure Hendricks hates reporting to you. Except he has to now that things are messy. And I'm the mess. A mess that Hendricks still hasn't cleaned up." I wrapped it and said, "Clearly you're in a terrible position."

I liked how it sounded. The idea that Vince Hendricks probably couldn't stand reporting to Price. I had no idea if it was true. But I sold the line best I could.

I stared across the table at him and tried to set the air between us on fire and said, "You're going to jail, Whitman Price."

He considered me seriously for a half-sec. Curled his lips and said, "You are clueless if you actually believe that."

"Oh, I'm not being stupid," I told him, "When I spread the word of Babi's murder. About how you murdered her the same night she formed a partnership with your fiancé. All for some family grudge."

Price was repulsed, "What can you possibly be talking about? There's no grudge and our family has done nothing but prosper since selling to JB Foster."

"I'm not talking real estate or buyouts. I think you blamed JB Foster for putting your sister over the edge. I think you think he's the one that put her in the mental institution."

"Now you're reaching," he said.

"It's the only thing that makes sense. You're right, the murder had nothing to do with the family business. You've got that covered," I said.

I specifically didn't mention the pending appeal.

Then I added, "You did a great job planning it. It only seemed to work since you had the perfect fall guy in Lenny. The role of the loser ex-boyfriend fit like a glove."

He nodded with each point. Not showing surprise or acknowledging where I got it right.

"Does dear old dad know about what you did?" I asked. I wanted to know if the rest of the Price Family knew about the appeal and Hendrick's plans for Monday night. Again, I couldn't bring it up because I didn't want the plan to change.

"What does *my dad* have to do with it?" Price replied unable to see where he fit in our conversation.

"He's the one who's going to send you to jail," I told him.

"Now you're absolutely out of your mind," he said and slapped a hand on the table.

"The North Shore Correctional Facility," I shot back.

He tried to figure out where that one was. Finally did and said, "There is no North Shore Correctional Facility."

"There is. And it's going to be worse than a Super Max for you, Whit. Your pops'll make you move to Kenilworth. Maybe Wilmette," I said, "Leave your penthouse in the city behind. Leave the clubs and the girls behind. Put you up in a big house. Make you buy a parking pass for the train station," I let that thought sit with him, "Dude, waiting on the platform every morning. Either that or sitting in whack ass traffic. Your wife — the one you marry after Ms. Constantini dumps you — will start wearing cardigan sweaters not silk tops. When I'm done with you you're gonna be a Eunuch."

I held my cupped palm up in the air.

"Oh, you're still going to make bank, Whit," I reassured him. "But the press will eat this story up. Whitman Price. Murder. Revenge. And abandoning his little sister."

He leaned back in his chair when I spit it like that.

"You can bet they'll also mention that you stopped visiting Jax. Jax's best friend Carly will see to it."

He leaned in, "I will silence you before you hit send on an e-mail."

I actually didn't think Price had his sister in mind when he went after Babi. He sent Hendricks in for a reason. Even if he knew Babi would be there. Even if he knew that Sophia left her at the loft earlier that evening. I didn't think Price had his sister in mind because he just didn't. She was a memory locked away in St. Charles — barely inside what you might call "Chicagoland."

But I believed it affected his decision about the timing to enter JB's loft.

"What if the recipient of my e-mail is Carly Marino?"

He leaned back a little and asked, "What are you going to get out of it?"

I know one thing. Craziness makes people uncomfortable.

My extended family was a joke. I hadn't seen them in over a decade. No distance between you and crazy was small enough. Shit, I stayed away from my own mom and she was all I had.

"There's only one thing I want out of this," I told Price, "Vince Hendricks on a plate. He's the only one that could absolve Lenny."

He said, "That's—"

"Not possible, I know," I jumped in, "But it's your only chance."

"You talk tough," he said.

"You haven't seen me at play yet," I warned him.

I faced the door. When I looked up Sophie stood near the hostess stand talking on her phone: calling in Vince Hendricks if he wasn't already here.

On the night of the murder, he already did the groundwork. Had Hendricks set Lenny up through Albert Brongel. Get the key, give the money. It was pure execution in Price's brain, no doubt.

But his sister lurked there, like a ghost.

The way I saw it, Babi Patras was a stand in for his sister. He could easily accept her as collateral damage.

I felt like I was making deep down connections — on the verge of putting it all together — when Whitman Price did it for me.

He asked, "How's Carol Fox doing, Michael?"

My mom. Of course.

I looked at him. The look on his face said he was the guy holding the fly swatter and I was the fly. Price was behind the shakedown of my mom.

It was Lenny all over again. On the South Side some drug lords were looking to skin my best friend alive. Sell his soul back to me. Up here on the North Side a real estate mogul was ready to toss my mom in the streets like a piece of trash.

I surprised myself when I felt a sudden flash. I wanted to protect her.

Felt a fire stoke inside me. Anger. But an even burn. It didn't flash uncontrollably and burn out. I had it under control.

'That Michael he's built like a tank,' my mom had always said. No matter how many Burger King refills I needed to get my calories. No matter how skinny I was or brittle my bones got. Always built like a tank.

If I didn't control myself I'd ram through that table and tackle Whitman Price. Probably hurt one or both of the people at the table behind him. Rip his face off and dent his trachea. I'd also wind up in jail.

Instead, I refused to play into his hand.

Played my own hand instead.

"Fool," I said, "I wrote her obituary a long time ago. You probably thought I'd waste my time trying to save her. Distract me. Make me work to keep her in her safe house. As if I had to protect her, the crazy woman who abandoned me. But you should be able to relate. It's more comfortable keeping crazy family members at a distance. Isn't it?"

He smiled beneath his white mane.

I wanted a drink of water.

"Carol Fox isn't going anywhere," I said not wanting to call her mom. "But it makes me wonder if anything you tried this week will work." Again I was chomping to tell him I knew about the operation planned for Monday night.

I asked, "You framed some ex-con loser? How'd that go?"

"Your friend is finished."

"Nobody will see Lenny again," I said. "Plain and simple. He'll never take the charges on this. And don't forget about me on your list of failures. You tried to get to me."

"You're as good as dead," Price said.

"Always have been, Price," I admitted, "It's part of my charm."

He puzzled over that one.

I finished, "Oh, wait. You did do something right. Babi Patras isn't breathing anymore. You're wife's new bestie and all," gestured a hand over his shoulder towards Sophie, "The same night they agreed to be business partners," flashed my eyebrows below my hat, "Yeah, I'm sure she's going to be real forgiving."

I said the last bit as I lifted myself up from the chair. Leveled a steady gaze on Whitman Price, wondered if he'd stew on that comment.

Couldn't care less if he did.

I was crazy, not stupid. I knew my tough words meant nothing.

His mom had a cancer ward at the hospital named after her.

My mom was about to get kicked off the lowest rung on society's ladder.

He wrote his own history.

I ignored mine.

We could've had a real talk if I scared him enough to serve up Hendricks. But he didn't play scared. I respected that.

I looked toward Sophie and gave her a gallant wave to come back to the table. As we crossed paths I didn't even look at her.

When I walked up to the hostess, she was touching useless buttons on her computer screen. I put my phone to my ear. It didn't mean anything.

The hostess looked up at me. Fear.

I muttered, "Bathroom," like I was asking for directions.

Vince Hendricks would be waiting outside.

I moved for the bathroom before the hostess said a word.

Glided through the restaurant. Stepped past the bathroom. And walked into the kitchen.

A team of kitchen guys — all Mexicans — looked at me. One guy kept singing along to the radio. Another guy sounded like he was finishing a story. The bus boy who saw me out front muttered something quickly.

I raised a finger to my lips. Shushed them with one hand, and pointed toward the back door with my other.

The ones who saw me went stone face.

I did an orangutan walk through the kitchen. Raised my arms up above my head to make me look non-threatening. Rolled my eyes at the oldest guy in the room. I held my arms high and stepped around the industrial sized pots and busy cook stations. Even with my arms all monkeyed up in the air I pointed at the back door again.

When I was two steps away from the door, I launched myself into the air.

seventy-five

Outside the restaurant a guy was on the phone. He stood at the corner of the building so he could see down both streets bordering the restaurant. It wasn't Vince Hendricks. I landed twenty yards down the sidewalk from him. Took me a click to realize it was the stocky guy from last Saturday at Red Rocks.

He hung up as I jumped out the kitchen door.

I didn't know the neighborhood too well. Got lucky that the kitchen door opened on the side street not across from the Lincoln Park zoo.

I ran.

Jumped across Clark Street half block later. Sprinted down Clark for a long stretch with no place to turn.

When the next side street approached, I looked behind me before I turned down it. The stocky guy was in pursuit. He was on the phone shouting instructions. I pictured a driver trying to get to our position; I pictured the driver keeping a special spot for me inside the trunk.

I could feel the fire that Whitman Price ignited. When my chest exploded like that it felt like I could do anything. This guy and his partner chasing me? Dust. They could be a distant memory in minutes.

But it had been a long week. I had spent the entire week in pursuit. First of Albert Brongel. Then Vince Hendricks and Whitman Price. But I also felt I spent my entire week running away from something.

I let the guy catch sight of me, and jumped down the side street. It was a great fake, NFL running-back-worthy.

I cut down the street fifteen yards. And then I stopped.

A restaurant occupied the corner. I stopped where the restaurant's windows ended. I peeked back through the windows to see the guy running his final steps on Clark before he turned.

I ran, crouched down, back to meet him.

People inside the restaurant looked at me.

I looked between their bodies, timed my steps. I kept that NFL analogy in mind. Used the restaurant and the people sitting innocently at the tables like my offensive line. I crouch-ran a few steps back toward the corner.

The stocky guy chasing me was one step from making his turn.

I drove my legs hard, and rose up.

His face turned the corner, his neck extended looking ahead, looking to spot me a half-block down and call in the coordinates of my next turn.

I launched. Tucked my right hand to my shoulder so my elbow stuck out. He was solid enough that trying to tackle and fight him would've been stupid.

My feet left the ground.

His eyes popped from surprise.

His nose popped from my elbow, and his feet flopped up in front of him while his head jerked back and smacked the sidewalk.

Out cold.

His phone slid across the sidewalk. I stepped to it, picked it up like a running back on a fumble—focused on the phone first. Thought about running next.

Then I disappeared.

seventy-six

I pulled my car over on the Inner Drive. Once I took the next left and jumped on the Drive it'd be all expressway and no stops.

I took the phone off the passenger seat.

Four missed calls.

I called back.

A guy picked up on the first dial and said a name.

"Yeah," I said, "No, not him. It's me."

"Who's me," the voice asked.

"Listen, it's just not going to work for you guys. Coming at me," I let out a big exhale, "Next time, how about this, you wait for me to come to you. Then see what you got."

I don't know why I called. I didn't have anything to say to them.

"You're dead," the guy said.

"I know, have been for a while," I told him, "Covered that inside with Whit Price."

It's true, and I never really tried to explain it to myself. I was dead. I don't even know what it meant to me, but it comforted me to feel like that. It felt more like being one with the universe than hating myself. But I think both applied.

"I'll keep the phone," I said, "Have Hendricks text me his number," even though JB had already given me his number, "We can stop all this cat and mouse."

seventy-seven

I woke up in a Motel 6 out by Midway airport.

The Historical Society loomed in my mind.

I kept thinking about it as I lay in that motel room bed. I kept expecting to get hungry again.

Blew past my check-out time, so I sweet talked the Paki dude at the desk into letting me stay until three. Dropped a twenty on him at four when I walked out the door.

I turned my phone back on when I sat in the rental car. The battery was almost dead.

Texted Dorothy: *Looking forward to tonight. Pick U up at 7?*

I left and found a Radio Shack on Cicero and bought an aftermarket car charger.

Further up Cicero ate a breaded steak sandwich with fries at Rico-benes.

By the time I finished Dorothy had texted back: *okay.*

seventy-eight

Detective Glenn took his time reading the Jardine-Hendricks text thread on my phone.

I had asked for our meeting — as long as he agreed not to haul me in. Surprisingly he said okay.

We met at the CPD's fleet services garage at Fifty-fifth and the Dan Ryan Expressway.

"Interested?" I asked.

"It was *interesting*," he said with emphasis, "Not much to be interested in."

It felt like I was chasing down a date; I wanted to know if he'd commit to backing me up Monday.

He set his head back on the headrest and looked out his windshield at the oversized doors of the fleet services garage. He had driven over in his personal car, a bronze Chevy Blazer.

I had to go. I didn't have time. I didn't even know if the Bears were home or away or if the traffic around downtown would slow me down when I drove to Dorothy's.

JB Foster would come through for me. I made sure of that during out last conversation. I had that at least.

"All right, then," I said, held out my hand.

"All right," Glenn said, put the phone in it.

"Tomorrow night."

"Tomorrow night," he parroted.

"You'd be neglecting your duty as a cop if you know about this and decide to do nothing," I informed him.

"You know jack shit about my duties, Panozzo," he said, and hit the button to roll up his window.

seventy-nine

Dorothy looked great, as expected. Skinny jeans tucked into knee high boots and a skintight grey cashmere sweater. Her green eyes popped against her pale skin.

I still rode that sweet spot with the Percocets, wasn't feeling much pain.

In our car ride over to the concert I was like a comedic fluffer getting us amped up. I went from picking her up, to driving to the Loop, to in our seats seemingly on a monologue. She laughed straight through.

Erykah Badu strutted out to that smooth Neo-Soul beat that defined her early years. The crowd hooked into her vibe from note one. Just like with her first single, we followed where she took us. Back when Erykah came up singing she wore Egyptian style headwraps and rocked the ankh. She channeled her African ancestors. She channeled cosmic currents like Sun Ra. Channeled anything she felt like. On her albums lately she got downright experimental. She did just about everything. Just like with Erykah's career, that night we went wherever she took us.

Live music was the ultimate catharsis. It just took me away.

I kept an eye on Dorothy.

She had never listened to Erykah before. I had checked out the music on her computer once. She had a lot of Sleater-Kinney on there.

I told her, "You can't deny the greats," when we stepped out to hit the bathroom and refresh her drink.

"Why would you want to?" Dorothy answered more with her eyes than her voice.

Looked like Erykah just got a new fan.

I bought her a beer in the wide mezzanine level lobby of the Auditorium Theater. Bought myself a water because the Percocets caused a little cottonmouth. We stood for a minute and made stupid faces at each other sparkling under the massive chandeliers.

The fat bass from "Bag Lady" kicked in when I opened the door to the theater. It felt like Erykah tailored up the music for our return to the show.

Dorothy bopped her head to the pulsing bass as she stepped through the door. She pursed her lips.

The ladies in the crowd screamed. They all shouted and jumped to their feet as we walked into the theater. "Bag Lady," had the ladies swaying their hips in time with Erykah's back-up singers. They extended their arms and pointed in unison too.

We paused at the top of the stairs, so I cupped a hand around Dorothy's waist and gave her a soft kiss.

The rest of the women in the joint continued ignoring their men in order to sing along.

Dorothy caught the groove, rocked a small pump action in her shoulders. She took the first step down the steep incline to our seats. After she stepped down she dangled her hand back over her shoulder. I grabbed it.

The night was set.

eighty

I had parked the rental over by the library.

"Let's warm the car up a minute," I said as I stuck the key in the ignition.

I kept my head still and savored the ringing in my ears. Then I asked, "You're gonna download some Erykah tomorrow, aren't you?"

She matched my goofy grin.

"Amazing show. She was spectacular," Dorothy said as I leaned in, "Thank you for taking mmmm–"

I kissed her.

I didn't know if I kissed her at the absolute cheesiest moment, or the perfect one.

Based on her reaction, it didn't matter.

The car heated up fast. I had been working my way around her waist all concert long. That skintight cashmere called for it. But at the show my touches were light and flirty. In the car I grabbed her at the base of her ribs while we kissed. Squeezed her hip with one hand. Then I pressed my hands firm against her body and rubbed them all the way up to her neck.

When I felt like we lingered too long there in the car — for two people with apartments of their own — I pulled back and smiled.

"Perfect timing," she said and giggled.

I kissed her lightly for a minute and rubbed her cheek with the back of my fingers. Then I sat up and readied to drive away.

"So?" she asked, "What's up with the car?"

"Oh, my car got stolen," I said and pulled off the curb.

"Stolen, holy shit!" she burst, "Why didn't you tell me earlier?"

"What's to say?" I asked.

I couldn't maneuver to where I wanted in the post-concert traffic. I caught the red light at Congress and had to go straight instead of right.

I couldn't tell her the truth. My stolen car was a lie, but it was better than saying I had been chased, shot at, and rolled in my old car before I jumped out and ran away as it exploded behind me.

As if I could say to her, 'That was Wednesday night, just down the road here.'

Sometimes I didn't talk because I felt like everything had a bigger explanation. Like holidays. I hoped she wasn't going to bring up Thanksgiving. I wasn't worried she'd invite me to her family's house. We weren't enough of a couple for that. But even if that innocent question came next weekend, I didn't like having to answer what I did for the holiday.

What did I do on Thanksgiving? Nothing. Absolutely nothing.

"Where we going?" Dorothy asked as we crossed through Printer's Row.

"Taking side streets," I said. I wanted to flaunt my mapping skills, so I ducked down some empty streets. There was this oddball block over there. At the end of it you had nothing but possibilities as a driver — north, south and west.

I turned right onto the block. At the far end a white utility van was set up and three ComEd workers stood around. One of them held an orange flag. They had traffic cones placed on the street and one of those three way portable fences surrounding a manhole cover.

Dorothy wiggled her hips in her seat. She looked out my window at the dark windowless side of a building, then up ahead at the flaggers.

Dorothy wasn't too interested in exploring new parts of the city.

I saw the sweep of headlights behind me and checked the rear view to watch another car turn in behind us.

It felt odd to have that much activity on this block: the flaggers with their white van, and another car leaving the concert behind me. The flaggers were three, four hundred yards up by the turn. I saw one guy point an instruction at the other two. It looked like he was telling one of his lazy co-workers to start working the flag.

Flaggers, I thought.

The lazy guy started flipping the flag in circles, like he could give a shit about work.

They all wore orange hazard vests with the ComEd logo on them. The three-way fence around the manhole also had the ComEd logo.

But there wasn't a light rig. They were working by streetlight.

I had never seen that.

That was the first thing I noticed. I took my foot off the gas, not enough to raise an alarm, just enough to give me time to think.

I let my eyes dart around, look like they were otherwise occupied. In reality I kept checking the foreman.

The white van was just that, white. No blue stripes. No ComEd logo. The back was open and revealed tool racks on either side. Again no light.

No blue stripes.

"Sit back," I told Dorothy and thought, *flaggers*, again.

"What?" she asked.

"Just sit back, okay."

We were fifty yards away from them and I felt like turning around.

"Why?" Dorothy asked, "Is everything okay?"

I locked eyes with the guy playing foreman and smiled large, "Everything will be fine," I said and looked over at her.

I wanted to turn around but the car behind me was riding in the middle of the street.

I didn't bother looking back to see what kind of car it was. I wanted to watch the foreman.

I recognized that I had a gun in my glove box, but didn't dare think about using it.

"What's going on?" she asked.

I doubted they had guns. I did wonder if they were in that spot just for me. It was random, but anything was possible. All the right names flashed through my mind: JB, Hendricks, Whitman Price.

Last time I was on this street was months ago. No way someone looking for Lenny could know this particular driving habit.

"Something's up," I said, "I want you to be ready, and when I say 'okay' you bend at the waist and touch your feet."

She didn't say anything.

If the car behind me was a part of their set-up, I hoped that meant there wasn't another car waiting on the far side of the van.

Thirty yards out. As if I needed any other proof, I looked at the van again. No license plates. They probably took them off when they set up.

Dorothy hadn't spoken again, so I gave her a one-line pep talk, "You got this, no problem."

When I was about fifteen yards out, I said, "Okay," to Dorothy.

She bent at the waist.

I raised a palm up to ask the pretend foreman if it was okay to pass. Then I put that hand back on the wheel while my other one fiddled with the door latch. Topped off my playacting with an over earnest suburban grin.

He shook his head in smooth little shakes. Repeatedly pushed his palm down like he kept time with the bass on a slow jam. No, it wasn't okay to pass.

I jumped on the gas.

Swerved my car right for his knees. I really wanted to crunch those things like chips at the bottom of the bag.

The fingers on my left hand caught the door latch. I thrust it open.

Pushed my elbow against the door to swing it out as hard as I could.

Extended my arm fully while throttling the car, and nailed him.

He hit the ground with a thud.

The kickback in the door jammed my wrist. I was still able to grab a hold of it and pull it closed.

Cut the corner to head north.

"WHAT'S GOING ON?!" Dorothy cried.

I kept repeating, "It's okay, you can sit up, it's okay, you can sit up," until I slowed down four blocks away.

I turned onto State Street where a cop was directing concert traffic. I parked in front of his squad so we could bask in the flutter of his flashing blue strobe.

I put a hand on her leg and said, "That was a set up."

"They wanted you?" she asked.

I paused for a minute. Her womanly intuition already grasped that there was a bigger game being played.

"For money," I answered and explained, "Better odds than a smash and grab."

"Should you tell that cop?" she asked.

"Nah, they'll be gone by now."

Like I've been saying to anyone who will listen, Chicago was a city on the make. City Hall and anyone with a connection was working hard to get rich as they sold off the city's greatest assets one by one. The cops wanted to work for Vince Hendricks. City executives wanted a VP position with a for-profit company that paid bonuses. Other less connected people took advantage of them being distracted. The guys in the white van were doing just that.

I couldn't tell Dorothy, but I kind of liked how they worked. Good set up. Good location. Took some thought and preparation. Had to appreciate the fact that they elevated their game past smash and grabs. They too were in search of a higher rate of return.

"Did you get their license plate?" she asked.

Nice question, Dorothy, I thought. On point, not too panicky.

"They didn't have one," I answered.

She was shocked, "You noticed that?"

"No license plate. No lights to keep the work area safe. Wasn't an official ComEd van. Work like that is official," I explained, "Guys earn double-time for that kind of work, and guys with seniority like double-time. They'd create a beacon in the night for their work area."

"You noticed all that?"

I nodded, and put the car into drive again.

"Well, you know what I say?" I asked her. I had wanted her to ask me if I was afraid. Just so I could say this. But in case she didn't ask that, I jumped in with it anyway.

She started to giggle.

I didn't see how I was being funny. Not yet.

"No, Bones," Dorothy giggled and slapped the dashboard of my rental car in frustration, "I actually don't know what you say because you barely say shit."

"Fuck the fuckers," I smiled and looked at her, "That's what I say."

She didn't laugh. She looked at me and said, "What does that have to do with any of this?"

"Those guys back there?" I said.

"Yeah," she answered.

"Fuckers," I told her, "And fuckers even if they're poor and desperate for money, and have a pathetic amount of employment options. When those fuckers come at me, they too need to get knocked with a door upside their head."

She laughed at that.

"That's what that was, Dorothy. Fuck the fuckers," I laid it out. "You need to know anything else about our evening?"

"Well. Yeah. For one thing," she said and chatted over the entire incident two or three times as we drove back to her place.

I put on music. I sang to her. I laughed. I did exactly what I always do, even if the scene back there left me thinking heavy on Lenny and Vince Hendricks, and Gesso on my back.

I answered her questions like we were going over a TV show plot.

I pulled up in front of her building.

"Who are you?" she asked. I was pretty sure it was rhetorical.

She didn't know I was being squeezed from the North Side to the South. That I ran around waiting for shit to drop. She didn't need to know either.

I put a funny fake whine to my voice and said, "Do we have to talk about that again?"

eighty-one

In the morning, after I got up to piss, I woke her up by going down on her again. Did about twenty minutes time to start the day right.

She wanted to take a shower before brunch.

My phone beeped as I lay in her bed. I picked it up. Ten in the morning. A fresh text from Gesso.

Dorothy was in the bathroom, so I opened the text.

Gesso: *You have a visitor.*

Me: *You?*

Gesso: *No. Hendricks.*

Me: *Where? My house?*

Gesso: *Where else?*

Me: *He going in?*

Gesso: *He's in.*

Me: *Okay, nothing I can do now. I need to stop back later.*

Gesso: *Not too late. We're meeting at nine o'clock.*

Me: *Give me a spot then, 8:00.*

Gesso: *See you then.*

eighty-two

My King Crush on Dorothy absolutely freaked me out. I had woken up with a weight on my chest. The weight pushed down on my ribs and when I breathed it felt tingly at my sides. Suddenly, I wanted to know how she and I would end — happy in love, or flame out lust. I wanted to know that morning. Right then. It could've been a reaction to all the other pieces in play that day. It could've been anything.

I've had these feelings before, but usually sorted them out before I slept with a woman.

No doubt, I should've just laid off. But when I felt something I needed to act.

At brunch we were sitting by the thin picture window of a local café. The window had duct tape keeping a triangle of glass in place in the upper right hand corner. I could feel the cool November air through the glass.

Halfway through brunch, when we were in the middle of our eggs, a truck pulled up. It was a Hummer.

I hated Hummers.

The guy driving was boosting "Give It Away," by the Red Hot Chili Peppers. His windows were down so the old glass in the picture window next to us vibrated. He was mouthing the words too, looked to be spot on. The comic book thought bubble above his head screamed, "I'm masculine and cool and rich!"

Dorothy giggled.

"You know, that's the difference between you and me," I said. Yeah, that's the way I started. It wasn't going to go well from there, no matter what I said. I continued, "You look at that guy in the truck and you see some Neanderthal knuckle dragger who's not smart enough to have good taste in music. I look at a guy with a fat truck. That thing cost bank. Probably a contractor with his own crew and driving around the city cranking the jams while he runs his business."

I could've ranted longer, but when I paused a fucked-up feeling took over.

Her eyebrows wiggled. She licked her lips. Did a micro jut of her chin while she shrugged one shoulder. She then looked me in the eye and rolled both of her shoulders back.

"You know what?" she said. She wiped her lips clean with a napkin.

She pursed her lips to prepare herself for what she had to say next.

She said, "You're an asshole."

eighty-three

Then she got up and left.

Monday afternoon at four-forty-five I pulled up alongside Grey Park in Evanston.

Three nut jobs with whacked out hair wearing Salvation Army discards sat in the park smoking.

Across the street from the park was Albany House where my mom lived.

Crazy people and their cigarettes, man. I used to stare at my mom every morning and watch her drink her coffee light and sweet. She'd suck two cigarettes down in a row. Even first thing in the morning, the coffee cup and those cigarettes were stained with lipstick.

Just a talk, I told myself. Just get out of the car and chat. Let her know she wasn't heading back to the streets. Have a word with her boss, Jerome Evon, so he knew my line was open (and still a little hostile).

That's the main reason I was here. I wanted my mom to stop freaking out. She hadn't slept more than an hour since she received the status change letter last week. Her haywired brain would be mush from the lack of rest.

I also wanted to move on. Didn't want to play a game with her anymore.

I must have sat there thinking about all that for ten minutes or more because the song switched a couple times.

Then she walked out the door.

Gained weight. Damn. She was fat. Her manic body had always kept her wire thin. Not anymore. She had a big gut sticking out of her pants.

She rubbed her hands through her frizzy hair. Her color was almost all grey.

She opened up and reached into her purse. I bet that purse was full of scribbled on scrap paper — no matter how much medication she was on.

She pulled out a cigarette.

Dangled it by a thread from her dry lips the way I hated.

Still, it warmed me to see her do that.

She spun the wheel on her cheap lighter a few times before it lit. Between tries she nodded and flashed "Hi" with the swollen fingers of her arthritic hands to the other crazy people walking in and out of the building.

When she pulled on her cigarette it was like she dragged me out of my car.

I opened the car door.

Crossed the street.

Walked up the sidewalk to her. She didn't see me coming.

Maybe this was a big moment in life — seeing my mom after deciding I'd never talk to her again. If it was a big moment, then so be it. I didn't give it much thought. Everything for me — since a very young age — was life and death. That's how I lived every day. Hell, I treated a bonehead in a Hummer like it was life or death when it didn't amount to jack.

I walked right up to her. I felt warm.

I stood close to her shoulder as she gazed out toward the park across the street.

When she looked up at me, I had a smile waiting for her.

I said, "Hi Mom."

eighty-four

My eyes hadn't adjusted from the lights inside my garage to the dark night. I stood still, slowly pulled the door closed behind me. Looked up the gangway thinking I should do a once-around-the-house before heading in.

Gesso was watching my place; but I thought about doing a circuit just in case.

The back of my house was covered in a deep shadow.

I saw a movement in there. Just a small blur like when you see a cat in the dark. Except this blur was five feet in the air.

As my eyes focused on the blur, everything around it got fuzzy.

I blinked and relaxed my eyes when they got watery. Then I saw the movement for what it was: Gesso spreading a piece of bubble gum over her tongue. Bored.

"Gesso?" I whispered.

She stood blanketed in the deep shadow, her body leaned against my brown aluminum siding.

She blew a bubble with her gum, and sucked it back in quietly.

I stepped up to her and whispered, "Need a half hour."

"Take it," she said, "You're clear."

She spoke so softly I could only hear her if I pointed my ear at her mouth.

Her chin lifted as if to point at my garage. She said, "I'm driving,"

She was tall. Must have been five-ten. We weren't quite eye-to-eye, but it wasn't like she talked into my neck.

"Sure about that?" I asked, extended my arm so it leaned on the brown siding.

I had expected to drive.

"I've got a car for the night," she told me. Then she said again, "I'm driving," to reinforce her stance.

We stood so close that I didn't quite get that this was teamwork, not intimacy.

"You sure you're in?" I asked, "There's not much in it for you."

Standing in the shadows the brim from my hat shaded my face pitch black. Still it was just an illusion, not truly dark like Gesso's skin.

She didn't say anything. She just moved her head aside so she could look at me.

I don't know why I did it. I was right up in her face whispering.

I put my hands on her waist and kissed her.

She kissed me back.

She didn't raise her arms and wrap them around me. She worked it out though. Felt like we had a decent connection. Or at least she made the effort for a nice kiss.

I pulled away slowly letting my lips linger for one last rub on hers. I felt her tongue flit in and out lightly. Nice touch.

Then she said, "There's nothing in it for me tonight. I'm getting out."

"And I'm your ticket?"

She put her hand on my chest and eased me back a half step. Then she said, "No fool, you're not the ticket. You're going to *buy* the ticket. You're going to create the ID that allows me to have a ticket in my new name."

I started to edge in slowly again and said, "I'm going to do all that?"

She put her hand back on my chest. Firm. "And then some."

"Tonight you're going to earn it then," I said and eased back further so she would know I wasn't just talking about sex.

Detective Glenn hadn't committed to working tonight. I didn't know how useful the guys from JB Foster's PI firm would be. He promised the best, but I'd have to see for myself. So I had to solidify as much as I could on my own. Worry about the others later. I didn't doubt Gesso's reputation; I just thought she might run her game differently working for me.

"Don't worry about me," Gesso said, "I take care of my people."

"You keep saying that," I whispered. "Maybe you're getting too empathetic at this phase in your life," I leaned back and taunted her, "Soft."

Finally. That drew a healthy laugh out of her. Her lips parted in the most heartfelt natural smile that exposed her every expression prior to that moment as fake.

She cut it off.

"Bones," she said, "Stop playing. You ready to take this to the end?"

I answered, "Oh, I'm ready to take this to the bridge," she probably didn't catch my reference — I had *Illmatic* on the brain.

eighty-five

Inside I put my phone on its charger, made coffee and took a quick shower.

I put on black pants and all black Jordans and prepped for the night.

I bolted downstairs and grabbed the murder weapon and diamond earrings from my stashbox. I had opened the panel so much this week, that I needed a plan to improve it.

I brought the gun and earrings upstairs.

Then I pulled out a hoodie — a zip up with oversized pockets up front.

This wasn't going to be easy. I had to put two guns on my body and still be able to move. Put the murder weapon in one of the hoodie's pockets.

Ran as fast I could from my kitchen to my front door.

The gun wasn't going to work there; it clomped around too much.

Checked the piece The Roach had copped for me. Fully loaded. Put another eight bullets in my front pocket. What to do with the guns? Tried The Roach's in the back of my pants. Nope. Front? Nope. Tried different pockets but none were big enough.

At each pause I sipped coffee. Jumped back into the flow. Electricity oozed off my skin.

It wasn't just the coffee; I knew that. I just felt amped. It was partly due to the quick nap I had earlier after leaving Dorothy. It was partly due to the quick tour my mom gave me of her living quarters. It was getting so close to finishing this. I mixed it all through the music in my head and kept working.

Drained two cups of coffee.

Put my gun—the one The Roach copped—inside the waistband of my pants so the muzzle ran along the grove in my hip like Johnny Too Bad. I liked that. Except I could barely button my pants. And when I tried running with the gun tucked in, my button popped. I grabbed a couple belts. Put one belt on regular, so it would hold my pants up. I had this canvas belt with double holes all the way around. I cinched the gun between the two belts and ran. Then when I pulled the gun out the belt fell slack, but the first belt kept my pants up. Perfect.

Took out a plastic grocery bag. I wrapped the bag around the gun that killed Babi Patras and Albert Brongel. The bag was supposed to keep any fibers or hairs from getting on the gun. Pulled the duct tape out of my junk drawer and taped the gun to my ankle. It fit under my pant leg without being seen. The earrings stayed in my pocket.

Timing might be a problem. I couldn't get the murder weapon out in a hurry. It'd take a minute to extract it from the duct tape and bag and plant it on Vince Hendricks.

The job couldn't be done in a hurry anyway. It could prove fatal to rush while planting a murder weapon.

My skin was wet. I worked up serious heat just getting ready. I decided I didn't need the hoodie tonight.

Put on a black t-shirt and tucked it in. Set The Roach's gun in place—I still couldn't think of it as mine. Slid a black long underwear, long sleeve T over it all.

When I jogged in the winter, I used a pair of football receiver's gloves. Had a black pair with a Bears logo on the Velcro wrist straps. The gloves had a thin tacky leather that made gripping things easier. Tonight that tackiness would come in handy.

I put the gloves in my back pocket. Took three hundred dollars cash, my license and a credit card.

Finally, I tried rocking a plain black skullcap. Looked in the mirror and just couldn't do it.

On party nights when I wanted to look nicer than normal I rocked a black on black White Sox cap. The logo was stitched in a shiny black thread that reflected more light than I would like for the night. But I certainly wasn't rocking my hat with the bright white logo.

I held the hat before me. Flipped it brim over bowl a few times. Spun on my heels. Stopped spinning when I set the hat on my head and pulled down.

"Formal wear," I said with a smile. Time to jet.

eighty-six

Gesso drove.

Nice car — an all-black Mustang Cobra. Leather seats with the white stitching. Six speed stick shift. Premium package stereo.

I pulled out the burner from Saturday night and dialed Vince Hendricks.

"Mister Hendricks," I said smart-assy when he picked up, "Saturday night. You picking up the tab for that guy's broken nose?"

"Get to it," Vince Hendricks said not wanting to spar.

I knew he'd be in the final stages of preparation for tonight. He'd be running through tactical plans with his team and handing out orders. I assumed he couldn't resist picking up when he saw the call come in.

I wanted Hendricks to keep his focus.

"Lenny's missing and I think you know something," I told him, "We need to talk."

"You're talking," Hendricks spat.

"Not now. Face to face," I told him, "In public."

"Call it," Hendricks said.

"Fine, tomorrow night, nine o'clock," I said, "And let's try that joint Red Rocks again."

"Anything else?" Hendricks asked. There was no noise in the background, no information to glean from his voice.

"Alone, Hendricks. I'll be ready for you," I said spitting at him, "You already know what I can do when you try to take me by surprise."

He didn't say anything on the other end.

I hung up on him. Job done. I didn't want to set up a meet with Hendricks tomorrow. I wanted him to think I was out of pocket tonight.

I put the phone down and whistled a long whistle, and said to Gesso, "This ride is nice."

We were already on the expressway. Gesso had black driving gloves on to match her all-black outfit. I glanced toward her feet and assumed she rocked black All-Stars.

"Let me guess," I said, "The car's not yours."

We were boxed in behind the car ahead of us and one to our right.

I added, "I can see why you wanted to drive it."

"I wanted to drive," she said like she was teaching me a lesson. Then she down shifted, jumped the car forward, slid it diagonally to the right, fit impossibly between the two slow pokes. She gassed the car. It responded perfectly in the lower gear. She jumped out ahead of them, upshifted, and finished her thought, "Because I know how to drive."

"So you do," I told her.

"Never catch me rolling a car on Canal Street," she added, "Any street for that matter."

"Let me guess," I said "This car belongs to a Liberty Finance customer. Some deadbeat client and you needed to repo the thing."

She shook her head at my hypothesis.

"Oh right," I corrected myself, "You take care of your people. So the car belongs to a legit client who falls behind on his payments. You convince the dude a stolen car getting totaled would be better for his credit rating than going into default. Insurance would cover it like he never could.

"Is that about right?" I asked and gestured toward the hot-wire contraption that sat in the Mustang's ignition.

Her eyes blinked as she sized up my game, then asked, "Talk to them? They on their way?"

JB Foster's PI firm had sent three guys in two cars for tonight.

"They're set and waiting," I said.

I had talked to one of them on my way home from my mom's; he knew his shit. We planned the tail of Jon Jardine together instead of me just making it up.

A block from Jardine's apartment we stopped at one of the PI's car's, a black Suburban. Two big white guys sat in the front.

Our cars were pointed in opposite directions so me and the other passenger were three feet from each other.

"He's in there," my counterpart said.

That was the guy I talked to. I reached out the window and took a walkie-talkie from him.

"Who's that?" the passenger asked as he leaned up trying to get eyes on Gesso.

I mimed his movement to block his view, "Secret weapon."

He moved and I turned my body sideways to take up more space.

"My driver, okay?" I said, "Nobody to bother with."

"And you said the PD is involved," the guy asked as his eyes jut around, looking for a way past my body, "We're clear on this?"

"They won't commit," I told him, "But we're in contact. They won't be able to ignore my call. I'm betting they'll show up sooner or later."

"The sooner the better," the guy obliged.

Gesso slid the car in gear.

"You guys are on contract with JB tonight, protecting one of his facilities," I clarified.

Gesso let up on the clutch and we nudged slightly forward.

I finished, "PD involvement or not. You guys are clear."

Gesso leaned over and forward to gain an audience with the PI in the passenger seat. She said, "You only saw Bones here," she told him.

His eyes bugged wide and shifted his ass cheeks.

"Nevermind about me," she added, "I find out someone even whispers about me, it'll be time to pay."

I saw the PI turn to his partner in the driver's seat as Gesso throttled the car and jumped up the block.

She kicked it around the corner and put us in position by Jon Jardine's apartment.

An hour later, Jon Jardine walked out of his Logan Square apartment building.

We never saw the second car the PI firm sent. He squawked in when each of us tested our talkies.

The three of us dragged Jon Jardine to the meet. That's how it felt. Our tail was so on top of him it curled around his head.

We hung back when Jon Jardine pulled into the warehouse district along Kingsbury. The quasi-industrial road paralleled the highway.

One PI car held the north entrance to the street while the other jetted to the south end.

Gesso let the drone of Jardine's engine fade out before she turned in behind him.

We came around a kink in the road and saw him stopped three blocks up. He was standing at the passenger side of a blue cargo van with tinted windows.

"Jump in back," Gesso said.

I jumped into the back seat and slid as far to the ground as I could get.

Gesso turned the radio on. The quiet storm played on V-103.

"Hold the button down on the talkie," she told me as I pressed myself down by the floorboards.

Then she added, "Jardine's standing at the side of the van. Van's got Missouri plates. The side doors are open and he's talking to the guys inside."

I felt the tug of the Mustang's brakes. Heard the driver's side window glide down. She turned the volume up on the radio station.

Gesso came to a full stop.

"Haaaaaeeeey," she said out the window, "You gentlemen looking to party?"

The North Branch of the Chicago River wound through here. The bridges crossing the river at Division Street, behind us, and Chicago Avenue, ahead of us, were the most obvious — and popular — places in the city to find faux fur and pleather clad hookers. The surrounding warehouse district provided plenty of nooks to complete transactions.

"Keep moving," a voice said.

"Have a good night, booiyyys," Gesso said as she pulled away.

"That was Jardine, right?" I asked from my prone position behind her seat.

"Uh huh," she said.

"Let's be careful now that they had eyes on you."

Gesso would be as memorable as the pristine Mustang. One glimpse by someone in that van in the next hour could prove fatal.

"Who'd you see inside?" I asked.

"Driver in plain clothes. Seat next to the door was empty. Saw four more guys, wearing all-black. By the looks of the van there were two more sitting way back there."

"Seven guys," I said.

"Eight with Jardine," she told me, "Looked like there was some back and forth between him and the guys in the van."

"A conversation?" I asked as I lifted myself up. Started climbing back into the passenger seat.

Gesso said, "He still wasn't inside by the time I turned," she said.

That made me think Vince Hendricks wasn't in the van. I thought if Hendricks was inside, then Jardine would've jumped in as soon as the door opened. Just to show his obedience. Instead Jardine stood outside and negotiated. Why?

I kept the button down on the talkie and explained to the PI's what just happened.

"We're in full communication now," I told them, "Cutting over to Halsted as planned."

The blue van with Jardine and friends made its way back to the expressway.

One of the PI cars rode their tail. The second PI car was out of position once Jardine started moving and needed to play catch up.

Gesso and I were expected to stay local until we knew which way they were going.

The PI's drove on the expressway calling out exit names when they passed.

We approached the dead president streets down in the West Loop.

The PI on the talkie rattled off the street names a mile behind us. They were catching up fast.

I pulled out my phone and texted Detective Glenn.

"Glenn's in play," I told her.

"Where?" she asked.

"On my phone. I'm setting him up now," I told her, "He'll bite later."

As Gesso drove and I ran maps in my head. I was trying to figure out which JB facility they were attacking. If they turned toward the Loop they'd be headed to JB Foster's office. If they headed west there was only one warehouse in that direction. If they headed south there were two warehouses they could drive to. Once they got past Forty-Third Street there'd only be one option left.

We approached the Jackson Hotel on Halsted.

The PI's tailing the van started barking out dead president names. In a minute they'd be at Jackson too.

"The van in an exit lane?" I asked over the talkie.

In the heart of downtown the highway exits came fast; a driver needed to jockey into position well ahead of time. For that stretch of streets they'd have to project their intentions.

"Negative," the PI said back, "No exit lane."

That eliminated JB Foster's office and the west side warehouse.

"Stockyards," I told Gesso, "Has to be the spot. Lets get there first."

JB Foster maintained a warehouse in the old Stockyards. It was one of the things that earned him the city document storage contract.

Whitman Price didn't have that. The other bids submitted had smaller warehouses in the city. But JB's was the mammoth kind you usually only saw in the far suburbs along major expressways.

Gesso whipped a U-Turn on Halsted. She had to jump back and grab a southbound on-ramp. The van with Jardine and Hendricks in it was coming up on our position fast.

Gesso shifted perfectly. The gears didn't click. The tires didn't squeal.

I barked into the PI's intercom, "The Stockyards. Stockyards. We're jetting ahead. Jump the tail, meet us there."

My grandpa had worked the Stockyards. Hell, my grandpa was even named by the Stockyards. But that was another story.

Gesso didn't want to talk. She didn't even flinch when I laughed out loud.

All these memories came rushing up. I could feel them like they stood behind a barrier. The Jackson Hotel. Orky, my grandpa. The Stockyards. I ignored them. The front of my brain focused on executing. But those memories lurked as we passed under the big stone archway of the Stockyards main gate.

Gesso took the empty streets like she was racing Grand Prix. The car gurgled and growled through straights and corners until we came to a stop.

I texted Detective Glenn again. Gave him our exact location.

"You switch the plates on this thing?" I asked Gesso.

"No plate," she said.

I double checked my gun, and felt around in my pockets to make sure I knew where everything was: spare bullets, Babi Patras earrings. Felt down my leg for the murder weapon.

I wiggled the gun down by my leg to make sure it could come out quickly but not easily.

"Some people," I said.

Gesso didn't respond. Didn't fidget. Didn't need to prepare anything.

"All this because Whitman Price has a boner for History. Legacy. But the greedy little fucker couldn't be happy with a billion dollar real estate portfolio. That bitch wanted an empire," I paused, "Whatever."

Gesso pulled up a street away from JB's warehouse. There were a couple low-slung warehouses. These were drab one-story brick buildings.

We peeked JB's warehouse between them. It was a white behemoth. It was well-lit and looked foreign on these forgotten streets.

JB's Stockyard facility contained city documents: marriage licenses, death certificates, and baptismal records submitted with various applications. It contained things like ancient construction and building permits.

In Whitman Price's view, Chicago was a city to be taken. He planned to roll up, wreak havoc and steal a city contract worth tens of millions of dollars a year. It was that simple. He couldn't care less about the shit inside. There were no top-secret medical formulas buried in there. Nothing like a hidden weapon of mass destruction. No buried skeletons of bureaucrats past. No ancient plan for world domination that would work if it got into the wrong hands. Inside the warehouse there weren't the type of buried family treasures that would be worth billions on today's market. There wouldn't be anything to do with old Nazi skeletons inside. Hell, the mob wasn't even battling over the place.

Nah, maybe the warehouse contained an old deed on a family home bought in nineteen sixteen out of a Sears mail order catalogue. The plot of land that went with it looking like every square plot around it.

That junk was only useful to historians or some layman with enough money and time to go looking for a tie to the past.

THE COME UP

That kind of stuff.

That's what Whitman Price was destroying tonight.

eighty-seven

JB Foster had bulldozed a new street into the Stockyards when he built his facility. Gave him naming rights. The new street made his building feel exclusive in this dingy cluster of warehouses and shipping docks.

Gesso and I watched the warehouse between the two low-slung worn-brick warehouses.

I radioed directions to the other cars. Texted Detective Glenn again with our position.

The streetlights were out. I wondered if Whitman Price had rented that service for the night.

Three minutes later the two cars from JB Foster's PI firm came barreling around the corner. The Suburban with the two guys we talked to earlier parked behind us. The other car, in front of us, was a full-sized Blazer that looked old enough to be the one OJ drove.

Every resource I could harvest sat in these three cars. If I had made the wrong call about the warehouse, it would be game over.

My phone rang.

"Ahh, Detective Glenn," I said before picking up the phone. I said to him, "You here?"

Glenn wanted to know about positioning.

I told him where to turn and where to park, finished by saying, "I'll call you when we move."

Gesso released the seat back. By the time I was off the phone she lay back in the chair like she was going to take a nap.

Detective Glenn's Crown Vic had its parking lights on as it drove. As I watched, I saw another Crown Vic — this one with no lights on — round the street behind Glenn.

The second Crown Vic freaked me out. I had images of Hendricks barreling down on my back on Canal Street. I hadn't said it yet, but I didn't think he was in the van. It would be smart for him to bring up the rear in a separate car.

I pulled the gun out of my belt, just in case the second Crown Vic wasn't friendly. If it was Hendricks surprising us, I wanted to be ready.

The second Crown Vic followed Glenn around the corner.

I called Glenn, "Did you bring friends?"

He did. When I asked how many he said there were four of them.

"That's the PD," I barked into the walkie. JB's hired guns would know, "There's four of them."

"That was Glenn?" Gesso asked.

"Yeah, they rounded that corner up there," I told her.

For the first time since I met her silence seemed awkward.

"Aahhh, Detective Glenn," I said, "*He's* your source inside the PD. Isn't he?"

She lifted her seat back up and said, "See Bones, that's what I'm saying. You've got the raw skills."

"And he can't see us together, can he?" I filled in the picture.

She shook her head.

I added, "Because he knows your bosses. Right?"

She nodded.

It made me wonder, "He clean?"

"For the most part," Gesso said.

I put the gun in my lap. Same gun I pointed at Gesso a couple nights back. I had a murder weapon taped to my leg. I was surrounded by cops and ex cops, and a street legend ready to leave the game. I learned one thing this week, when you stop running, you find yourself in interesting places.

I called the lead PI. Turned around in my seat so I could look at him while we talked.

"Cops brought four. We wait until everyone's out of the van," I told him, "Head between the warehouses, take them at the front door before they can do too much damage."

"If you're right," he warned, "About the location."

His chain-of-command mindset would have preferred tailing the van with Jardine and Hendricks. That would eliminate the possibility of getting the location wrong.

The PI behind me continued, "The guy ahead of you," he motioned up to the Blazer ahead of us, "He's going to head up the drive and block the van from leaving."

"Good idea," I said.

It all clicked for me. The two additional cops made our team nine strong. They either had seven or eight in the van.

I liked our chances so much, a bass line kicked in my head. It was that deep fuzzed out bass from the "It Ain't Hard to Tell" remix they put on the *Illmatic* Tenth Anniversary edition. The bass on that remix penetrated deep. Yet it didn't overpower. It was the kind of bass line that could knock the fuzz off a peach.

A light reflected off the warehouse behind us.

I watched the trajectory of the headlights approaching. I assumed everyone else did too.

It was the van.

It cruised up the drive and parked.

The driver got out and walked into the office.

The walkie-talkie squawked, the voice from the other end said, "Dan Daly, just walked inside."

Dan Daly? Dan Daly? I remembered and explained to Gesso, "The guy who went in was JB Foster's former head of security."

I knew something was wrong. I started to think my way through that instinct. I thought, no way Vince Hendricks would send that guy to the front door.

There were acres of aluminum sheets out there wrapping that building. City blocks — plural — to each side. And Vince Hendricks would send his only team — without backup — right to the front door?

Didn't buy it.

As if putting words to my thoughts, Gesso said, "Decoy."

"Let's move," I barked into the talkie. I called Glenn and said the same.

The beat-up Blazer in front of us kept its lights off and turned around.

Gesso stayed in the car.

The two PIs and I walked over to the nearest wall and used it for cover. I spotted Detective Glenn and his partner. They were against the wall of a loading dock. I didn't see the other two cops.

Four minutes later Dan Daly came out from the warehouse's office and climbed in the van.

The van started, and the lights came up. Seven black-clad soldiers hopped out the passenger side.

The van pulled off the curb and the soldiers started to trot—using the van for cover.

I couldn't tell which one was Jon Jardine.

That's when I knew it wasn't the real deal. Thoughts before that moment were just thoughts. Sometimes I could never know what I really understood or felt until I took that first step from around the building. When I started running, out in the open beyond the warehouse, that's when I knew.

Decoy.

There wasn't any new information. I just became certain that Vince Hendricks wouldn't use the front door.

On our left, the PI driving the beat-up Blazer sped up the drive into the parking lot. Just like Hendrick's car from Canal Street, the Blazer had a bumper guard made of thick metal piping.

The two PI's and I ran together around the right side of our cover building.

Over to our right, beyond Detective Glenn and his partner the other two cops came out from their cover. Everyone wore vests except me. Glenn and the three other officers wore helmets too.

Seven soldiers executed for Hendricks.

We had eight with Gesso in the car. I hoped she stayed there to watch—just in case she was needed.

The Blazer sped up the drive. We all slowed down, waiting for the Blazer to make its entrance.

Looked back at the black Mustang. I saw smoke poof from the tailpipes when Gesso started the car.

The Blazer caught its passing gear and revved hard.

I tapped one of the PI's and pointed at my chest. *No vest.* So I waved bye-bye. He gave me a thumbs-up.

I caught Glenn's eyes as I peeled off. He nodded as I motioned to my chest.

Gesso was turning the car around.

I sprinted in her direction.

Behind me a shock erupted when the Blazer rammed the blue van that Dan Daly drove.

I raised an arm in victory.

Gesso started to pull away.

"GESSO!" I yelled as hard as I could.

eighty-eight

"Where to?"

"JB's," and I paused. I had a minute while she drove towards the Stock-yards exit.

JB's loft? What could Vince Hendricks plant there to take down JB Foster? Hendricks wasn't about to try and pin the murder on JB with Lenny already hotstepping. JB's Kenilworth house? Again, no reason.

The Mustang roared through the barren Stockyards. The guy who bought the car may have slipped behind payments. But whoever he was, dude knew how to pick a fucking car. Gesso didn't grind a gear as she cut the corners at forty and jumped to eighty on the straights.

She came hard under the gateway at the exit.

"Office," I said, "Monroe between Clark and State."

Left. Right onto Thirty-ninth. Dan Ryan Expressway. Not a cop in sight.

Up to Congress and under the old post office. Made all the lights to Clark Street and she turned the wheel well before the intersection. Cut through four lanes of oncoming traffic. The lanes were almost empty. Two cars came right at us.

Those two cars were just like the others that night, an afterthought.

Three blocks up on Clark, I screamed, "Here, here, here."

Gesso screeched up to the curb.

"Let me out," I told her, "Park up there and meet me in the lobby."

I wanted to check the alley first.

I pulled out my phone and started running.

JB Foster picked up after the first ring.

I had just turned the corner into the alley and confirmed what I was about to say.

"Hendricks is in your office," I said.

The pock-marked Crown Vic that rammed me on Canal Street was parked in the alley.

Foster didn't say a word.

Of course. Hendricks had worked the building the entire week before. Today would have been his last day. He came in as the white knight
after Babi's murder. The flashlight wavers at the front desk either
feared him or worshiped him. He'd have easy access.

"Tell the security guard to buzz me in," I told JB, "Then tell him to forget what he sees. And no cops until I say."

I hung up.

I broke up the alley to the sidewalk.

Gesso was already there waving hard. She pointed at me. Apparently, the phone at the front desk already rang, because Gesso nodded
and pointed at the phone and then the doors.

Unlock. Now. Her point said.

I tried one set of doors. Locked.

The guard spoke into the phone, nodded as if JB on the other end
could see him.

I went to the revolving doors and started jerking them back and
forth.

With the phone cradled in his shoulder the guard waved us over to
another set.

By the time we ran past the front desk the guy was pointing at the nearest elevator bay.

I shouted, "Which floor?"

"Thirty-three!" dude shouted.

An elevator door was open and waiting for us.

As the door closed, Gesso said, "Didn't even need to ask," nodded at
the button panel.

I tried to decipher the code of the numbers. Looked for a star next
to one. Or some special colored button. But nah, I caught her drift quick
enough. Thirty-three was the top floor.

True, I could've figured that out. Glad I didn't try.

"I'm going to need that security guard's name," Gesso told me as we
rode up.

When I looked at her, I could barely see her breathing.

I first thought it was, like, elevator banter. Then I realized the security guard could put us together.

Gesso was thinking about her next play.

I wasn't finished with this one. Didn't say a word.

The elevator door opened on the thirty-third floor and we stepped out.

Which way?

Left. The left side of the building faced north. It'd offer a more commanding view of the Chicago skyline. JB's office was there, no doubt.

I pulled the thirty-eight I got from The Roach out of my waist.

Gesso held a forty-five. Or a nine. Couldn't tell.

The office door at the end of the hallway was open.

We walked in. Wasn't it. It was the secretary's office. I tapped Gesso, nodded toward the inside door that led into JB's suite.

Gesso reached for the knob.

Turned silently.

She turned the knob fully before beginning to push.

Open.

That's when my phone started buzzing. Of course I had it turned off. The ringer anyway.

Couldn't even swear.

Gesso couldn't even get a damning look at me.

Had to be JB, checking back to see if we were safely in.

We were in. But we weren't safe.

The buzzing phone shouted from my pocket.

Bullets answered back.

We dropped.

Slugs came right through the door, chest level.

I crawled back through the open door to the hallway.

Gesso jumped behind the desk.

Didn't know if I left myself exposed for a second. Maybe Gesso had the right idea to climb behind the wood and paper files for cover.

I looked down the hallway. Spotted a second door.

Caught Gesso's eyes and jerked my head down that way.

I crouched down and crab-walked towards the second door—it would lead directly into JB's office.

I wanted to attack. But I waited for a signal from Gesso.

Shotgun blast ripped from inside the office.

Another one. And another.

Heard a ton of bricks hit inside the secretary's office.

Two more blasts.

I quick opened the door leading directly into Foster's suite.

Hendricks was wheeling toward me, shotgun leading the way.

I dove away from the door.

The blast opened the doorway a little wider. Glass shattered into the hall and sprinkled my clothes.

I thought about phoning JB to call in the cops. The added numbers'd be nice. But the cops couldn't get here until after I had my hands on Hendricks. If they came too soon then I couldn't plant the murder weapon and earrings. They'd be found on me. There'd be too much commotion to sort out who was who. JB Foster wouldn't be there directing traffic to say — yes him, not them. Even if he was there, shots fired on the scene'd eliminate any chance of JB getting a favor from the PD until all questions stopped.

That meant if I didn't get to Vince Hendricks first, two murders would get pinned on me.

I thought about going back to check on Gesso, see if she was hit.

Couldn't hear a thing out of Hendricks. I assumed he was tiptoeing in the direction of his shots.

I crawled back to the doorway. Spun around. Landed on my back with the gun pointed where I last saw Hendricks.

He had his shotgun trained at the secretary's holding pen. Right where Gesso hid.

I leveled my gun, and tried to aim it.

Did the only thing I thought I could. I started squeezing. Five bullets came out as fast as my hand could work the heavy, resistant trigger.

I hit either his hand or the piece of the shotgun near it.

The shotgun smacked against the wall.

Hendricks didn't even watch it go. He started to reach behind him, grabbed his back-up piece.

That's when the ceiling crashed open and Gesso fell into the room.

She must've climbed onto the desk and up through the ceiling tiles. That big ton of bricks crash that I heard was the book case falling over when she boosted herself up into the panels. Smart move on her part. She sat up there while Hendricks emptied his chamber.

When I looked back at Hendricks he had his pistol out. He stepped toward Gesso.

I stood and entered JB's office in time to see Gesso swat at Hendricks hand.

Hendricks fired the gun.

Gesso had knocked it off trajectory.

She didn't scream so I assumed she wasn't hit.

Hendricks fought for an edge and shouldered Gesso to the ground.

I fired again at him. Missed.

Hendricks sprinted out the secretary's door.

"You okay?" I asked her.

"GO GO GO!" she shouted back.

I couldn't tell if I had bullets left in the gun. There's no way I was able to count in the middle of all that. There was no way I was able to reload while running.

I ran to the elevator bay.

Gesso bumped into me when I stopped.

The elevator lobby was empty.

No elevator was dinging down the floors.

"Stairs." Gesso said.

An elevator door dinged open. It opened and we both crouched on the ready.

Nobody came out.

"You, elevator," I said and bolted to the stairs.

Chances were Gesso could make it down faster than Hendricks could run thirty-three flights of stairs. Meant I could've made it down too. But I wanted to stick on Hendricks and make sure he wasn't heading roof-side.

Spun and caught the exit sign from my eye to the left. There was another exit sign to the right — on the far side of the lobby from JB's office. I took that one.

Put my head in and looked up. Listened. Silence.

Looked down.

Nothing.

Other stairwell.

I took the next stairwell's door full steam. Launched myself down the first flight. Practically ran sideways to make sure I landed a full foot on each step. Didn't want my heel to catch or the ball of my foot to slide off and trip me up. At first my feet did the ba-da-ba-da-ba-da as one foot took each step. Then I started taking them by twos: baa-daa-baa-daa.

It was just a matter of catching the rhythm.

Gregory Rossi

After four flights I started to lock in. I took the steps by threes. That meant two steps to each half flight, and then I hit the landing and pivot stepped to the next flight.

When I was down ten flights or so, I got eyes on Hendricks.

He was another ten ahead.

I thought about giving up and jetting to an elevator. I had given him too much time – took me too long to get out of JB's office. Took me too long at the elevator bay and that first stairwell.

I felt locked in enough that I could do my steps and my pivot foot while keeping an eye on him. I thought it was too much space to make up. He'd be outside well before me and I thought my only hope was Gesso being there waiting for him.

Then the rhythm inside me got stronger. Paid less attention to Hendricks and crammed the gun into my pants again so both my hands would be free.

Hendricks still pointed his toes forward and drilled his legs into each step: da-da-da-da-da-da-da – like some military drill all the way down.

I was all steps and pivots. I was pivot-sliding across each landing. I had all the steps strung together like the best kind of bass line. Like the one that pulsed through "NY State of Mind" on *Illmatic*. I strung every third step and the landing together and my body began pulsing boom-bip-ba-boom-boom-bip-bip. A couple flights on that rhythm like in a song – I needed to take it to a new level. I mastered this rhythm with these elements and just did.

I just did it. The clarity was sick. I was on the fourteenth floor. Hendricks was four or five flights ahead of me.

It wasn't like a thought that came in, and then I decided and then it was happening. I just did it. On the last stair of that particular flight, I gripped the hand railing. I didn't drop step down to the landing like I had been doing. I compressed my leg and jumped. Up over the railing, my body moving at a fierce velocity that might've scared the shit out of me except I was so fucking determined to land my Jordan on the correct step – three down from the landing – that I just noticed the force. It was like the air in that stairwell had been still for so long my body had to thrust up and over the railing and even feel a little resistance on down as I eye-guided my Jordan.

Nailed the step. Jumped down three, compressed and launched

again.

Used the railing like a gymnast and bounded down the flights.

I was all jumps and Jordans. Forgot about Hendricks. My eyes watched the Jordans, guiding them to the correct step. My body just worked from the legs, launching over the railing. While my arm stabilized everything by gripping the hand rail and taking it off after I landed the jump, then grabbing again as I took the second step.

I wanted to get eyes on Hendricks again. It had been four or five flights since I looked. I just wanted to be a few steps behind him when we exited the building.

Locked in to that rhythm, my body felt impossibly amped up. I saw the fourth flour and noted that I could still hear Hendricks running down the stairs.

All my anger and energy came out as focus; my whole body and my whole brain did this one thing.

It felt like I was just getting warmed up.

A primal yell started to build inside me, but I contained it. Kept the energy focused on my legs.

I had two flights left. Hendricks had one.

I started to think how soon I'd have to break form. *Hold it,* I told myself.

Keep it on repeat, I told myself.

Hendricks reached the bottom.

One more.

Hendricks pushed open the door.

The fire exit siren screamed and flashing strobes flickered into the stairway's echo chamber.

I swung over the last landing.

Strobe lights distracted me.

I almost landed it. It was that last flight of stairs.

My eyes couldn't focus on my Jordans and guide them to the step because the strobes threw my focus off track in the two seconds it took me to swing over the railing. My foot landed with the outside edge hanging off a stair by a half-inch. The force carried me off the step. My hand lost its grip on the railing. There was no continuation of the stairs to recover to. It was the last landing.

I dropped the rhythm.

Hesitated. Tripped myself up.

My feet flew out from under me, got caught in the corner of the stairs. My head whipped around and down as my shin banged the metal edge of a stair. My thigh banged the metal edge of the next one down. My hip slammed into the one after that. And my shoulder crammed into the final cement landing. Same shit as the car crash on Canal.

Couldn't even hear myself scream above the blaring fire alarm.

My body didn't stop moving once I hit the landing. My feet rose up, and tumbled over my head.

I couldn't control much, but I did tuck my knees in towards my body. All that energy and momentum from the thirty-three flights crumbled in upon me. It rolled my body until I came around and faced the ground again.

My knees hit the concrete and I was propped up on my elbows.

Sat there on all fours like a dumbstruck beast.

Groaned deep and low enough, just so I could feel the vibration in my chest. Still couldn't hear anything over the fire sirens in the stairwell.

I didn't let the momentum and energy stop there. Used it to propel my body.

Forced myself to jump up.

Threw my sore shoulder into the metal fire escape door.

It opened.

eighty-nine

The fire exit let out onto Clark Street, not the alley.

Hendricks sprinted through the empty intersection.

We were behind the First Chicago building — the one with the sunken plaza behind it. Parked up Clark Street just past the intersection was Gesso's black Mustang. I saw fumes coming out of the Mustang's pipes. It was running.

I grunted and groaned through the first couple steps. Pushed through the pain and ran on my tender ankle.

Hendricks was about to cut up Clark when Gesso stepped out of her car. Fired.

Hendricks fired back.

He got two shots from Gesso in return.

That was enough to send him down the steps into the plaza. The plaza sank a story below street grade. It had a fountain in the middle and was ringed by restaurants on two sides. The restaurants were below street grade too. At street level they only had the structure to house an elevator to run customers down to their dining rooms.

I edged along one of the restaurant's structures. Pulled the gun out of my waistband. I crept up to the corner and peeked around it. Plaza was empty too.

Out of the corner of my eye I saw Gesso.

I began jogging down the steps.

Gun fired.

I dropped my gun in surprise. Dropped myself too.

Picked up the gun.

Another round echoed through the empty plaza.

Heard a big whistle.

Looked up at Gesso standing to my right. She pointed to the fountain. Had to figure Hendricks took his perch on the other side of the fountain. He squatted so I couldn't see him. I ran back up the stairs and around the seafood restaurant. Sprinted to the corner of Dearborn, came back down the steps at a new angle.

Couldn't peep Gesso anywhere.

There was no movement in the plaza, but Hendricks was still down there.

I finally peeped Hendricks. He was at the far side of the plaza against the long swooping curves of the First Chicago building.

The base of the fountain in the plaza's center doubled as a bench where people ate lunch and talked on cell phones. He crouched low and used the bench for cover as he talked on his cell phone.

Then, I couldn't quite tell how it happened.

First I couldn't see Gesso at all.

Next she was standing in the still waters of the fountain.

Hendricks hung up his phone.

I heard the faint beginning of sirens in the background. They were far enough away that they could've been for something else. I wouldn't count on it.

Monday nights in the Loop were pretty quiet — not a lot of police assets dedicated to the empty streets. I had to believe every cop in the area was screaming towards JB's office at this minute.

I jogged down the steps into the plaza again. This time my shadow stretched from a street light behind me, right over Hendrick's face.

He rolled, came up pointing his gun right at me.

Hendricks couldn't miss. His life depended on it.

Mine did too.

I dove. I landed and rolled and realized I didn't hear a gunshot. By the time I looked back at him he was wrestling with a shadow.

Gesso stood on the fountain's bench and wrestled with him over his head. She was bent at the waist which made her balance awkward without the advantage of a stable stance.

I sprang up to help her.

As I jumped down the awkward steps Gesso lifted.

She left her feet without putting a spring in them first. Maybe she used her arms as leverage against Hendricks' body. Maybe she just did it.

She swung her feet up over his head. Kept her grip on Hendricks' wrist. She pulled a half-twist in the air and landed with a crunch. She had used the force of her jump to crack his wrist.

Hendricks screamed.

Gesso let go of his wrist and took Hendrick's gun away in one motion.

Hendricks instinctively hugged his wrist to his chest.

I sprinted down the steps.

Hendricks put a little bend in his waist to divert his eyes from us. No way he'd cower under the pain of a broken wrist, guy was tougher than that.

"Cops," he said.

He was right. There were sirens.

When I stood next to Gesso, both of us facing Hendricks, she handed his gun to me.

"Use this one," she said, "got about a half-minute, Bones."

I pulled out the earrings, and put them in his broken hand and crunched it all together while putting a good yank on his wrist.

He screamed again.

"What's that?" Gesso asked.

"Babi Patras's earrings."

"Forget accessorizing, Bones, just do it."

"Sec," I told her.

Pulled out the gun that killed Babi and Albert Brongel.

Held Gesso's in one hand, the murder weapon in the other.

"Bones. Now."

Sirens.

I didn't want to do it. I was afraid of what lay on the other side of the door. Justified or not, I was about to be a killer. The word could have a string of modifiers surrounding it. Any interpretation would mean the same thing.

"Don't do this for you, Bones. This is your boy Lenny. You decide how the game ends."

I put the murder weapon in my pocket. Took Gesso's gun, and used the end of it to lift Hendricks head from the under his chin.

As his head lifted his eyes came to mine as if we were going to have one last conversation.

Pop.

I shot him in that fleshy part under his chin. Behind him the surface of the fountain rippled as if I had thrown a hundred little rocks into the still water.

"Hold him," I told Gesso.

Threw the gun in the fountain.

Took the murder weapon out, and started to put it in his hand.

"Hold him," I repeated.

"Heavy Bones, can't," she said.

Pulled his index finger out from his good hand.

"Hurry," she said as the body started to slip, and added, "They're almost here."

Pop. Fired Hendrick's gun at the bank building behind us.

Gesso and I were already sprinting up the step by the time Hendricks's body splashed into the water.

"Stop," she said, put a hand to my chest.

Just as we crouched, sirens and flashers ricocheted off the glass buildings surrounding us.

We squatted lower.

A cop car came screeching to a stop in front of JB Foster's building.

I started to launch.

She braced me again. Five seconds later a cop screamed the wrong way down Clark Street only fifteen feet in front of us. Took the corner and fish tailed behind the first squad we saw.

"Now," she said.

We sprinted to the car.

ninety

Gesso was quick enough to turn off Clark Street before they were too close.

"They aren't stopping," she said. She had a squad in her rear view mirror, the third arriving after Hendricks called it in.

Gesso turned up an alley. Jetted up to the next street and turned again.

When we crossed State Street we saw the squads doing the same a block south.

"The security guard," I told Gesso, "It won't matter if we get away. He'll make us."

She jutted out her elbow and put it in my chest, "Lean back, can't see." Brought her arm back in time to shift.

The car jumped across Wabash heading toward the lake.

I saw a squad pass again a block below us.

She took a northbound alley before we reached Michigan Avenue. Cut a couple blocks up the alley. Turned onto Lower Wacker, the service street that ran underneath the city.

And gone.

The cop was too many streets down for quick access to the underground network.

Gesso navigated the underground streets of Chicago until we popped out into the sparkling world of River North. Cut back south once we were above ground — came back into the Loop and glided under the bright street lights. We avoided any entrance and exit to Lower Wacker and soon found ourselves a world away.

ninety-one

We swung past my house and parked in my garage for an hour.

Then, I trailed Gesso down the South Shore. At some point we turned down an empty street that led directly to the lake. There used to be an old steel mill along the lakefront. Now there were just empty fields. I followed Gesso to the end of a road where it practically butted into Lake Michigan.

I waited while she grabbed a gas can from the trunk. She poured some gas on top of the car. Most of it she reserved for the interior.

I put my car in reverse and backed up another hundred yards.

She took out a piece of white cloth from the trunk. When she held it up it looked like there was a weight on it so the cloth hung taught and swung like a pendulum.

She opened up the gas tank and snaked the cloth down.

The first match she lit, she threw inside the car. Flames curled up inside and the all-black cabin of the car turned orange.

She dangled the second match at the tip of the cloth. She stood there coolly and watched to make sure the flame caught.

Some of the gas had trickled down from the roof. The body of the car caught fire too. There was a thin blue flame smoldering along the car's skin. She watched as the flame grabbed hold of the cloth.

Then she ran.

ninety-two

"Wanna grab a bite?" I asked as I pulled up to the side door of a high-rise in Hyde Park.

Gesso had a hand on the door latch. Her body was already leaning to exit the car. She looked back at me over her shoulder.

Then she sat back into her seat.

I thought, *Yes, we can grab a bite. Maybe kick it at her place after.*

"Bones, you've got some serious skills out there," she said, "After hearing about Canal Street, I thought maybe you were a little more polished than you were. But you've got game, kid."

I just looked back. I couldn't give a shit. What did this have to do with eating and then kicking it?

"That said," Gesso added, "You've got a lot to learn."

Then she opened the door and left.

ninety-three

Woke up screaming.

Nah, not like that.

It sounded like, "Yeah!"

There was a quiet "Yeah!" that pulsed along at a low level on "It Ain't Hard to Tell," the last song of *Illmatic*.

That "Yeah!" punctuated my thoughts.

Time check said it was two in the afternoon. About right.

I was so amped up when I got home that I — of course — smoked up. I tried laying down on my couch to focus on the silence. Tried thinking about Lenny, and wondered if I could help him anymore.

Ultimately — of course — I took to the streets. The night ran late anyway. By the time I walked the streets the sun was coming up.

Pulsed "Yeah!" as the sky turned from pink to blue.

Sunrise as celebration.

Pulsed "Yeah!" through my walk. But I didn't walk long. I was hungry. Headed to the diner at the gas station on Thirty-First and ate the lumberjack breakfast — three of everything they had. I held off on the coffee.

Neither the greasy food in my stomach nor the long day behind me could tamp the "Yeah!" from pulsing through my body.

"Yeah!" as I paid my bill. And "Yeah!" as I walked home.

"Yeah!" as the last thing before I fell asleep at seven-thirty in the morning.

"Yeah!" was the first thing I heard when I woke up.

Two in the afternoon.

ninety-four

I thought about Dorothy again. I wanted to call her and tell her it was over. The past week I had been hiding my real life from her. I let it eat away at me — saw how I freaked yesterday morning just because I anticipated last night.

Texted her: *It's over*

Five minutes later I texted: *It was intense and I should've not spent time with you this weekend*

Four minutes later I typed: *You're wonderful*

It was Tuesday. She worked on Tuesday nights and wouldn't be at home.

Three minutes later I texted: *Let's get on the news later*

Finally, she texted back: *What?*

I typed: *Make our own headline: Panda Bear attacks pathetic idiot bearing flowers*

She didn't respond.

I typed: *I'll call you later. I have a couple loose ends to take care of*

Texted immediately: *You get formal apology*

Next text: *I get my shit torn up by a Panda Bear*

Kept texting: *I'm so sorry*

Again: *Later, Okay?*

She answered: *ok*

ninety-five

By four-thirty I still hadn't moved from bed.

I did the wake-and-bake thing and just laid for a couple of hours. I was thinking about sparking up again.

"It Ain't Hard to Tell," was a true last track. I loved those last tracks on great albums. They weren't always your first favorite. There had to be a great opening track in order to make for a great closing track. Truly great albums forced you to take them in their entirety. The music demanded it. The last track on a truly great album was special. They were a song unto themselves, no doubt, but they carried with it the entire experience before it.

As I lay there in bed I knew I still had to get paid.

My doorbell rang around quarter to five, just as I started brewing coffee.

Detective Glenn looked like a cartoon bloodhound. His cheeks almost flapped to his shoulders. The bags in his eyes could get dipped in tea cups.

"Just put coffee on," I said as I let him in.

"Stuff stopped working five hours ago," he said.

I knew Glenn was just leaving the station. If they stopped the raid on JB's warehouse around midnight, he'd need the fourteen hours of paperwork to finish.

I brought him to the kitchen. Put down a glass of water for him.

He sat down at the table, and I joined him after I mixed my coffee.

"If you smoke cigarettes," I told him, "Feel free."

Glenn leaned back in his chair and pulled out a pack of Marb Menthols.

"Ashtray?" Glenn asked.

I got up and took a saucer from the cabinet.

He looked down at it, then back at me, "You don't smoke?"

"Not cigarettes."

He ashed on my plate.

"What happened last night?" I asked him, "How'd it go?"

"No deaths," Glenn told me, "Which was a bonus in the whole deal. Damn murder capital has admin worried about bodies."

"Damage?" I asked.

"Minimal. They didn't put up much fight when they saw five cops with guns," Glenn said, and added, "A minute later we had four squads on the scene."

"And?" I asked.

Detective Glenn was here for some honesty.

He gave me a cool stare. He didn't like to betray the spirit of things so quickly into our conversation.

I raised my eyebrows, knowingly. The gesture let him know that there was honesty and there were murder charges. He'd have to understand I wouldn't talk about Hendricks at JB's office. I also wouldn't ask stupid questions where I knew the answer.

"I did know where Lenny was," I told him.

I nodded at him and gave him another set of raised eyebrows.

"I'll probably find him," I said as if it hadn't happened yet, "And I'll leave it up to him if he wants to come in." That was the truth, at least.

Glenn nodded to that.

"Lenny said he was never going back again," I offered, "No matter how small the bid."

Glenn drew off his cigarette.

I wanted confirmation on the night so I asked, "Charges final and approved by the DA?"

"Came wrapped in a nice pretty bow," Glenn told me, "Everyone in the van rolled over on Vince Hendricks, and we hung the murders on him."

"So Lenny's just left with his parole violation?" I asked.

Detective Glenn shook his head, "I'm keeping the warrant open too."

"I get that," I said.

Glenn put his cigarette out with a series of little dabs on my plate.

He reached into his pocket and pulled out a piece of paper.

Flung it across the table at me.

"Summons," he said, "You're due at 18th and State at ten a.m. tomorrow."

I didn't pick it up. I'd be lying if my heart didn't skip a few beats and hit extra heavy on a couple others.

"Summons," I said and clarified, "Not a warrant."

"No," Glenn said as he pushed his chair back, "Not a warrant."

"A'ight Glenn," I said to him, put a positive spin on my voice, "Thanks for looking out man," I put out my hand, "Solid."

He shook it then turned toward the front door.

"So, Bones," he threw casually over his shoulder, "What car'd you drive to the event last night?"

Chest got tight. The casual nature of his question covered his real intent. Gesso wouldn't get out of the car at the warehouse for a reason. That reason was Glenn.

I didn't think I could lie around this one, not with Glenn and JB Foster's PI's cooperating. They probably compared notes all day long. Glenn wanted to know.

"I think I'm going to bring my lawyer tomorrow," I told him all quick and breathy like the idea just sprang on me that instant. It was true, I did just think of it.

"Oh, yeah," Glenn asked, "Who's your lawyer?"

"My lawyer," I told him, "is the guy I'm going to bring with me tomorrow."

ninety-six

The last condition, number two, I stipulated to JB was me getting paid.

I sipped coffee and tried to remember when I had that conversation with him. The one where I asked him to hire the PI firm to help me out. Yes, Saturday after I stole Jon Jardine's phone and took his text stream.

Condition two was all about me.

I dialed JB's cell.

Working or not, at seven-thirty at night he'd answer my call.

Foster picked up on the fourth ring.

"Happy?" I asked him.

He paused. I think I heard a glass or cup clank down in the background.

"Satisfied," he answered.

"No regrets about the job and how it turned out?" I asked him.

Even longer pause. I imagined the pause was filled with regret — thoughts of how Babi could still be alive. Maybe he was strung out on a series of if-onlys.

"No," he clipped out, then it sounded like he puffed on a cigar, "The job was fine."

"So," I said, slowing down to his pace, "Condition number two. Need a reminder?"

My reminder wasn't going to be about condition two specifically. I was going to remind him how I was the one who saved his city contract. After that if he wasn't persuaded I'd quote the value of his city contract, multiply it over ten years so he'd feel the weight of the number. The fruit of my efforts.

"You want to work for me?" JB Foster asked, "Sure, what'd you say? Next Monday?"

"That's what I said," I answered.

As much as I harbored the thought of keeping Lenny's twenty-five grand, I couldn't. It was in that bag next to his sweaty, squirming body where it belonged.

"That all, Michael?" he asked, "Been a long day."

Been a long two weeks.

I thought of those two weeks I spent alone and afraid as a kid. I truly lost my mind. During these past two weeks I had lost my oldest friend. I felt like I won though, because my hunch was correct — it was my time to shine.

"Unnnnnnfortunately," I said with a reluctant smile to my voice, "as your future employee I need to ask for one more thing."

"You want me to issue you a formal Thank You?" he answered, "I didn–"

"I don't need a thank you," I told him, "A service to help me out."

"Oh, so another favor," he said, "What are you up to? Condition number three?"

"I have a summons for tomorrow," I said, "Ten a.m. at 18th and State. Just a summons. I'd like to have a lawyer with me."

"You're asking me," JB clarified with a hint of disbelief, "To use my lawyer?"

I wasn't sure what his angle was getting hung up this ask.

He chuckled into the phone, "I'm messing with you, Bones."

Desperation peeked through my voice as I said, "Just do me the solid, JB."

"You got it."

I said, "Thanks," and sat quiet. I assumed I wasn't supposed to get off the phone with JB, my new boss, until he was ready.

He must have felt it too, because it became slightly uncomfortable, he said, "Hey, Michael."

"Yeah?"

"Nice work."

Gregory Rossi's fiction has appeared in *The Missouri Review*, *The Brooklyn Rail, ShotgunHoney.net,* and *Danger City,* a crime fiction anthology. The reading series he co-created, *Dirty Laundry Readings,* was featured on WNYC 93.9 FM (NPR). He also reviews crime fiction and thrillers at blackoutbookreview. tumblr.com. Find him at gregorywrossi.com.

Gregory Rossi